FALSE WALL

Previously published Worldwide Mystery title by
VERONICA HELEY

FALSE ALARM

FALSE WALL

VERONICA HELEY

W💿RLDWIDE.®

TORONTO • NEW YORK • LONDON
AMSTERDAM • PARIS • SYDNEY • HAMBURG
STOCKHOLM • ATHENS • TOKYO • MILAN
MADRID • WARSAW • BUDAPEST • AUCKLAND

Recycling programs
for this product may
not exist in your area.

False Wall

A Worldwide Mystery/July 2019

First published by Severn House Publishers, Ltd.

ISBN-13: 978-1-335-45548-2

Copyright © 2016 by Veronica Heley

FALSE WALL

FALSE WALL

ONE

Bea Abbot ran a domestic agency from her London home. She was accustomed to sorting out other people's problems, but when she herself came under fire, it was her turn to call for help.

Friday, early afternoon

She didn't even have time to scream.

The sun had made her office unbearably hot so she opened the French windows and stepped out into the garden, intending to get a chair out of the shed and have her lunch in the shade of the sycamore tree.

Her eye was caught by a movement on top of the wall at the end of her garden. Because of the slope on which these rows of terraced houses were built, the plots did not dovetail exactly, and Bea's wall was shared with not one but two other gardens.

Someone was up a ladder on a neighbour's wall, tackling the ivy. Bea did not care for ivy and cut it back when it strayed into her space, but some of her neighbours had allowed clumps of it to dangle from their walls.

The waving strands of ivy disappeared.

A brick tottered and fell into her garden from the top of the wall.

Another followed...and another, creating a V-shaped gap in the top of the wall.

What…?

The house opposite her to the left had recently been bought by her friend Leon. It was surrounded by scaffolding, and workmen were swarming all over it. One of these men shouted the warning.

Too late!

Bea didn't even have time to scream.

She watched in horror as cracks appeared, working their way along the wall, travelling faster and faster… unstoppable.

The section between the gardens bellied towards her and flexed.

The Georgians had known how to build for the future. Their cream-painted terraces and red-brick walls had survived three centuries and two world wars, only for the result of their labours to be brought down through the carelessness of a jobbing gardener.

One moment the wall at the bottom of her garden was there…

…and the next, it was not.

It thundered down, bricks slipping, crashing, sliding, in a tangle of ivy…taking the man on the ladder down with it.

The wall fell on to the sycamore tree at the end of Bea's garden, shaking it to its roots.

A cloud of dust rose…

Bea was reminded, crazily, that when Joshua had fought the battle of Jericho, the walls had come tumbling down.

Pigeons crashed through the branches of the tree, escaping as it fell.

Bea tried to scream. Between one breath and the next

she realized that if the sycamore tree were to fall, its top-most branches might crash into her house.

Or annihilate her, where she stood in the doorway?

She didn't have time to move.

The tree shuddered, and slowly…so slowly…she couldn't take her eyes off it…the tree toppled over into her garden. Towards her. Blocking out the sky.

There was a thumping crash as the tree settled down into her paved garden, bouncing, and then flattening everything beneath its weight.

The topmost leaves brushed her skirt.

A cloud of red dust bellied up, hiding the sun. It reached her, overwhelmed her. She inhaled dust and choked, hands over eyes and mouth. Tasting dirt. Blinking to clear her sight.

The rumbling died away.

Coughing, Bea wiped dust from her eyes and looked up. Someone pulled at her elbow, trying to drag her back into the house.

'Oh! Oh! What!' Carrie, her office manageress, at a loss for words. 'Shall I ring the police?'

Bea couldn't look away. Where there had been a peaceful garden, there was now nothing but tree. Branches, leaves, tree trunk. Her garden shed was under that somewhere. And the huge stone pots which she'd lovingly planted up with summer bedding plants.

The tree had fallen straight down towards the house, grazing the garden walls on either side.

She coughed. Tried to catch her breath. Through bleary eyes, she looked up and up through the topmost branches of the tree. The spire of the church, which stood a couple of roads down the hill, seemed much closer than before.

The tree hid her view of Leon's house opposite.

Shock.

Someone was screaming. Several voices were shouting.

Still coughing, she tried to straighten up.

The man on the ladder. Was he all right? Had he been killed when the wall fell? She wiped her eyes, trying to see. Coughing.

She couldn't seem to get her breath. She couldn't see straight. Her eyes were streaming.

'Police!' Carrie was on her phone.

Bea wanted to say, 'Don't be ridiculous!' But couldn't get the words out. She tried to work some moisture into her mouth. Wiped her eyes. Dust, all is dust. From dust we came, to dust we will return. She croaked and coughed, convulsively. 'Fire…brigade.'

Carrie had caught on. 'Fire Brigade, please. And, possibly, an ambulance.'

Lots more shouting from the houses opposite. Houses, of which she normally could only see the roofs—and that only here and there. Now all she could see was the tree.

Presumably there had been some casualties? Luckily not on her side of the wall. No one had been sitting outside in her garden at that moment, although she had planned to do just that. Just as well the wall hadn't fallen then.

Her eyelids were gritty. She lifted her hands. They were red. A fine dust had settled on her hands and arms and skirt and legs.

She felt herself begin to shake and, coughing, reached for something, anything, to hold on to.

A growling red fury of an animal shot between her

legs and into her office. Winston, her cat? Her long-haired black cat? No longer black.

She tried to say, 'I need to sit down.' And only managed to cough harder. Her eyes were sore, eyelids gritty. Where was her box of tissues when she needed it?

She could hear Carrie on the phone, her voice high-pitched, reporting what had happened. Excited voices behind her...the news had reached her office staff and they were crowding into her office from the main room, to see the catastrophe for themselves.

Still coughing, Bea fumbled her way to her chair and let herself down into it. Tissues. And, she needed water. Her throat was raw. She couldn't stop coughing, wheezing...

Leon had wanted to cut a doorway through the wall between their two gardens. She'd not particularly liked the plan. She wasn't sure that she wanted him invading her space as and when he wished. Perhaps he'd been pushing too hard for a permanent place in her life?

Well, now the wall was down, there'd be no need to cut a doorway to link the two gardens because the only obstacle to negotiate would be a pile of rubble. He would have to take care that he didn't twist an ankle clambering over that, of course. And then the tree would be in his way.

What ridiculous things you think of when you're in shock!

'I've alerted the police and the fire brigade,' Carrie said, bending over her. 'And an ambulance. Are you all right?'

She shook her head. No, she was not all right. She wanted to say, 'People shouldn't employ gardeners who don't know what they're doing.' What she did say, or rather croak, was, 'Water…?' And even that brought on more coughing. Her eyelids were inflamed.

'Yes, yes,' said Carrie, lifting Bea to her feet. 'I'll deal with everything. How about a good wash and brush-up… perhaps a change of clothes? And then a nice cup of tea, don't you think?'

Bea wanted to say, 'Don't baby me!' But didn't. Shock, of course. She tried to speak. Could only whisper. 'Get… photos! Everything! Me, as well.'

'Understood.' Carrie had a smartphone, and took some of Bea, covered with dirt, before starting to photograph the tree in the garden. Bea made her way into the main office, through the shocked faces of the rest of her staff. She stopped in the middle of the room. 'Winston? The cat?' A hoarse whisper.

Someone said, 'He's hiding in the stationery cupboard.'

Bea nodded. 'Needs…brush!' If he was allowed to groom himself, he would ingest too much dust. One of the brightest of her girls dived into the cupboard for the cat.

Good girl, thought Bea. Worth watching. With a lunge, she made it to the door of the downstairs cloakroom.

Someone shouted, 'Tea for Mrs Abbot! Now!'

From the cupboard, 'Ouch! He scratched me!'

Carrie yelled to her staff, 'Answer the phones, why don't you?' Which indeed they hadn't. Three of their phones were ringing. The girls scrambled back to their places.

Bea turned on the cold tap. Gushing water. Lovely. Scoop into mouth. Rinse and spit. Again. Her eyes were raw, her throat was raw. More liquid. Splash water on face. Hands red with dust.

Face. She glanced up at the mirror and shuddered.

She looked as if she'd tried to paint her face red and then stood out in the rain. Ugh.

She needed a shower and a change of clothes. And a good sit down. She couldn't see properly. Her eyelids were puffing up, and her throat…

Don't think about her lovely garden. Aaargh! Her lovely, lovely garden.

All right, so it was lucky the tree hadn't fallen on her when she'd been sitting outside, but…

She was overtaken by a surge of rage.

How dared they! HOW DARED THEY!

She wanted to scream but didn't, because she was afraid it would hurt her throat. She wanted to hit something, hard. It would relieve her feelings. Except that she was too weak to lift her hand to her face.

Of course, she could always have a crying fit. Floods of tears might wash some of the dust out of her eyes. When she had recovered she was going to go round and give that neighbour hell!

She checked the smartphone in her pocket. No messages. Leon was due to return to London today from… wherever it was that a multibillionaire went to talk to people about money. He was supposed to be taking her out for a meal this evening. He would not be pleased to hear about his wall. No doubt one of his workmen would even now be trying to contact him by phone. Did they allow phone messages on planes? Probably not while taking off and landing. So, if he were still in the air, there'd be a flock of messages waiting for him when he landed. For the moment, she wouldn't try to contact him.

Carrie opened the door and thrust a mug of tea at Bea, who nodded thanks and took it. She leaned against the wall with her eyes closed, and forced herself to drink the tea, which was heavily sugared and tasted horrible.

Carrie's arm came round the door again, offering a bag of lemon-flavoured sweets. Bea took the bag, fumbled her way through a wrapping and put the sweet into her mouth. Bliss.

She sucked the sweet, and sipped the tea. Presently she felt strong enough to unstick herself from the wall and rejoin humanity. She wasn't going to get a headache, was she?

Ignore the symptoms. Rise above it!

The girls were all back at their stations, answering phone calls, consulting computers. Concerned faces turned to her. She tried to smile, and knew she'd only managed a grimace.

The bright young girl had Winston on her desk, and was brushing dust off his coat. He'd scratched her, of course. The girl had a plaster on two fingers, but would survive. Winston was lashing his tail, but he must have understood that she meant him no harm, and was allowing himself to be groomed.

Carrie bustled forward. 'The police are on their way. I've organized someone to take photos of the damage. We've tried to get through to the bottom of the garden, but it's not possible.'

Bea whispered, 'Police…know…who?'

'No one's been round from Them Over There.' Carrie tipped her head, meaning the neighbour who'd caused the problem. I'm trying to find out who owns the place.'

Bea nodded. 'Good.' She gestured upstairs. 'I'll shower. Change.' She avoided looking through the open door of her office to the mess beyond. 'Any questions?'

Carrie looked around. Everything seemed to be normal. In the agency, anyway. 'We can cope. I'll come up with you, shall I?'

Bea shook her head, and hauled herself up the flight of stairs to the reception rooms on the ground floor. Because of the slope on which the house was built, there was a short flight of stairs down from the street at the front, leading into the basement, which was where the agency was located. At the back of the house Bea's office led directly out into the garden. A circular iron stair curled up the back of the house from the ground to the kitchen and sitting room on the first floor.

Bea paused when she reached her living quarters. Because it was such a lovely warm day, the windows in the reception rooms, both front and back, had been left open; but, most fortunately, she'd drawn the blinds down at the back of the house to keep the rooms cool. So, the dust wasn't too bad up there.

Courage! Her bedroom, dressing room and en suite were one more flight of stairs up. She could make it! Of course she could. She held on to the banister and hauled her way up to her bedroom. She told herself that she was suffering from shock and that's why she felt so weak. She wondered how soon she'd be too decrepit to climb the stairs in her house. Would a stairlift look incongruous in these big, well-proportioned rooms?

She could still taste the dust. She realized it lingered in suspension in the air. Her eyelids were red and swollen.

She showered and dressed in clean clothes; a cool grey, short-sleeved silk top and a linen skirt in almost the same hue. She tidied her hair and attended to her makeup but couldn't do anything about her eyes. The lids looked and felt raw. Every now and then she blew her nose but it didn't seem to help. She was definitely getting a headache.

Did she feel strong enough to look out of the window? Because of the slope, her bedroom was two storeys above her garden, and she could now look down over the tree and get a better idea of the devastation below.

As she'd feared, her poor garden had come off worse than the others. Some of Bea's neighbours had called in designers to create mini-Chelsea Show gardens for them. Leon's garden had been neglected so long that it could hardly have been made worse by the catastrophe. True, trenches had been excavated here and there... something to do with the utilities? Oh yes, and the previous owner had buried her dogs there, hadn't she? Their bones were being removed as and when the builders had come across them.

There was no skip in Leon's garden, as the houses were joined together in one long terrace. As was the case with Bea's house. There was no convenient back alley down which refuse could be taken. Everything had to be taken out through the house itself.

Which meant, Bea realized with fury, that the fallen tree now occupying her garden would have to be sawn up twig by twig and branch by branch and carted away through her agency rooms, and up the narrow flight of steps to a skip in the road at the front. Aaargh! And getting a permit for a skip would take ages and cost a bomb! Unprintable words flew into her head. She repressed them with difficulty.

She noticed that the workmen in Leon's garden had clustered around the fallen wall. The bricks had mostly fallen inside Bea's garden. At some point in time, the wall on Leon's side had been reinforced with knee-high brick piers. Some of these had been forced out of the ground when the wall fell and the workmen were looking down into the disturbed area of earth.

As Bea watched, one of them bent down to manoeuvre something—a stick?—out of the ground. Another dog's grave?

Bea switched her attention to the house next door to Leon's, the one in which all the trouble had started. This one had been paved over. Low maintenance: no shrubs, no planters, no lawn. The only greenery to be seen was where curtains of ivy overhung the walls and still tangled with the bricks that had fallen down. Oh, and a tumble-down sort of shed that probably had been put there to contain gardening tools in the days when there had been any gardening done. The only wall that wasn't covered with ivy was the back wall of the house itself, where a balustrade protected some steps down to a basement flat. At least they'd had enough sense not to let the ivy attack the house.

The wall between Leon's garden and that of the troublemaker had also toppled down, ending up mostly on his side. Smothered in ivy. Yes, very little of the damage was going to affect the man who'd started the problem off. Even the ladder that the gardener had been using appeared to be unbroken, as someone had picked it up and leaned it against the shed.

Bea wondered if Carrie had yet discovered the name of the people who lived in that house. She trusted they were well insured because personally she was going to sue the boxer shorts off them. Hah!

A young man—the gardener?—was walking up and down, talking a blue streak, gesticulating. Probably saying it wasn't his fault. A dumpy-looking woman stood nearby, staring around her in dismay.

Suddenly Bea felt so tired, she had to sit or fall down. She let herself down on to her bed. Her head throbbed. The room swam around her. She would close her eyes for five minutes...

She started upright on hearing her front-door bell ring. Carrie called up the stairs. 'Mrs Abbot, it's the police.'

Bea pulled herself awake. How long had she been asleep? She tried to focus on her watch. Perhaps thirty minutes? Oh well.

She went out on to the landing and called out—or rather, croaked, 'Would you ask them to come upstairs? They can see what's happened better from here.'

Two members of the police force duly toiled up the stairs. One was a woman, a substantial blonde, sweating under the mountain of paraphernalia they all had to carry nowadays. With her was a slender Asian policeman.

The woman was in charge. She said, cheerfully, 'Mrs Abbot?' She flicked out some ID and gave her name. 'I gather there may be some damage to your property.'

'Come and see.' Bea led the way into the sitting room. She pulled up the blind and stood aside, to give the police a view of the damage. Carrie followed. Carrie did like to be in on everything, didn't she?

The two police crowded to the window and took in the fact that a fallen tree now occupied the garden below. Gaped. Said, 'Oh.'

'Yes,' said Bea, rubbing her forehead in an effort to ease the pain. 'Under the tree is my garden shed containing all my tools and garden furniture. Also various pots and plants that have been here for ever. Removing the tree is going to be...'

'Ouch,' said the girl, grimacing.

'Yes. Then the party wall will have to be rebuilt. I can't remember offhand whether it belongs to me or to the houses opposite.'

'You'll have to look at the deeds of the house. Your neighbours say it's your responsibility, that you neglected to maintain the wall.'

Bea told herself not to scream. It hurt to use her voice but she managed in a whisper, 'Look at the remaining walls in my garden…no ivy. We had a party here a while ago, in the garden. We took photos. They show what my garden looked like.' She put a hand to her throat. 'Sorry, can't talk. We took photos today, too. Carrie…?'

Carrie was only too eager to show the photos she had on her smartphone. 'Mrs Abbot was standing in the doorway downstairs when it happened, and it got into her throat and there's red dust all over everything, the back of the house, everywhere. It's going to take professional cleaners to get it off.'

Bea croaked, 'I have to phone…solicitors, insurance people.'

The policewoman had her notebook out. 'You'll need a crime number. And, if you'll take my advice, you'll get a doctor to give you the once-over. That'll help if your neighbour doesn't accept responsibility.'

Carrie said, 'Sir Leon won't cause any trouble, will he?'

Bea pointed Leon's house out to the policewoman. 'Sir Leon Holland, that's his house. He's got builders in. They saw what happened.'

She looked over the tree into Leon's garden. The workmen had withdrawn from the wall, but some strange men—and a woman—in uniform had arrived and were clustered around the spot where the latest dog's bones had been found.

'Who are they?' said Bea.

The policewoman tore off a sheet of paper and handed it to Bea. 'That's your crime number. Sir Leon's been out of touch for a few days, hasn't he?' A sideways look. 'They found some bones in his garden. Do you know anything about them?'

'The previous owners buried their dogs there.'

'It takes all sorts. My gran keeps the ashes of her cats in a row on the windowsill in her kitchen. I tell her that one of these days they'll end up in the soup, but she won't listen. Those bones in the garden…they have to be looked at, just in case.'

'In case of what?'

'In case they're human.'

TWO

ONCE THE POLICE had gone, Bea found herself dithering. Normally she didn't dither. What! Bea Abbot, whose efficiency was a byword, who had turned the Abbot Domestic Agency from a tiny, if tidy, little business into one of the top agencies in London...was she really unsure what to do next?

Yes, she was. Shock, of course. And her head hurt, as did her eyes and her throat.

She tried to act normally. Back in her office, she wiped off the red dust which had settled on her desk and chair, and attacked the phone. She rang her doctor, who listened to her tale and said she should make her way to the nearest Accident and Emergency department at once. Well, she would, once she'd set the insurance people in motion.

She took a couple of aspirin for her headache, which didn't seem to help. She made the first of what she feared might be many phone calls to the company which insured her property. They said she mustn't try to move anything till one of their agents had been round to assess the damage, but they did give her the name of a firm who might deal with the fallen tree.

She found and printed off copies of the photographs showing what her garden had looked like the previous month, and asked Carrie to print off some of what it looked like now.

She looked at the diary. At two she was supposed to

be interviewing a bumptious chef who thought he was
God's gift and who said that he was prepared to let her
represent him if he liked what she had to offer him, and
at half past she had an appointment with a customer who
imagined she could get her bill reduced by complaining
about something that hadn't happened. Routine matters.

She realized she couldn't cope. She asked Carrie either to take those two appointments for her, or to post-
pone them till she felt better.

There was nothing from Leon. He should have landed
by now, and be on his way back from the airport. He
ought to have rung her as soon as he touched down. Why
hadn't he rung her? Perhaps his plane had been delayed?
Perhaps there'd been a bomb scare somewhere and he was
still locked down at some airport with an unpronounce-
able name in Japan or the Philippines or wherever. Or
he'd been kidnapped from his hotel and was being held
by masked terrorists at gunpoint.

She told herself she was being absurd, and knew that
she was only just holding on to her sanity.

Nothing had happened to Leon. He would surface
when he could.

She could hardly breathe, and her eyelids were puffy.
She couldn't see straight and her headache was pound-
ing. She gathered herself together. She would take her
doctor's advice and get down to A & E at the hospital.

A tinkle on her internal phone. 'Mrs Abbot?' An agi-
tated voice. Carrie's? 'There's someone on the phone who
wants to speak to you about the wall.'

Bea said, 'Put them through.'

A woman's voice, sharp, backed by a Force Ten rage.
The rage was under control, but there was a thick layer of
ice on top. 'Mrs Abbot? I am your next-door neighbour.

I return from an appointment at the osteopath's only to find my garden wall in ruins. I understand that you are to blame. You will be hearing from my insurance people immediately, and I trust you will honour your liabilities—'

Hunh? 'And your name is...?

'You know perfectly well who I am.'

Public-school voice, upper middle class, accustomed to command. A bully. Not to be trusted. Manners? Pleasant with the few she might consider her equal, and condescending to the rest of the world?

Clearly, Bea came under the heading of 'the rest of the world'. A 'pleb', to use a pejorative term.

Bea coughed, tried to clear her throat. 'I regret that—'

'You must think I'm a fool. If you hadn't known who I was, you wouldn't have tried it on. Admit it!'

Bea smothered another cough in her handkerchief and tried to think. She didn't really know her neighbours to speak to. They might nod to one another in the street, but...which of her neighbours would this be? Both were elderly...no, one had recently moved away, hadn't she? Bea couldn't remember which one.

'Don't deny it! You planned the destruction of your wall, thinking I'd pay through the nose to have it fixed. Wrong! I'm going to sue you till you squeak! Punitive damages! Recompense for the suffering you have caused me and my family.'

Bea might have been amused by the woman's effrontery if her head hadn't been aching so badly. 'Do you really think you can bully me into accepting responsibility for something I did not do?'

'I have my builder working on the costs even as we speak.'

Bea sighed, coughed. Croaked. 'I regret, being a poor

widow woman, I can't negotiate. I've contacted my insurance company. They'll want to talk to yours. I'm off to the hospital now.'

'I suppose you're going to say you've got a whiplash injury? Pull the other one.'

Bea was fresh out of ideas. As a businesswoman who'd been on her own for many years, she rather despised those who dropped names to get themselves out of trouble, but in this case she considered it appropriate to do so. 'Are you suing Sir Leon Holland as well?'

'What!' That gave the woman pause.

'Our neighbour. The house with the builders in.'

'Never heard of him.'

Surely that was a lie? 'You swim in a small pond. Try an international one. Now, I'm gone.' Down went her phone.

Carrie peered round the door. 'Everything all right?'

Bea nodded and eased herself upright. 'I'm off to A & E. Can you cope? And would you get me a cab? I don't feel up to driving.'

Later that evening

SHE WOKE SLOWLY, turning her head towards the delicious aroma of…fried bacon? No, not bacon, but…she opened her eyes a slit and sighed. The drops the hospital had given her were in the fridge in the kitchen; she was under a duvet in the sitting room and there were about twenty steps between the two. Twenty steps were twenty too many. On the other hand, if she didn't make an effort, she wouldn't get any relief. Her headache had subsided—a bit—but her sinuses were still blocked. She sneezed, wholeheartedly, reached out her hand for the tissues she usually kept on a table nearby, found them, and blew her nose.

'Feeling better?'

She turned her head an inch to discover Leon sitting at the dining table in the front window, working on his laptop. One-handed, he was eating something out of a pile of takeaway dishes. Chinese? Taiwan? Not Indian. She tried to push herself upright and didn't make it.

He abandoned his work to help her. 'What do you want? A drink? Water? Something for your eyes?'

She nodded. Tried out her voice. It didn't come out full strength, but she managed, 'Kitchen. Fridge. Two small bottles. And water, yes.'

He obliged, even helping her to get the drops into her eyes and nose, handing her tissues to mop up the over-flow. And a glass of iced water. Her throat was still bad, but she nodded her thanks and tried to smile.

He said, 'I turn my back for five minutes…!'

She made a better attempt at a smile. 'No great harm done. Dust in my sinuses, that's all.' She tried to move and found she couldn't. Winston, her great big hairy lum-mox of a cat was lying across her knees with all four paws in the air. Fast asleep and too heavy to move. His silky fur shone with good health and a thorough grooming. Good.

She abandoned thoughts of getting out from under the cat and turned her attention back to Leon. 'You got back, then.' Stupid remark. Of course he had, or he wouldn't be there, would he?

His eyes were anxious, but he was trying to smile. A big man, almost handsome, fair hair turning silver. A man who looked easy-going, but wasn't. A man who usually kept his thoughts to himself. A man who'd had a deprived childhood and had made few friends. A man who ought to be taking more exercise than running up and down the steps of various aircraft. A man who had keys to her house but lived alone in a series of hotel rooms or in a penthouse suite in the City. A man who had planned to move into the house in the next street.

He'd intended to take her out to supper that night, hadn't he?

He said, 'We were delayed by a bomb scare. I tried to ring you from the airport, but you'd turned your phone off.'

She tried to remember. 'Ah. Yes. At the hospital. Notices to turn mobiles off. Yes, I did turn mine off.'

'I rang your landline and Carrie told me what had happened. She said she'd stay on till you got back. I arrived to find you had crashed out on the settee.'

Bea was annoyed. 'Carrie takes too much on herself.' She thought, Listen to me: Carrie's only trying to help.

At the back of her head a quiet voice said that Carrie was taking on more responsibility because she wanted to take over the agency when Bea retired. For some reason Bea didn't like the thought of it. It wasn't that she disliked Carrie. No. It was because…she couldn't think straight. She'd think about it on the morrow.

Leon gestured to the table. 'Could you manage some food?'

'Yes. No. I'm not sure. I don't think so.'

He propped her up with cushions, and brought the food over to her. 'Carrie also told me that your amusing and highly coloured lodger is away for the moment. Right?'

She nodded, managed to say, 'Working abroad. Back next week, I think.'

'So you're all alone in the house, and it's my turn to play nurse. You've looked after me so many times when I was down and out…' He held a spoonful up to her mouth. 'Open wide…that's it.'

She did as she was told, and managed to get it down. Delicious, actually.

He said, 'You look like a little bird, all ruffled feathers…open again…and not like the Ice Queen who is so self-sufficient and rules her kingdom with a rod of iron.'

She tried to say, 'I'm not an Ice Queen,' but he had another spoonful ready for her to take, and it was less trouble to eat it than to object.

He was enjoying himself. Smiling. 'I had a look at the damage at the back. I'll see it's put right, of course…open wide…though I can't imagine how you must feel about the tree, which meant so much to you, didn't it? Open… there's a good girl. No permanent damage to you, I understand? And one more…that's the last. Shall I get some ice cream out of the freezer for afters?'

She lifted a wavering hand to her head. Her hair…and no makeup! 'What I must look like!'

He bent over to kiss her, first on one swollen cheek, and then, gently, on her lips. 'You remind me of when I was little. I had an old wooden nutcracker doll. I loved it, scratches and bashes and all, because it had been through the wars and survived. It got thrown away when I went to boarding school. So, what flavour ice cream?'

He removed himself to fetch the ice cream and she closed her eyes again. Winston stirred on her lap and she buried her fingers in his fur. Winston wasn't going to move unless forced to do so. She didn't feel like moving, either. Did she really give the impression of being an Ice Queen? Perhaps she did.

She'd married straight from school, been abandoned by her first husband—who had had ambitions to be a portrait painter and who had found a wife and baby son a hindrance to his tom-catting ways. He'd left Bea to bring up their son alone, to work all hours, to find a niche in the Abbot Agency and eventually to marry its owner, Hamilton Abbot, who had inherited the business from two maiden aunts. Bea's second husband had adopted her son and then, following some years of increasing prosperity and contentment in marriage, there had come his long, slow decline and death…and the struggle to keep the agency going.

Yes, she'd succeeded, but it had cost her something, and it wasn't surprising she'd had to develop some kind of armour against the world. Ice Queen, indeed!

'One spoonful for me, and one for you,' Leon said, reappearing with a tray on which reposed two bowls and two spoons. Winston opened his eyes and lifted his head, interested in ice cream. Leon said, 'Not for you, Winston. I'll feed you later.'

With an effort, Bea said, 'I can feed myself.'

'Possibly, but I'm enjoying this. Indulge me. It's not often I am allowed to look after you…that's it, open wide…'

'Ridiculous!' she said, round another mouthful.

He'd put on a bit of weight recently, and now, when he smiled, a dimple appeared in his cheek.

She said, round another mouthful, 'Don't think you can get round me by—'

'I wouldn't dream of it. My wall knocked over your tree. And yes, the wall between your garden and mine is on my deeds. I looked it up when I bought the house. So it's my responsibility to make good any damage.'

She pushed herself more upright. 'But it was that fool of a neighbour of yours who started the trouble. I actually saw him, or his gardener or whatever, up on a ladder against the wall—'

'And that bit of the wall is his responsibility, yes. All the houses in my road are responsible for the walls as we look up the hill.'

'The insurance people will sort that out. What about your wall with the neighbour who started the problem? That's come down, too. That's his responsibility, too, isn't it?'

'Stop worrying about it.'

'I don't even know his name,' said Bea. She waved the last spoonful of ice cream away, while at the same time restraining Winston from pawing Leon's sleeve to attract his attention. 'I asked Carrie to find out, but I'm not sure she did. I don't think the man I saw attacking the ivy was the owner of the property. I only caught a glimpse of him, but the lad I saw was quite young— possibly even a teenager. He was wearing a T-shirt and ripped jeans. The usual gear.'

'A son of the house? Grandson?' Leon allowed Winston to lick the last of the ice cream from his bowl. 'The owner is one Admiral Sir something Payne. Apparently several generations of his family live together in that house. When I bought my place, I called on both my neighbours to explain what I planned to do by way of rebuilding and apologized for any inconvenience. My neighbour to the right has converted her house into three self-contained flats. All three tenants are working professionals, out all day. On the Admiral's side, I met a pleasant older woman…now, what was her name? I think she might have been the housekeeper. She explained that the family were anxious about my renovations but accepted that they were necessary. My plumbing was remarkable, all lead pipes, over a hundred years old, and nobody could tell me when the house was last rewired. Coffee?'

She put her hand on his arm to detain him. 'What about the bones?'

The very slightest of frowns. 'Yes. I had a message on my phone about those when I landed. We knew there'd been some kind of pets' cemetery at the bottom of the garden because the workmen had come across some engraved stones, "Nipper, 1928, RIP". That sort of thing. The workmen had turned up some of the bones before I left and asked what I wanted done with them. I said to ask the local vet, take his advice.'

'The police officer seemed to indicate that the bones might be human.'

'I bought the house off an elderly lady who said she'd lived there for ever—been born there, even. I can't see her murdering the butler, or whatever. If that bone is human, it's probably been there over ninety years.'

She frowned. 'Is the woman *compos mentis* still?'

'Very much so. She ran some kind of charity from the house for many years, and only stopped doing it a while ago. It's one of the reasons why I bought the house. The local council frown on any change of use, but if she'd been running a charity from it, then so could I.'

She knew that it had been his plan to take over and revitalize an ailing charity, but he hadn't mentioned it recently. Had he gone off the idea?

He said, 'I think her husband was lost at sea, so she started a charity in a small way, did well for a time but then…age…other charities doing much the same thing…'

'It would be a lark if it were her husband's bones that have turned up in her garden.' She grimaced. 'Sorry. That was in bad taste.'

He followed her lead into fantasy land. 'Or her lover's? Perhaps someone she was ashamed of, who died in her bed…? A toy boy?'

She giggled. 'You're as bad as I am! Oh dear, there's going to be a horrible fuss. Will it hold up the work on your house? Has it put you off living there?'

'I don't believe in ghosts. And,' as Winston pawed at his arm again, 'I'd better feed the animal, hadn't I? Where's his stuff? It's in the cupboard above the kettle, isn't it?'

He collected the empty plates and removed himself to the kitchen, closely followed and even hindered by Winston, who was determined not to be left out when food was going.

Bea sighed deeply, blew her nose again—ugh!—and forced herself to get off the settee. The blind was down over the French windows that overlooked the back garden, but it was still daylight outside, and she needed to check what was going on. She pulled up the blind, and winced. Her poor tree…

Because she was on the first floor, she could now see over the wreck of the tree and into the gardens opposite. Something was happening in the garden belonging to— who did Leon say owned the house?—an Admiral? Admirals normally acquired a knighthood when they retired, didn't they? She had a couple on her client list who were Admirals, and were Sir something something.

Amazingly, that ramshackle hut of his was still standing.

Bea noticed that two workmen in the Admiral's garden were shovelling debris from the fallen walls into tidy heaps, pushing them further on to her garden but leaving Leon's strictly alone.

Surely nothing in any of the gardens should be touched until the insurance assessor had been round? Another couple of men emerged from the Admiral's house, carrying…metal poles?

She didn't rush—she wasn't capable of rushing at the moment—but she found her handbag and got out her smartphone to take pictures of what was going on. It looked as though the Admiral was preparing to entertain in his garden and couldn't be bothered to wait for the assessor before doing some clearing up. Yes, a couple of men were working to build the top of some kind of structure—a marquee? She supposed that the sides of the marquee would hide the fact from the guests that one side and the end of their garden lacked walls.

The Admiral seemed to be using people experienced at erecting marquees. In fact—Bea squinted—did she recognize a couple of the men? Her agency often arranged for marquees to be set up for their events.

She turned her attention to Leon's garden. The workmen had departed for the night, but, as she'd feared, a tent—a very different kind of tent—had been erected over an area bordering the wall between her garden and his. Men and women clad in white coveralls moved in and out of the tent. A police tent? Forensics were digging up the bones?

Dem bones, dem bones, dem dry bones…

The presence of the forensic team confirmed to Bea that there were human remains in addition to those of various pets which had been buried there over the years. She wondered how many years it took for a skeleton to turn to dust. Hundreds. Thousands? Did it matter? No.

Leon returned, placing a cup of coffee on the table beside her. This was where she often sat in the evenings to play patience and to enjoy the changing of the seasons in her garden below.

He put his arms around her from behind. 'I told my foreman to take photos of what's happened, although I'm sure the police will do so, too. I'm glad to see you're back on your feet. I wasn't looking forward to hauling you upstairs to bed.'

She relaxed against him. 'As if...!' He was a big man, but she was not and never had been a pixie. She smiled to herself. She was accustomed to looking after other people, and it was a heavenly change to be looked after instead. She could get used to being cosseted like this.

Leon was not usually so demonstrative. He kissed the top of her head. 'I'll sleep here tonight, just in case.'

'I'm perfectly all right.'

'No, you're not. I'll sleep in the spare room next to you and we'll keep both our doors open, so that you can call me if you need something in the night.'

'Ridiculous!' But she didn't move, and he didn't release her.

'Zoe, my new PA, tells me that we have a last-minute invitation to a drinks party at the Admiral's house tomorrow evening. As new neighbours. Both of us. Do you feel up to it?'

She was not amused. 'You mean that the man who was responsible for bringing down our walls has invited us to a party?'

'That's right. Admiral Sir Whatsit Thingy. A gent of the old school who, according to Zoe, has manners to match. By which I suppose she means velvet gloves hiding the usual steel. If I'm any judge of the matter, he'll be asking me for financial tips in two shakes of a lamb's tail. Zoe says he rang again this evening to apologize for the problem he's caused with the wall, and to renew his invitation. Mending fences, if you'll forgive the pun. So, shall we go? It should be an interesting evening, and he is going to be my next-door neighbour, after all.'

And if you are a multibillionaire, you are never much inconvenienced by damage to your property, because you can afford to get other people to sort it out.

She sighed. 'I suppose it is a good idea to keep on good terms with your neighbours, and it wasn't he himself who caused the wall to fall. Yes, let's go to show there's no ill feeling.'

She took another couple of pictures of the work in the Admiral's garden. The metal framework of the marquee was now fully up, and the men were lifting up and then dropping the roof onto it.

Leon went back to his laptop.

Bea remembered something she'd meant to ask him. 'You mentioned someone called "Zoe" before. She's new, isn't she?'

'Fortyish, stylish, Cambridge degree, widow. Workaholic with a passion for maths. One child with asthma in private school. Has worked in the City. Despises me for not wanting to rule the world, but reluctantly concedes that I might do some good in the charitable area. She needs the enormous salary I pay her. Will be loyal unless I turn out to be an alkie, a druggie, or addicted to porn.'

'A puritan?'

'I suppose. She volunteered the information that she can work round the clock if necessary. I hope I never have to take advantage of her offer, but it's good to know I always have back-up.'

Bea registered that this Zoe might be worth inspection. Someone without many ties, available to work all hours…didn't she have a life of her own? But perhaps Leon was sliding into the mind-set of the multibillionaire and thought that level of service normal. Perhaps it was, in his field.

There was some coming and going down the path that had been beaten through the scrubby grass in Leon's garden. Forensics. Men and women in onesies with hoods over their heads were carrying away sealed boxes of… whatever. They were taking the bones seriously, weren't they? Bea shivered. The bones were nothing to do with her, of course, but she couldn't help wondering how long they'd been there. Had they been there throughout the many years she'd lived in this house?

Bea checked that the grille was locked over the window and pulled down the blind, wondering what she should wear tomorrow, and whether she could fit in a session at the beauty parlour first. It might help to reduce the swelling on her face.

THREE

Saturday, late afternoon

BEA LOOKED AT her watch. Leon had said he'd pick her up at six forty-five and she was ready with only a few minutes to spare. She'd spent most of the day trying to repair the damage to her system with a facial, a manicure, shampoo and set. The swelling around her eyes had subsided, and she could now speak without coughing. She wore a brand-new outfit in oyster-shell silk, which did justice to her figure and screamed 'expensive' to those who would know about such things.

Some time ago Leon had given her a diamond pendant on a fine chain, but it didn't look right with this particular neckline, so she left it on her dressing table. She exchanged her everyday watch for a pretty trifle that had once been her mother's, and which she only wore for parties since it wasn't digital and needed constant adjustment.

She also put on the diamond engagement ring which her second husband had given her. Leon didn't like her wearing it because it reminded him that she still carried a torch for Hamilton... Well, tough!

She felt some guilt about having left agency affairs to Carrie for the day, but she promised herself that she'd make up for it on Monday.

As she pulled down the blind over her bedroom window, she noted that the forensics team was still in Leon's garden; that the fallen tree still occupied hers... And the insurance man wasn't due till Monday.

Music from the Admiral's garden drifted across the gap where the wall had been. She and her neighbours did occasionally have evening parties, but their high walls had done much to muffle and deflect noise. She realized that she was going to get the sound full blast this evening, and so was the rest of the neighbourhood.

Leon rang the bell and she went down to let him in. He was wearing a white dress shirt under a blue cashmere sweater over designer jeans, and looked a bit of all right.

He said, 'I thought we could walk round there, stay for an hour and then go on somewhere for a bite to eat.' He smiled. 'You look good, Bea.'

She ought to be accustomed to compliments at her age, but he wasn't lavish with them and his eyes told her even more than his words did. She touched his cheek in a rare caress, and smiled back. 'So do you.' She checked she had her house keys, set the alarm and shut the front door behind them.

Steps matching, they walked round the block into the next road. This terrace of houses had been built a little later, and to a different design from hers. The houses were larger, and a glass and ironwork porch protected the steps leading up to the front doors, whereas those in Bea's street were protected by stucco-covered pillars and a solid roof. But there were some similarities. At the front of the Admiral's house, there were steep area steps leading down to a basement, and Bea had already noticed that in his garden at the back, a balustrade protected a shallow flight of stairs leading down to similar semi-underground quarters.

Before they reached the Admiral's house, Leon paused
to check on his own property next door. The board was
still up giving details of the architect and builder who'd
been responsible for the restoration of the building. The
front door was shut and a policeman stood on guard.
Yellow incident tape prevented access to the basement.

The scaffolding had been taken down at the front.
Mouldings had been carefully restored, window frames
attended to, roof tiles matched and replaced. After which
the whole front had been painted cream to match the rest
of the terrace. Only the front door, and the iron railings
that guarded the stairs down to what had once been the
servants' entrance, had been painted black.

Bea scanned the house. 'The builders have done a
good job, haven't they? A fitting residence for a tycoon.
I wonder how many births and deaths this house has seen
in its two-hundred-odd years. Babies being born, growing up, dying. Servants arriving and leaving. Coming-
of-age parties, tuberculosis, the Spanish flu. Young men
leaving for the wars: the Boer War, the First World War,
the Second. You're not afraid of ghosts, are you?'

His grip tightened on her arm. 'It took me ages to find
this place. Large, well-proportioned rooms, high ceilings,
good neighbourhood. I planned to use the basement for
offices, and have the garden made over as a place to relax
in. And, you were just over the wall.'

'But?' she said, noting his use of the past tense.

'Mm. If someone has died in this house and been buried in the garden, I'm not comfortable about it. Was it
murder? If it wasn't murder, why would anyone want to
conceal a death? Can I live in a house where murder has
been committed? I'm not sure. That's why I want to go
to this party. I know there'll be the usual Barbie dolls

wheeled out to try to catch my eye, and I know that some business people will want me to give them tips for the stock market. I'm used to deflecting both. But I'd like us to find out as much as we can about the people who used to live here.'

'You met the woman who used to live here, didn't you?'

'Briefly, yes. I thought she was the genuine article, but maybe I was wrong. Will you help me find out more about her?'

She nodded. Of course she'd help him.

They turned their attention to number fifty-three, the Admiral's house. Here was a different story. The plaster and the paintwork looked tired; the glass in one of the windows at the top of the house had been cracked but not replaced. However, well-dressed people were converging on the front door from all directions. Leon frowned. 'Do you think the Admiral is short of money?'

'Then why entertain on such a large scale?'

He shook his head. 'I suppose it depends on what he hopes to get out of the evening.' They joined the queue to the door, moving into a cloud of strong perfume and aftershave.

Bea noted teeteringly high heels, micro skirts, enhanced boobs, facelifts, wigs and dyed hair. Lots of Botox, not only for the women. There were quite a few examples of arm candy…women looking for a millionaire to take to the cleaners?

The men wore expensive casual clothes but looked as if they'd be more at home in suits. Bankers? Financial gurus? Ahead of them in the queue, Bea spotted a well-known television personality, flashing charm around.

Whitened teeth, false smiles, wary eyes. A general air
of...what? Desperation?

She couldn't see a kindly expression on anyone's face.

She sighed. She was being taken out of her comfort
zone. She knew Leon was right and that as soon as they
got inside he'd be surrounded by people all wanting
something from him. She also knew she'd be separated
from him and, yes, she probably could find someone interesting to talk to, but she could think of more pleasant
ways to spend an evening. Scrubbing floors, for instance.

Leon narrowed his eyes at her. 'Are you not feeling
up to it?'

'I'm thinking: piranhas, sharks and vultures.'

'Agreed. We'll leave the moment you've had enough.'

A large man—a bouncer? no, no; surely not!—checked
that their names were on the guest list, and they were ushered through into a spacious hall. Bea's hall was a mere
corridor compared to this. Black-and-white tiled floor,
chandelier; broad oak staircase straight ahead. Half-open
doors allowed glimpses of a library and a dining room
on the left before they were ushered into a huge sitting
room on the right. This room ran from the front of the
house to the back. Another chandelier—no, two. Furniture and furnishings were out of *Homes & Gardens*, all
in pastel colours. Slightly grubby? A stain or two on the
matching settees?

A few easy steps down into the garden, and they were
out into the marquee which had been dressed with roof
and side canvas panels to turn it into a giant tent.

Trays of drinks were offered. A not particularly good
Prosecco. Nibbles had been turned out of packets into
large bowls. Food and drink were by courtesy of the
nearest supermarket.

The waiters and waitresses, however, were by silver service. Bea recognized the head waiter and a waitress who had used her agency in the past. The man—what was his name?—was currently off her books because…? She'd had a sharp word with him about something, she couldn't remember what for the moment. He hadn't taken it well.

They arrived in front of their host, the Admiral; spare as to figure and sharp as to nose, retired but still going strong. He had an expensively cultivated Imperial beard, very pale blue eyes and the air of one accustomed to getting his own way. A bully?

The Admiral looked Bea up and down, dismissing her as unimportant. 'So glad you could both come. My wife's somewhere… Sir Leon, have you met…?'

Leon was passed on to a sleek, expensively dressed man with more paunch than hair, while his free arm was commandeered by… No, this girl was not one of the usual lovelies with false eyelashes, hair extensions and amplified bosoms, who hung around such parties hoping to attract a free-spending protector—Bea noted that several of those were dotted around the room. For hire? None of them were wearing much in the way of clothes, and what they did have on looked as if it would come off in a trice—no, this girl stood out from the crowd.

Bea didn't need the Admiral to say: '… And this is my granddaughter, Venetia.' The very pale blue eyes and platinum-blonde hair of the girl, allied to a sharp nose, gave Venetia's bloodline away, but she had something the Admiral lacked. She had sex appeal. And, although she was fashionably dressed in an outfit which left little to the imagination, she had not darkened her eyelashes and eyebrows, which in itself was a statement of nonconformity. This girl was not trying to make herself look like everyone else's idea of beauty: she was a personality in her own right.

Just like her grandfather, Venetia looked Bea up and down, and mentally wrote her off as she turned back to Leon. 'Oh, I have been so looking forward...'

A cut-glass, high voice.

Bea's elbow was taken by the Admiral, who moved her around to introduce her to another of his fruity-voiced businessmen. This one wasn't interested in her, either. His eyes skittered around, looking for someone more important than Bea to talk to. Within two minutes, he'd stepped away to speak to someone else, and Bea was left on her own.

Leon had disappeared.

Bea spotted a face she knew, that of a long-time client, but before she could make a move, she was swept aside by an influx of newcomers. The hubbub was intense. Some tables had been put out, covered with paper cloths and drinks, but there wasn't a chair to be seen. The marquee was crowded. Probably chairs would have taken up too much room.

Muzak, courtesy of a ghetto blaster. A trifle on the loud side. A couple of lively young men were in charge of the Muzak. Noisily laughing. Drinking hard. Leon had said that several generations lived in this house. Bea wondered whether these two also belonged to the Admiral's family? Neither of them had the pale blue eyes and platinum-blonde hair of his granddaughter, but they had the same air of...what was the word...? Entitlement. That was it. They considered themselves special because of their birth and upbringing. Didn't they used to be called Hooray Henries? Most apt. They were both older than the lad who'd brought about the Fall of the Wall.

The sun beat down on the marquee. Bea had not really recovered from inhaling so much brick dust yesterday, and felt slightly sick.

A big-boned woman, who probably starved herself to get into her expensive silk dress—from Harrods?—extended her hand to Bea. Diamonds flashed. 'I'm Lady Payne, your hostess. Call me Edith.'

'Bea Abbot, from the next road.'

The woman bared perfect teeth in a social smile. 'It was your wall that brought ours down, right?' A superb haircut and tint; one if not two face-lifts; diamonds round her neck; a tan which had not come out of a bottle but which had done some damage to the skin of her chest. Her handbag would be by Mulberry, wouldn't it?

Bea said, 'Not quite.' The heat was getting to her.

Edith's smile lost its warmth and the ends of her mouth turned down. 'I gather you work, don't you? Some kind of agency? My husband thinks you're letting the side down by running a commercial proposition in this exclusive part of the world. He's going to raise the matter at the next Council Meeting.'

All Bea wanted to do was to go home and lie down, but Leon needed some information, so she made an effort to be civil. 'The agency was started by my husband's aunts long before either of us was born. We have all the permissions we need to be there.'

A shrug. 'I suppose you'll also say your wall was in perfect condition before it tumbled down.' A smile that looked genuine again. 'Ah well, I suppose we ought not to discuss it in case we get quoted by the lawyers or the press.'

A charm offensive. One that worked. Bea said, 'No, best not.'

Edith said, 'You look a little pale. Are you all right?'

Bea put a hand to her head. 'I'm afraid the heat is getting to me. I swallowed too much dust yesterday and it's knocked me out, rather. Is there anywhere I might sit down?'

'Come inside.' Edith led the way down some unobtrusive steps at the back of the house and through French windows into a basement flat. She closed the doors behind them. Oh, what bliss! The Muzak dwindled to a mere rumble. The room faced north and in winter you would probably have to turn lights on, but in high summer it was pleasantly dim. There were William Morris covers on furniture which must have been handed down through a couple of generations, shelves of paperback books on either side of a blocked-off fireplace, and a free-standing heater which would supplement the central heating in winter.

The paintwork was chipped and the carpet worn but, all in all, it was a pleasant room. There was a *Radio Times* beside a small television set, fresh flowers in a cut-glass vase, and a bundle of knitting on a coffee table. This was the nest of someone who had no intention of keeping up with the Joneses.

Edith said, 'Take a seat. I was just thinking about a nice, cold fruit juice to drink. How about you?'

'You're very kind. Yes, I would, indeed.' Bea wondered if this offer to her of a non-alcoholic drink at a party meant that she was showing her age, and thought she probably was. What a tiresome thought. Had she gone from being a femme fatale to Old Age Pensioner in a day? She sank into a chair, abandoning her glass of wine.

Edith bustled about in an adjoining, old-fashioned, but practical kitchen.

Bea pulled herself together. It was time to tap Edith about the house next door. 'It's been quite a day. Have you had the police round about the bones they found next door?'

'Indeed. I felt sorry for that young policewoman, having to cart around all that equipment in this heat.'

They'd met the same policewoman. 'Me, too,' said Bea, relaxing. 'I've lived in the next road for forty years, give or take. It's the first time I can recall a body turning up in the area. Or of being invited into a house in this street. We Londoners tend to keep ourselves to ourselves, don't we?'

Edith placed a glass of juice on the coffee table in front of Bea. 'I suppose we've been here about the same length of time. Between postings abroad.'

'Do you remember the people who used to live next door?'

Edith took her own glass to sit on a chair with a rug draped over one arm—for use on chilly evenings?—and smoothed her skirt over her knees. The skirt was fashionably short, revealing knees which were not Edith's best features. She was wearing a chunky gold bracelet in addition to a large number of rings. A superfluity of bling? Making a point? The cold drink was delicious, though Bea wasn't sure what was in it. A mixture of different fruits? Something with a kick in it.

'Yes, but they were a good bit older than us and didn't have any children, so we didn't socialize much. I remember their dogs were an awful nuisance, barking all the time when they went out for the day, but if our kiddywinks raised their voices in the garden, we heard all about it. Ah well. Time passes.'

'You knew them quite well at one time?'

A shrug. 'Just to say the occasional "hello" in the street, and chat about the weather. I remember she had some funny ideas about germs. If we came back from anywhere in the Caribbean or the Southern Hemisphere, she'd say she was afraid we were going to go down with malaria and give it to her. Very odd.'

Bea sipped some more juice. Most refreshing. She must ask for the recipe some time. 'They buried the dogs in their garden when they died?'

'We never had any pets, moving around the world as we did. In the old days it was thought perfectly all right to bury your pets in the garden. I don't suppose it would be allowed nowadays. Health and Safety, you know. She went a bit strange after the dogs died and her husband was lost at sea. Alzheimer's, poor thing. Didn't know what day of the week it was. That's why she had to sell up. Had to go into a home somewhere. Tragic, really. I suppose the human bones—if they are human—were put there long before her time and we'll never know who they belonged to.'

'Do we know if it's a man or a woman?' She saw that Edith was watching her every move. Why?

'I've no idea. It must have happened long before our time.'

There was a tin with a picture of two kittens on the lid on the coffee table. Bea had an inexplicable desire to laugh. Kittens. Too, too cute!

As—now she came to think of it—was dear Edith, who definitely didn't belong in this slightly out-of-date room. Edith was Mrs Admiral, and belonged upstairs in those pastel and cream rooms with the enormous television set over the Adam-style fireplace, with hefty, glass-topped coffee tables placed in front of matching settees, no books, and an orchid in the window.

And yet Edith had behaved as if she had every right to commandeer this flat. Perhaps this was the lair of the off-duty Admiral, who liked to be quiet and comfortable in the evenings?

Bea took another mouthful of the drink. It might, perhaps, have some brandy or perhaps vodka in it? No doubt Edith had added something to the juice to relax her visitor. With the best of intentions?

Or, possibly, not.

Was Edith, perhaps, not the innocent and helpful hostess that she was pretending to be? Why, for instance, had she abandoned her guests to attend to Bea? Was it to give her husband time to talk to Leon about business without interference? Or to allow their grandchild to vamp Leon?

Bea felt her eyes close. She felt the almost empty glass lifted from her hands and heard the 'clink' as it was set down on the table.

'That's it! Put your feet up. Have a little nap.'

Her feet were lifted up and set on something…the coffee table? A stool? Her shoes were eased off.

Bea wanted to resist. She wasn't a baby to be put to bed for a nap in the middle of the day… Or whenever it was. But it was true that she was slipping away into sleep…

She tried to fight it. She could hear sounds, people coming into the room, talking, several voices. Men's voices. Not the Admiral's. Talking over her head. She nestled back into the deep armchair in which she was sitting. Ah, that was better…

Her purse was removed from under her arm. Good. It had been digging into her side. A tiny thought wormed its way round from the back of her head and insisted on being considered. She'd been drugged.

No. Really?

Yes.

But...why?

Could it be something to do with the fall of the wall? Had Bea been led into a situation in which she might say something to incriminate herself, perhaps to admit that the fall of the wall had been her fault? No, that didn't make sense.

A confusion of sound, people moving around, talking to one another... Something heavy being dragged across the floor.

A strong light was switched on. Really bright. Bea tried to protest, tried to lift her heavy eyelids. Failed.

She felt her skirt being lifted above her knees and something cold and wet splashed upon her top. Something that stank of gin. She didn't like gin.

A sharp voice. A man's. 'Where's her purse? I could look around...'

A girl's voice, high and sharp. 'He's out for the count, but...'

A sound, as of something being thrown...and caught. A ball? What ball? She couldn't make sense of it.

A hand messed her hair and smeared her mouth. Bea wanted to resist. Couldn't.

The woman said, 'Hurry up. I don't know how long she'll be out for...' The voice faded.

Bea was drifting...one part of her mind tried to process what was happening...

Her arm was lifted, held in the air and dropped.

The light went off with a 'ping'.

Good. It was pleasant in the dark.

A man's voice. 'What the—!'

The woman, angry. 'I told you not to bother bringing in an extra light. Now look what you've done! Blown a fuse!'

'The overhead light will do!' Click, click. No light.

'Don't tell me!' Really angry. 'You've blown the whole system! Now what do we do?'

'Don't fuss. I'll replace the fuse!'

'You don't even know what a fuse looks like!'

More bad language. Retreating voices…

Now! Bea commanded her body to obey her. Managed to prise her eyelids open.

Bleary-eyed. Semi-darkness. No lights.

She looked down. Her top was soaked. Her skirt was up around her waist. Her shoes were missing. So was her purse. And her watch. No mobile phone, no keys!

She'd been set up for something…not sure what… Danger! She had to get out of there!

She staggered to the French windows and fumbled for the catch. Could she make it up the steps and into the marquee, looking like…

She drew in her breath. She'd been set up to be raped. Or just to be shown as having passed out from drink? Why?

She couldn't think straight. She must find Leon and…

A fearful thought. If she'd been set up, then *what about Leon?*

The same thing? What was it someone had said about him not being out for long? Or her? Or too long? Or… She couldn't think straight.

She staggered to the inner doorway and hung onto the frame. She was looking down a corridor which led from the back to the front of the house. Light trickled through transom windows over some of the doors that led off the passage, but some were dark. She felt her way along to the front of the house, coming across a bathroom and toilet, a couple of cupboards, a bedroom which must look out onto the road and a very solid door which must lead up to the street. She tried the door, but it had been double-locked. So near and yet so far. She set her back against it.

If she couldn't get out that way, she must try another. There was no sign of anyone on this floor.

She worked her way back down the other side of the corridor. A couple of closed doors, locked. Storerooms? Then a door gaping on to darkness, and beyond it, hurray! A staircase leading up to the ground floor and the light. These stairs were not as imposing as the ones above. Domestic staff, stairs for the use of. This basement flat would once have been the kitchens, larders and laundry areas for the servants.

The staff had lived in a windowless, twilight area. Bea ran her hand over the wall nearby, found a light switch and clicked it on. Nothing happened. The power to the whole house was off? Maybe they'd have to get an electrician? It gave her a chance to escape and find Leon. But…how?

She couldn't walk into the party looking as she did. They'd think she was drunk, although she wasn't. They'd call the police to remove her. The police? Yes, it would be good to contact the police. But how?

Find Leon.

She pulled herself up the stairs to the ground floor. The bouncer—if that is what he was—still occupied the hall. He had his back to her. If he saw her, he'd no doubt summon Mrs Admiral and her male accomplices. How could she get past him to the open air? And if she did…no keys, no mobile phone, no shoes…where would she go?

Panic. Where could Leon be?

Furious voices came from the room to her right. Kitchen quarters? Arguing about fuses? Not having much luck with them?

The main flight of stairs beckoned her upwards. Polished wood. No carpets. Bea crept up them to the first floor. If she could find a landline, she could summon the police.

No landline. Well-furnished rooms, somewhat sterile. A study. A master bedroom, large, en suite. Beyond that were two smaller bedrooms, one of which had a small en suite and the other a shower cubicle and washbasin fitted rather awkwardly into a corner.

Could she tell by the contents who lived here? Mm. On the dressing table in the master bedroom were silver-framed photographs of the Admiral in dress uniform, of his wife in a large hat, and various people whom Bea assumed were relatives.

The second bedroom: to judge by various articles of clothing left around, a man occupied this one. Would this be the Admiral's son? And the son's wife—presumably it was his wife?—occupied the smallest bedroom, the one with the shower cabinet in it, which was littered with cosmetics and smelled of a ripe perfume? So, whoever they were, those two didn't sleep in the same bed. Man and wife? Brother and sister?

There was in fact plenty of room in this house for a large family, especially if the Admiral's kith and kin had a second home somewhere else and only used this address for weekends or for entertaining.

The house was definitely bigger than hers. Perhaps

there'd be a fire escape? Yes, there was. It led out of
the master bedroom at the back and descended into the
patio, its exit blocked by the marquee, which snuggled
up against the remains of that length of the party wall.
The drinks hadn't run out yet, judging by the sounds that
rose from below, though the roof of the marquee hid the
guests from her view.

*Perhaps Leon was still there, enjoying himself, with
the Admiral's luscious granddaughter on his arm. Bea
didn't think Leon liked that type much but...perhaps he
did?*

One more flight up...though why she was doing this,
she couldn't think. Would Leon really be up here? Another floor, a different set of occupants. Younger. With a
shower room and a bathroom. Was this where the granddaughter and those two young men whom Bea had noticed at the party hung out?

Bea caught sight of herself in a full-length mirror, and
shuddered. She looked like a bag lady, plucked off the
streets, complete with an aura of gin. She was offensive
to herself. She couldn't bear it.

She sponged her top down, trying to remove the smell
of gin—which persisted.

Shoes. She must have something to wear. She sought
for flip-flops or any sandals she could wear, and found
some in a heap at the bottom of the girl's wardrobe. It
must be Venetia's. Only one female occupied the back
bedroom.

She used the comb on the dressing table, but didn't
touch the cosmetics. Venetia was untidy, careless of her
belongings. Expensive clothing had been thrown on the
floor. Cosmetics left uncapped.

No Leon. No landline phone.

She looked out of the window. Could she manage to attract the attention of the police working under the tent in Leon's garden? She looked out over the marquee to where her own garden lay, engulfed in the fallen tree. However was she going to get out of the house and back home?

If she had a phone she could ring…

Then it happened. Boom!

A burst of flame.

No, it couldn't be!

Her house was on fire!

FOUR

Saturday evening

BEA SCREAMED. SHE couldn't help herself, though there was no one to hear.

The noise from the party overrode everything. The police in their tent at the bottom of Leon's garden couldn't hear her, either.

She had no phone!

She could see flames rising up the back of her house. And she could do nothing but watch. And scream!

As if her screams would be heard by anyone who would help!

In fact, they might bring members of the family up to see who was making all that racket.

Flames licked around the window frame of her office, spreading...

She sobbed. 'Dear Lord God, dear Lord God...!'

Someone lifted up one of the canvas sides of the marquee. One of the waitresses looked out to see what that weird noise was... Sophy? Bea recognized her. She was one of the waitresses who used to be on the agency books. Milk-coffee coloured, fortyish, sensible.

What would Sophy do?

Hesitate? Call for back-up?

Phone the fire brigade, Sophy! Now!

Sophy yelled something back into the tent and got out

her mobile. One of the other waiters—one whom Bea didn't recognize—joined Sophy outside the marquee. He had another idea. He scrambled over the fallen wall into Leon's garden and yelled for help to the police inside. No one responded. They must have gone home for the day. Evening. It was getting late.

Bea checked her wrist. No watch.

She leaned against the window in tears, willing the partygoers to take action, thinking it was going to be difficult for the fire engine to deal with a fire in the back garden of a locked house. There was no access to the garden, except through the house. And they couldn't get into the house because the front door was locked and the alarm was on.

Some members of the party crowded out of the tent into the ruined garden to see what was going on.

Excitement ruled. People climbed rubble the better to see. Smartphones took photos. The fire engines would be there soon but too late, too late…

However much damage had been done?

Bea realized that even if she were on the ground at that moment, she couldn't get back into her house.

And Leon had disappeared completely and might be goodness knows where…

Find him!

Yes, but how?

A disguise. Bea grabbed a brightly coloured short kimono from the stir-fry on the floor and pulled it on. It wasn't silk but nylon, produced for sale in markets and cheap shops. She fumbled her way down the stairs as quickly and as quietly as she could till she reached the turn in the stairs to the ground floor. The big bouncer was still in the hall, facing away from her, on his phone…

getting orders? Gesticulating. Angry voices, down in the basement. Edith and a man? Had they discovered their prisoner had disappeared? The lighting had not yet been restored.

Guests crowded into the hall, excited.

Did you see? What a thing! Some entertainment that was! We would have stayed to watch, my dear, but now the flames had died down, the show was over, and it was getting late, and they were due somewhere else, what an eventful evening, my dear...

Lady Payne appeared, bidding farewell to her guests, trying to say the right thing, air kisses, Mwah! Mwah! Agitation showing through her party manners... Every now and then she hissed some words back to a young man at her elbow... 'Look again! They can't have gone far!'... Before turning smiles on to the departing guests... 'So sorry you have to leave so early. Yes, we must lunch, do ring me, and give my dear love to...'

More and more of the guests pushed into the hall, checking their watches, ready to move on to the next entertainment.

Bea couldn't think straight. Did the departure of the guests mean that the fire had been put out? Surely they would have stayed to watch till the excitement was well and truly over? She'd seen with her own eyes...whoosh! Flames. Surely, her house was doomed!

She slipped down the stairs to mingle with the guests moving into the house from the garden, wondering if she dared walk out of the front door with them... Keeping her eyes open for Leon...who was not with them.

He wasn't in the house. She'd have seen him if he had been. So out into the marquee she went, against the flow, no one recognizing her in her borrowed kimono.

Some guests still hung around. They'd pulled up the sides of the tent to see the fire better. Leon wasn't there.

Almost, she despaired.

Then she had an idea where he might be.

She ducked under the canvas to get out of the marquee, and scrambled over the debris of the wall into Leon's garden. Other people had done that, too, so she wasn't alone. A couple still lingered there, looking over at her house. Bea didn't give her house more than a glance. The flames did seem to have died down but...

It was more important at that very moment to find Leon. That must be her priority. There was a shallow patio and balustrade at the back of Leon's house, similar to the one at the Admiral's house, and a similar shallow flight of steps leading down to an identical set of French windows.

Someone shouted something.

Had she been spotted?

No. She breathed lightly, stilling her heartbeat. If they found her now...panic!

She must keep her wits about her, although she felt wretchedly ill and sleepy. If she allowed herself to relax for a minute, she'd be out for the count.

She crouched down under the remains of the wall... and crept like a crab, sideways, down the steps to the French windows.

It was no good. Leon's builder had done as she and all her other neighbours had done. He'd installed a grille inside the windows to deter burglars. So she couldn't get into the house that way. And, if she couldn't, then neither had he been able to do so.

She peered in through the window. A large empty room, wooden floorboards. Freshly painted. Unoccupied.

Almost, she despaired. She'd guessed wrongly. She'd thought he would have made for his own house.

The fire. The fire...

Her own house, gone up in flames. She couldn't bear it.

Forget the house. It is more important to find Leon.

Perhaps he was still in the Admiral's house, with unmentionable things being done to him? But where?

She sank down, huddling against the window.

He'd said once that her house was like a sanctuary to him from the world.

Don't think like that. That house is no more.

Find him.

If he'd got as far as her house, he might have been caught up in the blaze...

Don't think that way.

Pray.

Our father...

Anguish. She would sleep for a bit and then...

She heard a rough purring noise. Nearby.

Leon didn't exactly snore. He purred. Like a cat.

She dragged her eyes open again. The sound was coming from a heap of builders' planks, the ones the workmen had used to sit when they had their tea breaks in the garden. She dived for them. Leon had dragged a couple of planks over himself, and curled up against the remains of the wall to the next house—a wall which remained intact.

She pulled the planks away and shook him.

He was in a bad way. Scratched and bruised. Dishevelled.

Jeans dirtied, stinking of gin, no shoes, his shirt a mere rag.

Pockets? He might have his mobile?

No, of course he hadn't. No keys, no wallet, no mobile.

She shook him again, but he was too deeply asleep to waken.

If they'd given him too much of the drug he might die!

She had to get help.

How?

She sat back on her heels, head reeling, eyelids wanting to close, forcing herself to think! She drove her nails into the palms of her hands, the pain reminding her to keep awake. She couldn't afford for the Paynes to find them there when all their guests had gone...

Why! Why had the Paynes done this? Or was it just Edith who...?

Don't think about that for the moment.

I've got to get us out of here!

The sides of the marquee were being rolled up preparatory to removal, so that Bea could see the hustle and bustle within. The last of the guests was departing. The Muzak had been turned off. There was no sign of the Admiral or Edith...or of the two young men who'd been enjoying themselves in the corner. The waiters and waitresses were beginning to stack used glasses in cartons. Miguel was in charge. Yes, that was his name: Miguel. Well, he wouldn't help her, not after that incident in the embassy last month. But Sophy might.

Bea unstuck herself from the floor and made her way unsteadily back up the steps, calling out, 'Sophy!'

Sophy looked up, her ready smile changing to a look of concern.

'Mrs Abbot? You here? But...'

Bea clutched at one of the poles which held the frame of the marquee upright. 'Sophy, don't tell anyone, but I need help. I came here with Sir Leon Holland, who has been taken ill. I can't rouse him. He ought to be in hospital, but I don't know how to get him there because I've lost my mobile and my keys.'

'What's that!' Miguel. 'Sophy, I need you to... Oh!'

Bea despaired. He wouldn't help her.

Surprisingly, he said, 'Mrs Abbot, you don't look too good. Shall I fetch Lady Payne?'

'No, it was she who gave me something strange to drink.'

'Why would she do that?'

'I don't know why!' Bea almost cried with frustration. 'All I know is that she gave me a drink and I fell asleep and she took my keys and mobile and my shoes—'

Sophy broke in. 'And then someone threw paraffin at the back of your house? Miguel, I know you said you wouldn't work for Mrs Abbot again, but—'

Miguel stroked his chin.

Another waiter came up... Asian? Bea didn't recognize him. He said, 'What's going on?'

Sophy said, sharply, 'Mind your own bizz, Fahad.'

Miguel said, 'Hang about. Mrs Abbot, you've always been straight with us, no messing, paid on the nail. I know I was annoyed when you ticked me off over that business at the embassy, but I have to admit I'd taken my eye off the ball, and you were right, I had got careless. Now this lot here... Admiral he may be, but he's not treated us right. He's cut our money to the bone, we've had to serve inferior wine and nibbles and got nothing but abuse for it. Sir Leon's a bit of all right, too. We've done receptions for him a coupla times, been paid extra, always been well treated. Question is; shouldn't we call the police?'

Bea's head was spinning. She made a big effort. 'Agreed. It will have to go to the police, but for now, can you get us out of here without telling Lady Payne or causing any fuss? Sir Leon is unconscious. He's been dowsed with gin, which I know he doesn't drink. He ought to be in hospital.'

'We've not been serving gin. Prosecco and red and white wines, basic.'

'It was inside; they threw some over me, too, though I tried to wash it off. I don't understand why this is happening, any of it. My house attacked, too. But the important thing is that Leon needs hospital treatment, now. Could you—I know it's a lot to ask—but could you put him on one of your trolleys and wheel him out of the door and then I'll get a taxi or something to take us to hospital... except that I haven't a penny or a mobile or...?' Bea was afraid she was going to cry. She took off her diamond ring and held it out. 'Take this, in exchange for helping me get Sir Leon to hospital. If you bring it to the office next week, I'll redeem it for five hundred pounds.'

Sophy looked at Miguel. For permission to take the ring? She said, 'I'd like to help.'

'We'll do it,' said Miguel.

Sophy took the ring, saying, 'I'll bring it back. Promise.'

Miguel swung into action. 'Fahad, you help me. Sophy, get those cartons off the trolley. Mrs Abbot, show us where Sir Leon is.'

Bea led the way to where Leon was lying. He hadn't moved since she'd left him.

Miguel lifted Leon's eyelids, and recoiled. 'You're right. His pupils are enlarged. He's been drugged, and yes, he ought to be in hospital.'

He and Fahad carried Leon between them into the marquee, put him on a trolley and placed boxes of drinks on either side of his head. A length of paper tablecloth was stretched over him, and the used lengths of paper from the serving tables placed on top.

Sophy took off her own black jacket and helped Bea into it. 'People like Lady Muck never look at our faces. Wear this and become a waitress, one of our team, brought in to help us clear up.'

Bea gave one longing look at the back of her house, which still seemed to be standing, though heaven only knew what damage had been done…but that wasn't so important as getting Leon to hospital. 'Show me what to do.'

'Carry this. Follow me.' Sophy dumped a plastic container into Bea's arms, took another herself, and indicated that they follow the men with the trolley.

Into the house they went, the men easing the trolley up the two shallow steps into the big sitting room, and wheeling it along through the house. Edith was in the hall, arguing with the bouncer, while a couple of young men hung around in the background, one biting his fingernails, the other necking back a can of beer.

Edith glanced at the waiting staff as they went through and shot a few words at them. 'Hurry up! I'm not paying you overtime!' She barely glanced at Sophy and Bea, bringing up the rear. The men eased the trolley down the front steps on to the pavement, and Miguel indicated their van, which was a couple of doors down the road.

Bea was weak with relief. They were not out of danger yet because if Edith looked out of the door and saw…

Miguel opened the passenger door of the van and, with Fahad helping, got Leon into the front seat. Sophy got on her mobile, speaking fast but clearly, asking for an ambulance. Bea felt her knees buckle.

Miguel propped her up, 'Whoops, now! Careful!' He

took the plastic container off her and stowed it in the back of the van. 'You look like you need the hospital, too. Sit inside, in the front, next to Sir Leon.'

Bea let the tears fall. Couldn't speak. Could only nod. She got her arms round Leon, but he was too far gone to respond.

A sharp voice, 'What are you doing out there? I thought I'd made it clear I wanted everything cleared away by...' Edith was approaching along the pavement. In a moment she'd see them and then... Bea closed her eyes.

Miguel slammed the door on Bea. 'One more trip, Lady Payne, and we should be out of your hair.'

'I should think so.' The voice receded, saying something about it being a disgrace.

The car door opened. A mobile phone was dropped into Bea's lap together with a couple of twenty-pound notes. From Sophy? The door closed before Bea could say, 'Thank you.'

Bea prayed that Edith Payne would be safely back in her house before the ambulance arrived...and here it came, gently easing itself down the road, in which cars were parked both sides. They would be looking for someone at number fifty-three, which meant Edith would realize...

Bea opened the door and collapsed on to the pavement. She struggled to her feet, trying to see where...?

A passer-by caught her arm. 'Steady, now!'

Bea managed to say, 'Ambulance! For us!' She heard someone... Sophy?...telling the ambulance men to hurry, two guests at the party had collapsed, very ill, they weren't drunk, honest, although it looked as if they...

And that was that.

FIVE

Saturday evening

'THAT'S IT, NOW. Open your eyes…!'

Bea wandered up out of the depths, recalled that something terrible was hovering over her, decided she couldn't cope and sank back down into the darkness.

Slowly, slowly, she came back to consciousness. Feeling dreadful. Knowing that she had to do something, urgently, that it was important…

She cried out and made a convulsive movement.

'Take it easy, now!' A woman's voice. Kindly but firm.

Bea tried to open her eyes. Made it halfway. A stranger. A nurse. Bea looked beyond and above the face and whispered. 'Hospital?'

A smile. 'Good girl. Now, just you relax and—'

Bea remembered. 'Leon! Is he all right?' She tried to sit up, but the nurse pressed her back.

'Your husband, is it? Did he come in with you?'

'My fiancé. Leon Holland. I couldn't wake him. They poured gin on his clothes, but he doesn't drink gin any more than I do!' She heard her voice climb. Hysteria. That wouldn't help. Quivering, she fought for self-control. 'We went to a party. We were given something in our drinks. We passed out. We were robbed.'

'You'll want to report it to the police, then.'

She nodded. She thought, This is a nightmare. It's

not really happening. Is anyone going to believe that the Admiral and his wife would drug two of their guests? It's ridiculous. They'll think we're mad, have taken hallucinogenic drugs or something. We'd better say it must have been a foolish prank on somebody's part.

Frantic thoughts skittered through her head. Her lost keys and phone, Leon's lost keys and…was this a plot to interfere with one of Leon's business projects? That would make sense. Yes, it was the only thing that made the least bit of sense.

Her house! Her wonderful home! Her whole adult life, her business, everything. She wanted to wail and tear her hair. *There'll be time to think about that later.* She said, 'Leon?'

The nurse said, 'Relax. You're going to be all right. I'll see if I can find out what's happened to your fiancé.'

Bea closed her eyes again. Would Leon object to her calling him her fiancé? Well, he'd asked her to marry him a couple of times, so… The nurses probably wouldn't tell her anything at all if they didn't think she and Leon were related, or about to get married.

She'd lived in that house for so long that… Don't think about what's happened there, or you'll break down. Push it to the back of your mind!

We were drugged and robbed. Why?

The only answer must be that someone wanted Leon out of the way, someone who was planning an attack on his business empire, and had got the Admiral to help. She remembered the slightly neglected air of the house. Was Admiral Payne so short of money that he'd agree to lay a trap for a wealthy guest? Using his granddaughter as bait?

If so, then the attack on Bea and her house would be collateral damage, to get her out of the way. She was not

important in the scheme of things, but he was. If someone had set out to ruin him…? Yes, that's what this was
all about. And she so helpless, could do nothing to help
him or herself!

An idea trickled to the forefront of her mind. She'd got
Sophy and Miguel to help them get away and…

She jerked upright again. Vertigo. She set her teeth
and hung on to the bed.

When the ceiling had stopped slithering sideways,
she moved her eyes around. In a heap by her legs were
a mobile phone and a black jacket which was not hers.
Also not hers was the garish, short kimono which she
was wearing over her own clothes. Her tights were lad-
dered and holed. No shoes. Flip-flops.

She reached out a wavering hand and, at the second
attempt, picked up the mobile phone. *Thank you, Sophy.
I owe you one.*

The battery was low. She might only be able to make
one call. So who…? She needed someone whose phone
number she knew off by heart, who lived close by, was
intelligent enough to grasp the situation quickly and was
free to help her. Someone who knew that she and Leon
were good friends.

She discarded a number of names. Not in the country,
not in London, not available, not sharp enough…and dialled the number for that well-known portrait painter and
unreliable gift to womankind: Piers, her ex-first-husband.

She'd married him straight from school, borne him a
son and divorced him when it was clear he was incapable
of remaining faithful to anyone for more than a week. In
spite of that, in recent years they'd become good friends,
and she thought she could trust him to help her.

He answered, 'Yes?' Meaning, I'm busy, so make this quick.

She must keep this short and to the point. If she let herself think about what had happened to her house, she'd break down and cry. And then where would they be?

'Piers, I hope you're not just about to get into bed with someone but...' To her horror, her voice broke.

'Bea?' Alarmed.

'I'm in hospital, don't know which one. Charing Cross, I think. I'm on a borrowed phone and the battery is running low. Piers, I need help. Leon and I went to a party, our drinks were spiked, he's unconscious—'

'I've got someone here at the moment, but—'

Well, he would have, wouldn't he! 'Listen! We've been robbed. Money, cards, mobile phones, keys and shoes. I think my house may have been set on fire, too, but that's not important—'

'What!'

She was tempted to scream *My house! My house!* But managed to control herself. 'I think this may be an attack on Leon's business affairs. Can you get through to his PA, name of Zoe, to let her know what's happened, so that if there's a run on his shares or something, she'll be able to soothe the market?'

'Do you have his office number?'

'I have the clothes I stand up in and that's it. Can you get her through his office or on the Internet?'

'You said your house—'

She choked back a sob. Her voice was going to break up, she could feel it. 'Well, afterwards, if you have time, you still have keys, haven't you? Would you take a look? But the alarm should be on.' She hit her head. Tears flowed. She needed to blow her nose. 'What's the number, I can't have forgotten… Oh, I remember. My birth date. Sorry, sorry! I can't stop crying.'

'Hold on, Bea. I'm on to it. I'll ring you back, right?'

'Now, then,' said the nurse, bustling back in. 'Put the phone down, there's a good girl. The doctor's here.'

'Leon?'

'Coming on fine.'

Bea wasn't sure she believed the nurse but, when the phone was lifted from her hand, she didn't try to hang on to it. She thought she ought to do something about cancelling all her credit cards…and Leon's, too. But the important thing now was to persuade the doctor that she was well enough to see Leon.

BEA SAT AT Leon's bedside and held his hand. The nurse said he'd been pumped out and they hoped he'd regain consciousness soon. At the moment he was still deeply asleep.

A stir, and Piers brushed past the nurse to get into the cubicle, saying, 'It's all right. I'm her husband!' He handed a black plastic bag to Bea. 'Clothes and shoes for you. I hope they're all right.'

'But—' said the nurse.

Bea tried to smile. 'Complicated situation, nurse. Piers was my first husband. Leon is my fiancé.'

'You're not wearing an engagement ring,' said the nurse.

'No watch, either,' said Bea. 'I'm not looking forward to telling the insurance people about everything we've lost.'

Piers pushed the nurse out. 'I promise not to stay long.' Piers was dark, with a slightly twisted nose and enough charm to launch a cruise ship. It didn't surprise Bea that the nurse had let him in. He said, 'Leon's not come round yet?'

Bea shook her head, steeling herself to appear optimistic, trying not to cry. 'Thanks for the clothes.'

He magicked another chair from somewhere and seated himself beside Bea. 'I got hold of Leon's PA, Zoe something. She doesn't panic easily, does she? She says that there *is* something strange going on and she wants to know if Leon can go into the office to deal with it. I told her he was in no condition to leave hospital. She insisted it was important that she see him, so I told her to come here. I hope that's all right.'

They looked at Leon's calm face. His cheek had been badly scratched but he hadn't needed stitches.

Piers said, 'I told Zoe that all his things had been stolen, including his keys. I thought the motive behind the assault might be to rob his flat, but apparently he's staying in some posh hotel or other. I suggested she rang the hotel to explain what's happened and ensure that the staff don't let anyone but her into his suite. I asked if she could cancel his cards, find him another phone and some clothes to wear, and she said she didn't think she could do that without his permission. I suppose that's reasonable. When she comes, she can see how he is for herself. I gave her my mobile number and she's promised to keep in touch.'

Leon was wearing a hospital gown and nothing else. Piers frowned. 'He doesn't look too good. Have they pumped him out?'

'Yes. He'll have a sore throat when he comes round. At first they thought we were both drunk. Understandable. So they breathalysed me and took blood samples from him. I was way under the limit, which made them more inclined to believe me when I said we'd been drugged. If they knew what we'd been given, it would be a help.

They say we did the right thing, coming in to hospital straight away. Everyone reacts differently to drugs. As you can see, I'm more or less all right.'

'You look pretty awful.'

She tried to smile. 'Thanks.'

'Yes, well. You'll bounce back. You always do.' He cleared his throat. 'Are you ready for the bad news?'

She steeled herself. 'The house?'

'The firemen were still there when I arrived, coiling up their hoses and all that. They had to break in the front door to deal with the flames at the back of the house, which meant they'd had to cut off the alarm, too. I told them you'd landed up in hospital. I showed them my keys and told them the code for the alarm, which convinced them I could be trusted to a certain extent, so they let me go in to fetch some clothes for you, under supervision. I had to itemize and sign for them. Nobody has been in, as far as I could make out.'

He shot her a wary glance. 'The agency office in the basement was flooded with water, which means that the electrics for the whole house are out. They turned off the gas, too. The fire officer said it looks as though someone tried to break through the French windows into your office at the back but couldn't get past the locked grille inside. So they chucked a can of an accelerant, paraffin or the like, into the room and threw a match in after it. The curtains inside caught fire which spread via the carpet to your chair and desk.

'The flames might have got much further into the building if the door to the main office hadn't been closed, and what with that and the sprinkler system, the damage was contained. Forget your office. It is no more. The big office where the girls sit is mostly out of commission but the house itself is safe. The flames went up the back of the building but burned themselves out without causing too much damage. I'm afraid the firemen caused more damage by putting out the fire than the fire did itself.'

Bea let his words sink in. Her house, her beautiful house. Her home. Her refuge from the world. And the agency, which was her life. She made no comment. She was *not* going to cry again. But what of Winston, her much-loved, difficult, food-stealing cat? Had he perished in the flames? Almost she broke at the thought. Somehow she must hang on to the hope that he'd survived.

He sighed. 'That's the bad news. The good news is that although the hall is a mess and the agency rooms unusable, the rest of the house is OK, apart from smelling of fire. Even the kitchen doesn't look too bad, though the back door is almost burned through and you'll need to replace that and the glass in the windows at the back.'

Bea tried to smile. 'Thank you, Piers. You've done wonders. I think the plan was to take my keys and break into my house while I was out for the count. I'm a bit hazy about who did what to me, but I heard a man's voice—a young man, I think—enquiring about my purse. I suppose they thought they could get into the house through the garden, but when they tried my house keys, they realized they wouldn't work on the doors into the agency at the back. I don't carry those keys around with me. So they decided to break the window and set a fire instead. It doesn't matter.'

Houses can be replaced. Leon can't.

Piers pinched in his lips. 'The firemen did a temporary repair job on the front door, which means no one can get in at the moment. You'll have to get a builder on the job first thing tomorrow. You can sleep at my place tonight. I couldn't cancel your credit cards, since I don't know which bank you're using and they wouldn't accept my say-so, anyway.'

'Bless you, Piers.' She continued to hold on to Leon's hand, and he continued to sleep.

Piers stroked his chin, already dark at this time of the evening. 'Do you want to phone Max?'

She shook her head, and he didn't press it. Max, their son, was a hard-working, self-important but self-centred Member of Parliament, who would not wish to be bothered with other people's troubles. She said, 'Parliament's in recess, isn't it? He'll be back up north in his constituency. I'll ring him tomorrow.'

Piers folded his arms and leaned back in his chair. 'My successor in your life doesn't look too chipper at the moment, does he? You know he's asked me to paint you?'

Bea shot him a frown. How irrelevant was that!

Piers grinned. 'I told him I'd been meaning to get round to it for years. And, looking me straight in the eye, all mild-like, he said that this time I was going to manage it. And, would you believe, I found myself saying that I would?'

Silence.

'Well, what do you know!' said Piers, mock serious. 'I make a play for his woman, and he doesn't even have the courtesy to wake up and challenge me for possession!'

Saturday night to Sunday morning

LEON FAILED TO regain consciousness. The doctor said Leon had to stay in overnight.

Bea didn't feel any too good herself, but they said she could leave if she wished to do so. She didn't wish. She wanted to stay beside Leon's bed, holding his hand. But, as the minutes ticked on, she began to fret. Someone had launched an attack on Leon and it had almost succeeded. Why? She could feel in her bones that things were happening out in the great wide world and that time was of the essence, but she couldn't think what action to take.

Perhaps Zoe would know?

Piers decided to stay with Bea, and every now and then he tried to contact Zoe, whose phone was solidly engaged.

Saturday night in Casualty meant drunks, druggies and accidents. Also, two stabbings and a shooting. Noise. Confusion. People screaming, blood; paramedics, doctors, nurses working flat out. The police moved in and out of the chaos, taking notes, trying to record what had happened to this person or that.

When they got round to her, Bea told the police that they'd become ill after attending a party. Perhaps they'd eaten or drunk something that had disagreed with them? Perhaps a silly prank on someone's part? The police asked if Bea and Leon wanted to take the matter further and said that, if so, they should report to the police the following day.

Bea changed into the blue cashmere sweater and jeans which Piers had brought her, together with a pair of brogues. Fortunately, Piers had a good eye for colour, and she felt comfortable in these clothes. They didn't smell too much of the fire, either. She only wished he'd thought to bring her some makeup, too. She thought she looked a shadow of her usual self, but Piers didn't comment.

At last, Zoe arrived. Thin, perhaps over-thin, she was exactly as Leon had described; fortyish, tough and humourless. She didn't look a happy bunny, but then who would want to visit an Accident and Emergency ward on a Saturday night? Her manner was chilly to freezing. 'Sir Leon? How is he?'

Leon didn't stir, even when Bea pressed his hand and called his name.

Zoe narrowed her eyes at him. 'What happened?'

Bea shrugged. 'We went to Admiral Payne's drinks party. We were separated. I was given a spiked drink. Someone tried to pose me with my skirt up around my waist, for a photograph. I could hear them talking but I couldn't move. A light fused and while they were trying to deal with that, I went looking for Leon. I found him in his garden next door, deeply asleep. I couldn't rouse him. I got some of the waiting staff to smuggle us both out, and to call us an ambulance. We were not drunk. The hospital checked. They pumped Leon out. They say he'll come round in due course, but...' Her voice broke.

Zoe, tight-lipped, said, 'His face is scratched.'

Bea shrugged. 'His clothes were torn, as well. He must have struggled to get away.'

Zoe's expression indicated that she was not amused by the situation. 'I really don't know what to think. At seven this evening a reporter rang to ask Sir Leon to comment on a news item that is due to hit the headlines tomorrow. His story is that Sir Leon had been arrested for molesting an under-aged girl at a party.' Her manner indicated that she was more than halfway to believing it, and for two pins she'd resign her post.

'What!' Piers guffawed, then saw that Zoe was serious.

Bea clutched her head. 'I'm beginning to see. We were drugged and set up to be photographed in compromising situations. That's why Leon's face was scratched.

They used the Admiral's granddaughter—who is, incidentally, quite something, but not under-age, no, not by a long chalk—to lure him into a honey-trap. She's got Leon's DNA under her fingernails, *and they're holding that as evidence against him!*'

'Ouch!' Piers was quick on the uptake.

Bea looked at Zoe. 'What did you tell the reporter?'

Zoe thinned her lips. 'I denied everything, but I was worried because that sort of thing can destroy a man's reputation. For the following hour or two I monitored the markets and there was nothing. Absolutely nothing. The rumour seems to be confined to that one reporter.'

Bea said, 'Do you think Admiral Payne is the source of the rumour?'

Zoe frowned. 'Why should he be?'

'I don't know. I'm just asking. What happened next?'

'Your friend Piers rang me to say you'd both been drugged and that Sir Leon was in hospital. I didn't know what to think. Then came another phone call from the reporter, again wanting to speak to Sir Leon and saying that if he wasn't able to come to the phone, they were planning to print the story. I told him I'd have something to tell him within the hour. I grabbed a taxi and came here to see for myself what's going on. The only thing that can save the situation is for Sir Leon to speak to the journalist—' she looked at Leon's calm face—'and that does not seem to be going to happen.'

'You said there was no panic in the markets?'

'Not yet. But the story is out there, waiting to break.'

Leon was not one to talk freely about work, but Bea did know he'd been working on a big deal. 'Ah, you think that Leon's work on the Far Eastern project is at stake?'

'Sir Leon's been working on the sale of Holland Holdings' Far Eastern branch for six months but, if this news breaks, the deal's off.'

Piers whistled. 'Someone with insider knowledge wants to upset the deal?'

Zoe stated the obvious. 'If Sir Leon is arrested, or even questioned about the rape of a minor, the shares in Holland Holdings throughout the world will drop, wiping millions off his fortune. The Far Eastern sale itself would have to be renegotiated, probably on less profitable terms. Or called off. There'd be a knock-on effect throughout the whole organization. Untold damage could be done—'

'And Leon might well end up in prison,' said Bea. 'Unfortunately, people are only too willing to believe the worst of those who are successful in life. Envy. Jealousy. They want to destroy anyone who's worked harder or been luckier than them.'

Silence, while they all thought about it.

Zoe stared down at Leon with narrowed eyes. She was clearly not going to initiate any course of action. Her job was to take orders and obey them. Bea wasn't even sure that Zoe believed their story, and if Bea couldn't convince Zoe to clear Leon, then tomorrow's papers would destroy him. She sought in her mind for something to help them. 'Zoe, you said you were contacted at seven o'clock. How long before that had they had the information?'

'My contact rang to ask for my comments on a tip-off they'd just received. I don't know exactly what time they'd been given the information.'

'But at seven o'clock, Leon and I were still walking round the block to get to the Admiral's house. We didn't arrive there until some time after seven, and I suppose it was half past, or maybe even a quarter to eight before we were separated and the stage was set for the compromising photographs. And, so far as I know, the police were not summoned to the party while we were there. I suppose the conspirators abandoned that part of their plan when we managed to escape. So, my question to you is, how come the reporter was informed that Leon had been arrested, *before we had arrived at the party?*'

Zoe's mouth snapped shut. 'I ought to have seen that.' Her eyes skittered around the room as she rethought her position. The frost in her manner thawed a couple of degrees.

Leon's calm demeanour never altered.

Bea sighed. She wanted nothing so much as to get into her own bed and go to sleep, and that was out of the question. 'Zoe, I think we must try to stop the rumour in its tracks. You told the reporter that you'd get back to him within the hour?'

A nod.

Bea hit her forehead. 'I wish I could think straight. Ah, I know what might work. Sitting here in A & E, hearing people throw up… Why don't we put a different slant on the truth? The key to eternal damnation in the eyes of the public is the reference to "under-aged girl". Those words are just floating in the ether at the moment. The reporter might well use Leon's disappearance as evidence of guilt unless we give them some part of the truth. Why don't you tell him that, following a drinks party, Sir Leon was taken ill and removed to hospital? The reporter may then try to find out which hospital he's been taken to, and they might or might not find him. But it doesn't matter if they do, because the hospital will only give out information to family members.'

'Do we allege that he's been drugged?'

'No, because we can't prove it until the hospital have

analysed the blood samples they took from us. I think we act bewildered. We say that he must have eaten or drunk something at the party which made him very ill. We say he had to be pumped out, which is true. We don't *swear* that it was food poisoning, but we do wonder whether it might have been. No one who's got food poisoning is going to think of having his wicked way with an under-aged girl.'

Zoe's face cracked into a thin smile, and she reached into her bag for her smartphone. 'That, plus the fact that the timing is wrong, should scotch the rumour... I'll have to go outside to use my phone, won't I?' She strode out, as neat and self-contained as ever.

Piers said, 'You're a diamond, Bea. Zoe, on the other hand, is a poor man's diamond—a zircon, in fact.'

'Bother diamonds,' said Bea, wincing at the thought of how easily she'd parted with the engagement ring that Hamilton had given her. 'Now, let's think what we do next.'

Piers said, 'Should we try to get Leon into a private room? Get specialists on the case?'

'The doctor says they're doing all they can and all he needs now is rest. Besides, I've no credit card at the moment. Which reminds me...'

Piers said, 'Surely the next thing to do is to inform the police?'

'Don't be daft. Mention "under-aged girls" to them, and the newspapers will be on to it straight away. No, it's obvious. We need to get our lost property back.'

'You've lost your marbles. How?'

She said, 'They've got Leon's DNA to back up their claim that he molested someone at the party. It might not have been Admiral Payne's granddaughter because, if I'm not going bananas, that girl is well over the age of consent. If they did use an under-age girl, then Venetia was there to act as cheese for the mouse, and they must have brought in someone else to take her place once the trap was sprung. Somehow we have to prevent them telling the police about it until we can sort that out. We need some evidence of the Admiral's wrongdoing so as to have something on them in return.'

She held Leon's unresponsive hand to her lips, noting that he still had his watch on. So, the Admiral's team had left Leon his watch, but taken hers? Why? She put that thought aside for the moment. 'I don't particularly want to leave Leon, but he's in safe hands here. I suggest I return the kimono I borrowed, saying that I don't want to make a fuss but something we ate or drank at their party put us both in hospital... Which means they won't know whether I'm on to them or not. Then I ask Admiral Payne nicely for the return of various bits of lost property which we "accidentally" left in their house.'

Piers frowned. 'Haven't you cancelled your cards yet? Has Leon?'

'You asked Zoe to do his, and she refused. Maybe she'll do it now she's seen what state he's in. As for me: no. Sophy's phone ran out of juice after I rang you and, to be frank, I wasn't feeling bright enough to tackle the issue. And yes, I know I ought to have done, but now I see that the time lapse has given them the opportunity to misuse our cards. And, if they have misused our cards, we can turn that fact to our advantage. If we can find even one fingerprint on them, we have them by the short and curlies.'

Piers stared at her. 'You think they'd hand them over, just like that?'

'They will if we can push them off balance.' She looked at her wrist. No watch. 'They also stole my watch. What time is it?'

'Half past eleven.'

'In a little while, when they're tired and hopefully have retired to bed, I shall call on them and see what I can do to stir the pot. But first I need you to find me someone's phone number. Leon's not going to be able to give it to me. Leon retains a man called Hari Silva for security purposes. With any luck, he'll be at my friend Anna's house. They're partners. She owns the Training College which used to be part of the Holland Holdings empire and she's a good friend of mine. She lives in South Kensington, not far away. I can't remember her phone number offhand, but I'll write down the address for you and you can find it out for me, can't you? Hari's just the person I need in this situation.'

Piers said, 'Why do you need him?'

'To find the container of accelerant which the firemen say was used to set my house on fire.'

'Ah-ha. Come to think of it, the chief said he'd have to get someone round the following morning to do a proper search for anything that might help them decide what started the fire. Your garden's full of tree, but it is just possible to get through to the house by climbing over and through the branches. It must have been done that way, because there's no access through the house itself. He probably threw the empty can into the branches.'

'Or,' said Bea, 'took it back with him into the Admiral's house and hid it. I'd suggest looking in the dustbins around and about, before the binmen collect on Monday morning. It's the weekend. No self-respecting refuse collector is going to remove rubbish on a Sunday, and I don't think anyone's going to start looking into the start of the fire on a Sunday, either. But, someone from the family might decide to dispose of the can in the morning, so let's get to it first.'

'If I'd been responsible,' said Piers, 'I'd be getting rid of the evidence tonight.'

'Yes, but you think things through. These are amateurs; gifted amateurs, I give you that. But there's a number of people involved in this and it seems to me that not all of them are singing from the same hymn sheet. I'm thinking particularly of whoever it was who gave the wrong information to the press too early, and the fact that they left us alone when the lights fused, so that we managed to escape before they could photograph us. They've been busy little bees today and are probably thinking they've done enough to knock us out of the ring for the time being. They'll be looking forward to reading tomorrow's newspapers and celebrating the success of their coup. So let's hit them now, because tomorrow, if the news item they've planted fails to appear, they'll start thinking how else to bring pressure on us.'

Piers had an amused gleam in his eye. 'Now why didn't you want to ask Zoe for Hari's phone number?'

Bea had to smile. 'Because he has all the skills of a private protection officer, plus those of a burglar. If I asked Zoe to get Hari to help me recover our lost property, and to search the Admiral's house for a container which might have been used to torch my house, she'd put on an icy smile and say that two wrongs don't make a right, and why don't we leave it to the police to sort out…which I would do if I thought we weren't up against time. Am I going to ask Hari to do something against the law? Mm. Yes. Possibly. And yes, ordinarily I don't believe in taking short cuts, but we're about to go into the lion's den and I want to make sure an angel is on hand to rescue us if anything goes wrong.'

Piers grinned. 'You said "we" and "us". Are you so sure I'm coming with you?'

'I rather hoped you would. But first, let's get hold of Hari.'

SIX

Saturday night

IT WAS NEARLY midnight when Bea and Piers decanted from a taxi three doors away from the Admiral's house. Leon was still asleep, but Zoe had effectively silenced her contact at the newspaper by telling him that, far from molesting a young girl, Sir Leon had been hospitalized with gastroenteritis.

One part of Bea had wanted to stay by Leon's bedside and hold his hand, while the common-sense part told her he wouldn't be pleased to find she'd been weeping over his body if his career were at risk.

Piers looked around. 'I remember this street. I've painted a major and his lady at number thirty-three. Very stiff upper lip, mountains of medals, third son of an earl—or was it she who was the third daughter of ditto? If my memory serves me right, the major said that one of his neighbours, a Rear Admiral, also wanted his portrait done. I put him off because he wanted to haggle about the price. Do you think it's the same one?'

'I think ours is a full Admiral.' She looked around for Hari. The streetlights were efficient in this part of London, but Hari could imitate a shadow better than most.

Then he was there beside them. 'Twelve o'clock and all's well. Whoever lives in the basement is fast asleep and snoring. A security light has been left on in the cor-

ridor outside his or her room; another has been left on in
the hall on the ground floor, and a third on the first-floor
landing. I suspect some members of the family are still
out enjoying the nightlife, won't be back for a while, and
when they do return they'll enter through the basement
and traipse up the stairs to the top floor where they live.'

'The fuse has been replaced and the electricity is on?'

A nod. 'There's no other lights showing on the ground
floor, but there's some on in the master bedroom at the
back of the house on the first floor. There's also a light
and the flicker of a television set coming from one of the
bedrooms on the top floor. Possibly left on by mistake
when the young things went out clubbing?'

'The three ages of man?' said Piers, being facetious.
'The oldest sleeps at the bottom, Mama and Papa Bear
in the middle, and Baby Bears at the top?'

Hari didn't dignify that comment with a reply, but
said, 'You can see there used to be an alarm on the front
of the house but it's been removed. They probably haven't
paid this year's bill. There's a poor lock on the door into
the basement, but two good locks and a bolt on the ground
floor. Windows are open a crack on the bedroom floors,
but they've been fixed with restricted opening, can't be
forced. If you like, I can go in through the basement,
take the stairs up to the ground floor, and let you in at
the front door.'

Bea shook her head. 'It would be more useful if you
would go through the basement and out into the garden at
the back to see if you can find the can of accelerant they
used on my house. Piers and I will mount an assault on
the front door, see if we can get them to give up our belongings without bringing the police into it.' She counted
on her fingers. 'How many people do you think are in the

house? There's someone asleep in the basement, and I assume it's the Admiral and his wife on the first floor. You say there's no one in the other bedrooms on that floor?'

'Dark and silent. A son and daughter-in-law who are not always here?'

'So at the moment there's only three people in the house and one of them is fast asleep. That's not bad odds. We'd better go in now, before the youngsters come back. Here's hoping we don't get arrested.'

Hari melted into the shadows.

Bea mounted the steps to the front door with Piers at her back. She put her finger on the doorbell and kept it there, while Piers found the knocker and rapped out a rhythm on it.

Nothing happened. 'Don't give up,' said Bea, through her teeth. The night was chilly, and she'd left Sophy's black jacket with her ruined clothes in a bag at the hospital. And the borrowed kimono. Bother!

Rat-a-tat-tat! Rat-a-tat-tat!

Bending sideways from under the canopy, Bea tried to see if the Paynes were responding to the assault on their bell and knocker. Yes, a light had gone on in a first-floor bedroom. Curtains swished open at a neighbour's house. A man in pyjamas looked out. Next door. Not the Admiral.

Bea said, 'Keep at it. Somebody's stirring.'

Rat-a-tat-tat! Piers changed hands.

'Hello, there!' Bea stepped back on to the pavement, clear of the canopy, and cupped her hands to call out, 'Lady Payne? It's only me! I didn't think you'd be in bed yet.'

Curtains moved wider apart. A man's head appeared beside a woman's at the window.

Rat-a-tat-tat! 'Is anyone coming?' Piers continued to work on the knocker.

The woman disappeared, but the man stood there, gesturing to them to go away.

'She's coming down,' said Bea. 'Don't stop now.'

Piers said, 'Let's hope they don't call the police.'

No, they didn't want the police, yet. They needed to get hold of their belongings before they'd been wiped clean of fingerprints.

A bolt was withdrawn with a grating sound. Keys turned in locks. The door opened to reveal Lady Payne in a padded purple dressing gown, minus her eyebrows and with grease on her cheeks. Surprise! 'What! Where have you been?' She looked past them, up and down the street. 'That's not Sir Leon with you?'

'No, he's in hospital, very ill.'

Lady Payne's eyes narrowed. 'The ambulance! You got away in the ambulance?'

'Kind of you to ask. He's in a coma. They don't know if he'll survive or not.'

The woman clutched the doorframe. She seemed genuinely shocked. She didn't fancy a murder charge, did she? Had never planned for that. And Bea could see her wondering what this news would do to their plan to incriminate Leon. Wheels were frantically turning in Lady Payne's head. She would need time to recover.

Good.

Bea pushed past Lady Payne into the hall. 'So sorry to disturb you. Didn't think it was that late. You know Piers, of course? The portrait painter? My first husband. You asked him to paint you once, didn't you?'

Lady Payne glanced back and up. Was that the shadow of the Admiral at the bend of the stairs? Checking on the invasion, but leaving it to his wife to do the dirty? And was the Admiral as shocked by the news of Leon's condition as his wife appeared to be?

'Yes, I think… But… It's… I don't understand why…!'

'So stupid of us,' said Bea. 'The food poisoning has thrown me completely. Boy, was I ill! Though not as bad as Leon, of course. The police were asking where we'd been but we didn't want to put you in the frame if Leon survives so, trust me, your name wasn't mentioned. But when I pulled myself together, I realized we must have abandoned our bits and pieces here and, well, that's rather inconvenient, isn't it? So I got hold of Piers and he came to my rescue, found me some clothes and said he'd come with me. My bag's the main thing; a sweet little thing, on a chain, silk with a rose on it, and it matches my shoes, which I must have left here, too? I'm not usually so careless, but I can't get back into my home till I've got my keys, can I!'

Bea could see the woman processing this information. Slowly, thinking it through, Lady Payne said, 'I don't think we've found anything—'

'And my mobile phone, too! Can you believe how absurd? Now, where was I last? Downstairs, I think. That's right, isn't it? You took me downstairs to give me a cold drink, which was so kind of you…although there must have been something in it that made me ill? Or something I ate? Perhaps it was the Prosecco? You really ought to be more careful who you get to do your catering. If Leon dies, I expect his family will be suing the socks off you. Such a shame for him to be ill when we've just got engaged.'

'Engaged?' That hit Lady Payne hard, because it made a nonsense of their story that Leon had been pawing an under-aged girl. Or did it? She made a quick recovery. 'Oh, I'm sure he'll be all right. Now, if you'll come back in the morning—'

'I can't, can I? Not without my keys. Now, Piers, there's a love. Go downstairs and see if you can find my things for me.'

'No!' Lady Payne was sharp. Then she made herself smile. 'What I mean is, that I'll go. My sister's down there, she's not well, she goes to sleep early. I wouldn't want her disturbed at this time of night.' She shot a look back up the stairs where, yes, a shadowy figure darted out of sight. The Admiral didn't want to get caught up in this, did he? Someone above, a long way above, called down, 'Is everything all right?' A young man's voice?

Not the Admiral? One of the young men? Oh. That was bad news.

Lady Payne called back, 'It's nothing. A guest who thinks she's left some of her belongings here. I'll deal with it.' And to Bea, with what could pass for a smile, 'Suppose I go downstairs quietly, so as not to disturb my sister, and have a look around while you wait outside?'

'No, no,' said Bea, flinging open the door to the sitting room and turning on the lights. 'It's cold outside. Did I have a coat with me when I arrived? No, I don't think so. It was such a fine evening. I'll wait here for you, shall I?' She sank into an easy chair.

Piers was rubbing his hands. 'I'll come down with you, shall I, Lady Payne? I know what Bea's things look like. It's the pale gold sandals is it, Bea? Or the grey slippers?'

'Cream sandals, darling. And the bag is the one you gave me last Christmas. The one with a silk rose on it, remember?'

He ticked items off on his fingers. 'Shoes. Watch. Bag. Phone. Keys...'

'Makeup,' said Bea, running her fingers through her hair. 'Oh dear, what a sight I look.'

'No need for you to come with me,' said Lady Payne, blocking the doorway as Piers started for it. 'We wouldn't want to scare my sister by introducing a strange man into her bedroom.'

'True.' Piers strolled around the room till he stopped before a portrait on the wall. 'Is that an early Lenkiewicz? Worth something, nowadays. Shall I poke around on the ground floor, then? Bea, didn't you say that Leon left his wallet, phone and keys here as well? What about his shoes? Have they gone missing, too?'

'No! Stay here!' With force. Lady Payne's colour had risen. She was very angry. Perhaps she hadn't realized how light-fingered her assistants had been? 'Ah, here's my husband. He'll stay with you while I investigate. Not that I think for a minute that I'll find your things here.'

Admiral Payne was also wearing a purple dressing gown, but he'd taken care to brush his mane of silver hair before descending to join the fray. 'What? What? What's going on? Who are you two, and what are you doing in my house at this time of night?'

'Looking for lost property,' said Bea. 'Lovely party this evening, Admiral. Shame about the food poisoning. Leon's very ill with it, you know. I'm afraid we left in rather a hurry and forgot to take all our belongings with us. Your dear wife is going to find them for me, and then we'll be off.'

Lady Payne sent her husband a meaningful look and disappeared. The Admiral shot his cuff to look at his watch. 'I don't think I know either of you, do I? Did you gate-crash the party earlier?'

'Piers, portrait painter,' said Bea. 'Bea Abbot, neighbour. Invited with Sir Leon Holland.'

Piers extended his hand with a smile. 'Delighted to meet you, sir. I believe you asked me to paint you some time ago, but I was in the middle of preparing for an exhibition and had no time to spare. We must discuss it again some time.'

'What?' Thin lines of red veined his cheeks. Was he, perhaps, not quite as sharp as he used to be? Or had he never been all that intelligent? 'I don't remember your name being on the list—'

'I expect your secretary issued the invitation,' said Bea. 'Or your wife, perhaps? Wanting to be on good terms with your neighbours?' She almost missed the look of calculation that slid behind his eyes. She decided that, appearances to the contrary, he was fully aware of what had been going on, though perhaps he was not as quick on the uptake as his wife...who now powered back into the room, bearing a pair of cream, medium-heel sandals.

'This is all I can find. There's no bag down there. It was really careless of you to leave your things around although, I suppose, under the circumstances... And now I really must ask you to leave.'

'Oh, many thanks,' said Bea. 'They're my favourites and almost new. Now about the purse—'

'No purse.'

Bea smiled. 'I expect one of the youngsters found it and put it somewhere safe. Perhaps you could ask them.'

'They're out. Clubbing. Won't be back till dawn.'

'Then perhaps you'll give them a ring? They'll have

their smartphones with them, won't they? And they can tell you where they've put it.'

The Admiral and his wife stilled for a moment, but as usual she took the initiative.

'Are you trying to suggest that one of our grandchildren might have stolen—?'

'Not at all. How could you even think such a thing! But I am suggesting that my bag may have become…misplaced. Let's say that one of them—your granddaughter, perhaps?—thought my watch pretty enough to try on and somehow or other she forgot to return it to me. And that my purse was thrown around the room like a tennis ball. By a young man. Or, perhaps, two young men? While I was incapacitated.'

There were red patches on Lady Payne's cheeks. 'You are mistaken, madam. And I think we have been kindness itself in allowing you into our house at this time of night, and finding the shoes which you so carelessly shed when you were here earlier. Food poisoning? What nonsense. I saw for myself that you had been drinking before you ever arrived, and shortly afterwards I came across you laid out in a chair downstairs. Snoring. Drunk as a skunk!'

Bea said, in her smoothest tones, 'That's not what the hospital said. They breathalysed me to make sure.'

Silence. The woman's mouth worked while she tried to think how to get round this unpleasant fact. 'No doubt you staggered out while my back was turned, and have abandoned your property in the street, where it has been picked up by some homeless beggar. And now, I think it is more than time that you left.'

Piers, hands in pockets, leaned his shoulder against the fireplace. 'Ah, I see it's not a genuine Lenkiewicz, now

I look more closely. Someone's sold you a pup, Admiral. And, late as it is, we really think you ought to make more of an effort to find Bea's things.'

'You see,' said Bea, smiling brilliantly, 'I can't get back into my house without my keys.'

The Admiral's eyes widened, and his lady became very still. Bea could see them wondering, suspecting, coming to the delightful conclusion that Bea *didn't know her house had been torched that night!*

'So,' said Bea, 'if you will just ask the youngsters where they've put my things, we'll be on our way.'

Admiral Payne said, 'As my wife told you, they're out, and I don't know when they'll be back.'

'In that case,' said Piers, 'we'd better all go upstairs and have a look around for the stuff.'

Lady Payne jerked. 'How dare you! I'm going to call the police, if you're not out of here in five minutes.'

Bea smiled. 'A good idea. The police can help us search for my bits and pieces.'

Checkmate. The woman knew it, too.

A stir in the doorway to the hall. One of the youngsters? No, it was an over-thin teenage boy, wearing ill-fitting glasses, boxer shorts, a creased, cheap T-shirt, trainers, and the sort of expression that made Bea think he was accustomed to dodging fists. He looked very different from the self-assured young men who'd been so raucous out in the garden earlier that evening. Much younger than them, for a start. A poor relation?

His appearance altered the balance of power. It had been two against two. Now it was three against two.

'Rollo?' Lady Payne, not pleased. 'What are you doing down here?'

'Th-thing is,' Rollo pushed his glasses back up his nose. 'S-someone's in the garden.'

Lady Payne said, 'Rats, probably.'

'N-not with a torch. Would they?'

Bea refrained from pressing a hand to her heart. With difficulty. The lad had seen Hari searching the garden? What to do? Bluster, or retire? Or, perhaps...? She shook her head. 'With the wall down, you can't tell one garden from t'other at the moment—and what a to-do that's going to be to sort out.'

Lady Payne's mouth worked. She shot a keen glance at her husband, and then rounded on the boy. 'Yes, of course, that's it. Don't be so stupid, Rollo.'

'I'm not s-stupid.' A note of defiance in his voice. 'I heard what my c-cousins were s-saying and I s-said it wasn't right to lift other people's th-things, and Venetia went off c-clubbing wearing the watch she s-said she'd b-borrowed but I bet she didn't have permission—'

Lady Payne gasped, and her husband said, 'What, what!'

Bea paid attention, fast.

'—and I may be younger than them and not allowed to go c-clubbing yet, and I get that, but it's not right that they should t-take my iPad to play with and b-break it, and then laugh—'

He held out a shoebox. No lid.

'—so I collected all the stuff they left lying on her bed and I was going to give it to you in the morning, but then these people came and I heard them say they'd come for their things, so here they are.'

Lady Payne made as if to take the box off him, but Piers was quicker and snatched it from the lad. 'Thank you, Rollo. That's very good news. Here you are, Bea;

your little bag…keys…mobile phone and cards. And are
these Leon's?'

A man's wallet. Leon's? Another phone, and a second
bunch of keys. One bunch of keys and one smartphone
looks very much like another, but Bea had given Leon
the angel tag which adorned the bunch of keys, and the
smartphone cover with another angel on it. These items
definitely belonged to Leon.

'Yes, those are Leon's,' said Bea, heart banging away.
'I'll see that he gets them back.'

Now, could they get away before anybody else arrived?
If the youngsters who'd gone clubbing returned now,
there might be some unpleasantness…to put it mildly.

She said, 'I'm truly grateful, Rollo. Now, Lady Payne,
as you say, it's getting late and we'd all like to be tucked
up in bed, don't you think? With a few prayers that Leon
is going to make it. As my watch appears to have been
borrowed by your granddaughter, perhaps you'd get her
to return it to me tomorrow, to avoid any further unpleasantness. Also Leon's shoes.'

She moved to the door, which Piers held open for her.

'What? You're going?' The Admiral, looking to his
wife for instructions.

Lady Payne appeared to be concealing amusement. No
doubt she was thinking Bea had a nasty surprise waiting
for her at home. 'Yes, yes. So glad it all ended well. I'll
send my granddaughter over with your watch tomorrow.
Naughty girl. What are the young coming to nowadays!'

Piers opened the front door and they descended into
the night air. As they walked away, they heard keys turn
in locks and a bolt shot home.

Piers said, 'Bolting the door, while the young ones
are still out? I suppose they get in through the basement

flat when they condescend to return. Or are they used to staying out all night?'

'I don't know and I don't care,' said Bea, clutching her arms around herself. 'I'm cold and miserable and… and I'm not going to lie down and cry, but…has Hari got away safely, do you think?'

A shadow drifted up the area steps and joined them. Hari was carrying a large plastic bag from which came the unmistakeable whiff of paraffin. 'The old dear's still snoring in the basement. I followed my nose around the garden. Nothing. Nada. Only tree. Then I waited downstairs till I heard you were safely out of the way and almost fell over the wheelie-bins they keep in the area outside the sleeper's bedroom. And there it was, next to today's newspapers. So I took a couple of photographs and, wearing gloves, put both newspaper and four-litre can in a convenient plastic bag. Hopefully, the arsonist left his prints on the can somewhere. Now, would you like to sleep in your own bed tonight, Mrs A?'

Her knees gave way and she caught at the railings of the nearest house.

Leon!

Piers put his arm around her. 'Hold up! You've done brilliantly so far. Come home with me. I promise not to molest you.'

She tried to smile. 'Thanks, but no thanks. I ought to be with Leon, but I'm so tired I can't think straight. Hari, I know you can probably get me back into my own house, but without electricity…and oh, what am I going to do on Monday? The girls will be arriving at the agency and… Winston! My cat! How could I have forgotten him?'

'Electricity and water's off, but it's no great problem. It's a warm night,' said Hari. 'We have torches. Maybe you keep a candle or two for emergencies? I'll sleep downstairs, see you're not disturbed.'

Piers was on his phone. 'Checking the hospital…' He moved away, talking into his phone, asking after Leon.

Hari said, 'Mrs A, you need to rest. Shall I get Anna to come and look after you? She'll come like a shot, if she knows you're in trouble.'

Bea slid down the railings and ended up sitting on the pavement.

I look like a drunk. I feel like a drunk. Disorientated. If Leon dies…dear Lord above! I haven't exactly been myself, have I? I forgot to ask you for help. For advice. I'm asking now. I'm praying, please save Leon…at least, I know I ought to be praying that your will be done, but… please, please! Look after Leon.

Hari knelt beside her. He put his arm around her. He was warm and comforting. She let herself relax, thinking that just for a moment she could stop being the one in charge.

Piers walked back, holding out his mobile. 'They wouldn't give me any information. You speak to them, Bea. They know you're his fiancée.'

Bea spoke and received reassuring words. No change. Leon's vital signs were OK. Breathing, heart, all OK. He would wake when he was ready to do so.

She returned the phone to Piers. 'No change.'

Hari eased her to her feet. 'Come along, now. Let's go and look for Winston.'

He seemed to think this was the right thing to do, so she let him drape one of her arms around his neck, to help her along the pavement. Piers took her free arm.

She stumbled and they held her up. She said, 'Winston ought to be all right. He's got more than nine lives, you know. I mean, he flew into the house when the tree came crashing down. Through my legs, nearly had me over. When he's frightened, he gets into the stationery cupboard. He claws the door open and gets in, and it shuts automatically behind him. The fire won't have got that far, will it? No, of course it won't. And as for the water the firemen have pumped in, he'd have jumped up on to something out of the way, wouldn't he? I mean, he wouldn't have drowned. No, of course he wouldn't.'

'No, of course he wouldn't.'

They turned into her street. Two men, supporting a drunken woman home.

Home was looking all right, if you hadn't seen the sheet of ply nailed over the front door. Access denied. Enter at your peril.

SEVEN

'CAN YOU HOLD her for the moment?' That was Hari, handing her over to Piers. Bea staggered but remained upright, more or less. She was so tired...

Wrench, wrench. Squeal of nails. Her poor door. Her poor, poor door...

'In we go. Mind the step. Yes, it's dark. Piers, take my torch.' A beam of light illuminated the hallway. The furniture was still there. Her coats still hung on the rack behind the door but everything was covered with a layer of...grit? The air was damp. She inhaled the scent of a bonfire. Everything stank.

Something attacked her shin, and she yelped. Something yowled.

Piers angled the torch beam down. An indignant, furry monster butted her leg.

'Winston!' She scooped him up into her arms. He smelled of smoke. 'Oh, Winston! I thought you were dead!'

'He's hungry, I expect,' said Piers. 'If I remember rightly, he has a habit of tripping people up when he wants to be fed.'

Bea closed her eyes and opened them again. The lamps in the street outside sent a weak light through the transom over the front door. The doors to the sitting room and to the kitchen were open, and more light came in that way because she hadn't drawn the curtains before she left for the party. Long ago and in another life. Making her way along the hall, she saw that the door leading down the stairs to the agency rooms had been levered open. It was normally kept locked, but presumably the firemen had had to get it open, to access the blaze in the rooms below. Oh well. Don't think about that now.

She managed to get into the kitchen with Winston in her arms. The back door had been forced open and was hanging off its hinges, but a piece of ply had been roughly nailed into place over it and another fitted over the missing pane in the adjacent window. The farthest section of glass was cracked but intact, though cloudy from soot.

Bea deposited the cat on the barely visible central unit. Cat food. Top left-hand cupboard. Everything felt gritty. Soot, probably. One sachet or two? Two.

Scissors...where had her scissors gone? She knew perfectly well that she couldn't open the cat-food sachets with her teeth. She'd tried that in the past and it didn't work. People who took other people's scissors and hid them should be consigned to the lowest region of hell. She tried the cutlery drawer and felt around inside. With care, so as not to cut herself.

The men had disappeared. Where did men go when you needed them? They were calling to one another, fumbling around in the dark.

Winston was alternately growling and yowling, informing her that he was seriously distressed. He'd had an abominable day, what with the tree falling when he was in it, the fire and the water and then her not being there. She knew she was crying, but hadn't time to find a hankie. Or a tissue. Let the tears come. What did it matter?

She abandoned the cutlery drawer to feel around for the knife rack over the sink. She located a sharp vegetable knife, and slit open the first sachet. She couldn't remember where the cat's dishes might be, so emptied the contents out onto the central unit. So what if there was soot on it? Winston fell onto the food. Of course he could see in the dark, couldn't he? Not that it was ever that dark in London.

That morning there had been blinds at the window and in the top part of the back door. Gone. All gone. The flames had found and destroyed door and window but hadn't been able to get as far as the units. Perhaps the gas cooker might still work. No, of course it wouldn't. The firemen had turned the gas off, hadn't they? As a precaution.

Winston butted her hand. He wanted the second sachet. She managed to get that open, too. She knocked into a stool and sat on it. It felt gritty but she couldn't have cared less.

She supposed she ought to find out what the men were doing and tell them to stop it. No, not stop it. Or, did she mean…? She didn't know what she meant.

Someone was knocking at the front door. What…?

Then there was a rush of footsteps, and she was in someone's arms. A woman's arms. Someone who loved her. Hari had said he'd called her…?

'Oh, Anna!'

Tears.

'You poor thing. Come on, now! Up to bed with you.'

Torchlight in the kitchen. A male voice. Hari. 'Ah, there you are, Anna. I'm not sure I can get the power back on, but with luck there'll be some hot water in the tank if she wants a shower.'

A lovely word, shower. Raindrops are falling from heaven…

Pushed and pulled, she managed the stairs. Still in

the dark. But not so dark, really. Into her lovely big bedroom. Nothing much seemed to have been affected here. The window was cracked but not broken. The blind still worked. Hallelujah. The stink was not as bad up here.

Anna helped her undress and get into the shower…but oh dear, a power shower can't work without power. Oh, well. Run water into the washbasin. Hari was right and there was still some hot water in the tank. Slosh, slosh, rub rub. That was better. A bit. Even if she did feel so unsteady that…

'There you go! Into bed. Sleep tight, don't let the bed bugs bite.'

'But you…?'

'I'll be next door in the spare bedroom. If you need me, just call.'

She knew she wouldn't sleep.

Leon, *Leon*, LEON! The agency. Her garden. Only yesterday…was it only yesterday or was it the day before? She'd thought that the fall of the wall was a tragedy. Now, she knew better.

She couldn't possibly sleep. Her eyes were wide open. She couldn't close them. A great furry lump landed on her legs and worked his way up to her chin. Purring loudly. Settled down to wash himself. With every lick of his coat, he shook the bed.

If she slept, she'd have nightmares. She knew it. Just knew it…

Sunday morning, breakfast time

AND THEN, IT was light.

Someone was at her bedside, shaking her shoulder, calling her name. What was Anna doing there?

Daylight. The blind was up and daylight flooded in. Winston had disappeared. What time was it?

She smelled fire.

She remembered and shot upright. 'Leon?'

'No, no. Don't panic. So far as we know, he's all right. Look, Hari's got you a takeaway tea. Drink it before you do anything else.'

Anna was fully dressed but looking anxious. Bea took the cardboard cup of tea and sipped it. Ugh. Sugar. Sugar was given for shock.

'You're sure Leon's all right?'

'I rang and said I was his fiancée. He's still in the land of the living. I'll phone again in a minute. Winston's all right. I've just fed him. Piers and Hari stayed the night here in the top flat, but Hari can't get the power back on. It's a job for an electrical contractor. So we can't even boil a kettle.'

Bea sighed. 'The freezer. The fridge. Everything in them will be spoiled.'

Anna opened drawers, looked into the dressing room. 'What would you like to wear? The smell's not so bad up here, and the clothes in the drawers should be all right. It's early still. Do you want to ring your office manageress to give her the bad news? Your landline doesn't work…surprise! But I brought up your smartphone. Want to ring her?'

Bea tried to switch it on. 'This isn't mine. It's Sophy's, and it needs a charge. Mine is downstairs with the other stuff we retrieved from the Admiral's last night. I suspect someone will have run up a bill on it. I'll look at it in a minute.'

She could imagine the Admiral's granddaughter, that bright young thing, amusing herself, using Bea's phone to ring contacts in far-flung corners of the globe. And, when the power had began to run low, deleting everything in sight. But maybe not. Maybe Bea was maligning the girl. 'The Paynes have a granddaughter who took part in the scam last night. Was it only last night? I seem to have lost track of the days. I think she may have "borrowed" my watch as well.'

Anna laid out some clothes. 'Bea, we think you ought to move out for the time being. If Hari can't reconnect the electrical supply, it's going to be a major job to get you back on line. There's hot water in the tank at the moment, but the boiler won't work without the pump and the pump won't work without power. Ditto the gas stove. Windows and doors are going to have to be replaced, and everything in the house professionally cleaned. We think you should move in with me. And don't argue.'

Tears threatened. 'I hear what you're saying, but I can't just abandon my home. I've lived here for so many years... Then there's the agency. What am I going to do about that? No agency, no income. I need to decide all sorts of things, but I can't think straight.'

'You're strong. You'll survive.'

Bea wasn't so sure about that. She got out of bed. Her body was reluctant to move. Her joints were stiff. Anna vanished, leaving Bea alone. She went to the window and looked out through the cracked glass. More devastation. Tree in garden. Some of the branches nearest the house looked as if they'd been scorched, but at midsummer the leaves were full of sap, so the wood had hardly burned at all.

The party wall was still down. The tent was still poised over the graveyard in Leon's garden. No policemen had turned up yet. Well, it was Sunday morning, wasn't it? Or was it? Yes, it was Sunday.

The scaffolding around the back of Leon's house was still in place, but through it his house gleamed bright in the morning sun. A bigger house than hers. With blank eyes for windows, no curtains, no blinds. Empty.

Dear Lord, what would you have me do now? The agency—gone. My home—destroyed. Oh, they can both be built up again, I suppose. But...it's as if everything's been wiped away. The past. Gone. What do you want me to do?

Leon. Always and forever. In my heart.

Dear Lord, you're not going to let him die, are you?

The woodwork on either side of the window felt cool to the touch. The flames hadn't done much damage up here, but the woodwork would probably have to be replaced and repainted. The flames had risen up the wall from the patio below, seeking anything that would burn until, meeting an expanse of brickwork, they'd died. The whole back of the house would have to be attended to. Brickwork cleaned, possibly repointed. Window frames replaced. Glass renewed. And that was just the start of it.

Hold on to the thought of Leon. He's not dead. Anna said he wasn't.

I do love him. I hadn't realized how much until last night.

I can't think straight. That threat to Leon's reputation... Did I do enough to stop it? Zoe! I must ring her, straight away. Wait a minute, I don't know how to contact her. Will her number be on Leon's phone? Never mind that. Piers has her number. I must get dressed, get moving, get to the hospital...

She clutched her head with both hands.

I'm being torn in different directions. I don't know what to do first.

Go to Leon? Or do something about the agency and this house?

And what about the Admiral and his lady? What they tried to do to us was horrific, and if Leon dies... Don't think like that. He's not going to die. But I shall have to deal with them some time.

Dear Lord above...

Everything that she'd relied on was in disarray. Her home, her business.

Was God telling her that her life was to take a new direction? That she must move on into uncharted territory?

She'd heard it said somewhere that now and then God shuts one door in your life before He opens another. The idea was that He shuts the first door—which can be very painful—to make sure you go through the new one.

If that was so, then her old life was dead. She must let it go. She must step forward into the new. She stood there, praying for strength, for wisdom to know what to do, until she realized she was repeating the same words over and over, whereas what was needed now was action.

She could, with difficulty, discern what that might be...provided Leon lived.

She washed as best she could in tepid water, and dressed in the clothes Anna had laid out for her. Normally she would take time to make up her face, but today she looked at herself in the mirror and decided that she was looking her age, but so what! She was sixty-plus. Why bother to look fifty? She'd never gone in for Botox or face-lifts. Hadn't thought it was a good idea. If it ain't broke, don't meddle with it. Enhance with makeup, but

don't interfere with what's under the skin. If this was the
new face she presented to the world, then so be it.

Her hair had always been a natural ash-blonde and
she did like to spend money on a good cut. She brushed
her fringe sideways over her forehead. Yes, her hair still
fell into the right shape.

Her skin was good. Her eyes were unusual. Hamilton
had been used to call them her 'eagle' eyes, because they
were large and long-tailed. So, a swipe of mascara and a
sweep of lipstick would have to do.

If she was leaving, she needed to pack a few things.
She took down a suitcase. Her bible went in first. She
picked up her jewellery box. Ah…she stood stock still for
a moment, remembering how quickly she'd exchanged
her exquisite diamond engagement ring for Sophy's help.

Would Sophy bring it back? Perhaps. Perhaps not.
Sophy could sell the ring for far more than Bea had offered to give her.

She'd told the hospital that she was Leon's fiancée, and
made up a tale of having been robbed of her ring. So, it
would be best to let her finger go bare. She did, however,
hang the diamond pendant Leon had given her round her
neck, and put her everyday watch on to her wrist. She
slapped the jewellery case shut, and locked it.

In went a pouch of basic makeup. Some all-purpose
clothes were next. A holdall took some of her favourite
shoes and boots. She'd always loved boots.

She looked around. She'd loved this room. She'd loved
this house. She'd be back, some time. Perhaps. But now
she must move on.

She took her luggage downstairs and left it in the hall.
The air was surprisingly clear for a house that had been
the subject of arson. Ah, now she could see why. The tem-

porary fittings over the kitchen door and window were
no longer there, which allowed a pleasant breeze to con-
tend with the stink of fire. Hari and Piers were sitting in
the kitchen, both on their phones, while Anna emptied
the freezer and fridge into insulated boxes.

Anna looked up and saw Bea. 'I'll take this food and
put it in my freezer, shall I? I hate waste.'

Winston was winding round Anna's legs, reminding
her that he didn't like waste, either. Anna duly fed him
some titbits.

Bea said, 'Thanks. Many thanks, to all of you. As you
see, I'm on my feet again and ready to face whatever the
day holds. Anna's quite right. I shall have to move out
of here for the time being. I am truly grateful to you for
all you've done but I don't want to ruin your weekend.'

Anna said, smiling. 'Oh, no you don't. I seem to remember that some time ago when I was in a bad way,
you took me in and looked after me like a mother hen.
So now it's my turn to look after you, and no arguments.
It's Sunday morning, and I've found enough in the fridge
for breakfast. I've got milk and orange juice, bread and
butter and cheese. Oh, and some ham. That do you?'

Piers clicked off his phone. 'I've nothing on for today.
I was going to take a prospective client out for lunch, but
I've postponed it.' He took a good look at Bea and stilled.
'I'll paint you like that. Showing your age, showing your
integrity.' He flexed his fingers.

Bea was by turns annoyed, touched and amused. 'I
haven't any time to sit for you now, Piers. Even if you
meant it, which I doubt.'

Piers was off his stool, fiddling with his smartphone.
'I'll take some preliminary shots…just stand still for a
moment…there! And now move around, turn around,

to the left…and now to the right! Got it. I'll paint you as
the three ages of woman: the girl I met first, the woman
you became and the crone that you will become. Perhaps
with a door between, coming and going… I'll make a
start after breakfast.'

Bea didn't know whether to laugh or to hit him.

Anna was wiping down the surfaces, putting food out.
And, yes, Anna was actually laughing. 'I think you look
fantastic, Bea. You look real.'

Bea managed a smile. 'You mean that I look my age?
Well, so I do. I have more important things to think about
for the moment than how I look. What is the latest on
Leon?'

Hari picked that one up. 'Anna rang again just now;
they said it looked as if he were slowly coming out of
his coma.'

Bea felt a flood of gratitude. Praise be, Leon was going
to live! She accepted a glass of orange juice. 'Do we know
if Zoe managed to stop the papers printing that awful
story about him?'

Piers said, 'I've been in touch with her. She sounded
pleased with herself, and I suppose she should be. She
says there isn't a sniff of trouble in the newspapers or on
Facebook this morning. I told her you'd recovered some
of Leon's belongings but that he'll need her to get him
something to wear. She said she'll meet you at the hospital when she's picked some things up from his hotel.'

Hari indicated a large plastic bag on the floor. 'Bea,
I've got your purse and phone here. What do you want
done with them?'

'Can't think. It would be easiest to hand them over
to the police and tell them what happened to us at the
Paynes' the other night. They have the facilities for tak-

ing fingerprints off the cards, and they can demand that the Paynes give them their fingerprints, too, which would help to substantiate our story that we were drugged and robbed. But then they'll ask why the Paynes should do such a thing, and I'd have to say that I really don't know. And the Paynes would bring out their story about Leon trying to molest an under-aged girl, and offer his DNA by way of evidence. I worry that if I go to the police, the moment the Paynes say "under-aged" sex, the police will focus on that to the exclusion of all else.'

Hari helped himself to bread, butter and cheese. 'I put on some gloves and had a look at your bits and pieces. Everything has been well handled. If you would like to spend a few quid, I know who could get us the finger-prints. We must already have a few of the family Payne's prints on various items. Your shoes, for instance, will have been handled not only by the boy, but also by who-ever took them off you. Also the box everything came in.'

'That would be Lady Payne and her grandson, if that is what he is—name of Rollo.' Bea had a second glass of orange juice. She wasn't sure she could tackle solid food.

'Your house keys, too. I wonder how many sets of fin-gerprints are on them?'

'You mean they should have the fingerprints from whichever of the young men tried to break into the house last night and then set it alight?' She tried a small piece of bread and butter. That went down all right, so she took some cheese as well.

'Your makeup bag won't have taken any prints, not that soft silk, but the makeup inside has been handled. I assume you don't usually leave your lipstick lid off? No, I didn't think you did. The lipstick's smeared all over the inside of the bag. So someone else has handled

it since you last used it. And if they've used your compact, there'll be a perfect set of prints there. I'll need to
take your prints for comparison, right?'

Bea helped herself to milk. 'It'll be the Admiral's
granddaughter, by name of Venetia. I'm trying to get
the generations straight. The Admiral and Lady Payne
are the oldest and they occupy the master bedroom and
en suite on the first floor. I don't know his first name,
but she's Edith, and she has a sister who lives in the basement, name unknown. Then there are two other bedrooms on the first floor which show evidence of people
staying there, though they were not occupied on the night
of the party. A man and a woman. Members of the family
whose main property is elsewhere, but who use the house
when they need to stay in London, perhaps?

'At the very top of the house there's evidence of a
number of young people staying. I saw two young men,
probably in their twenties, at the party. They were not
in a group of their own kind, but they were in charge of
the Muzak, and I think it's a fair assumption that they
are part of the family and that they also took part in the
honey-trap. And then there's the granddaughter, Venetia, who was definitely involved. It was she who helped
set the trap for Leon, and it was she who borrowed my
watch. In turn, I borrowed her kimono and flip-flops to
help me get away. And lastly, there's the young lad, Rollo,
who retrieved my property for me.'

Should she try a ham sandwich next? 'I think, though
I can't be sure, that it may have been Rollo who attacked
the ivy and brought down the wall. Right size and shape.
Much younger than the others. Nervous. A bit of a stam-
mer.'

Anna said, 'No, Winston!' And lifted him off the table.

The men had both built themselves ham sandwiches. Piers said, 'So how many of the family do you think are involved in the plot to destroy you and Leon?'

'I really don't know,' said Bea. 'I suspect that the original idea to discredit Leon was thought up by the Admiral and his lady, and the only reason I can think of for them to do this is that in some way they believed they might gain financially by ruining the deal Leon had set up. Then they brought in the granddaughter, Venetia, to bait the honey-trap and the two young men to set the stage and take some photographs. So far so good.

'But, after drink had been taken and Leon and I were put out of action, I think the youngsters took the bit between their teeth and ran with it. Why else bother to torch my house? Did they do it out of sheer devilment? And why steal my purse and watch, and use my makeup? Just because they could? Do they think they bear charmed lives, that they can be as destructive as they like and get away with it?'

Anna said, 'I've met the attitude before in public-school kids. They think they are the elite, and therefore untouchable.'

Hari drained the second bottle of milk, which reminded Bea that she must stop the milk and the newspapers being delivered to an empty house…and Carrie! She must get hold of Carrie and tell her the agency must be closed down for a while. Only, how could she ring Carrie when Sophy's phone was dead, and Hari would need hers to trace fingerprints? She straightened her spine. There must be a way…

Hari said, 'So, I'm to send all this stuff to the lab to get the fingerprints?'

'Right,' said Bea. 'But, even if we're lucky enough to

get their fingerprints off my bits and pieces, we keep the information to ourselves. We don't tell the police, but we do tell the Paynes to prevent them repeating that story about Leon and an under-age girl.'

Piers said, 'The police may visit you, in a follow-up to your appearance in Casualty.'

Bea nodded. 'They may. I think Leon will be safer if we avoid making a complaint about stolen goods for the time being. As for our landing up at the hospital, unless we file a complaint, surely they'll write that off as a prank that went wrong at a party? True, they breathalysed me and took blood samples from Leon, but they'll take ages to get the results and in the meantime we can work out how to checkmate the Paynes.'

'And the arson? The fire brigade are going to pass a note about this on to the police. They have to.'

Bea thought about that. 'You have the can. Any prints on it?'

'The lab could find out. We have the photo I took of it nestling in the wheelie-bin at the Paynes' with Saturday's papers, but I suppose the Paynes could say that anyone might have dumped it there. So, do we give the police the can?'

'If asked, we do. And let them follow it up. If not, we hold on to it for the time being.'

Anna said, 'It's Sunday morning. Surely we have at least twenty-four hours' grace to think how to handle this? What about your credit cards? Do you want me to find out if they were used when you were hospitalized?'

Bea said, 'Without knowing my PIN numbers, they wouldn't have been able to use them. Not like my phone. I'd better see what damage has been done there. Can I borrow yours to check?'

She walked away from them into her living room. It stank of fire and there was a fine dust over everything, but a good clean would soon put it right again. 'Hello, is that…yes. I lost my phone last night and only recovered it some hours later. I'd like to check if it was used while it was out of my possession…' While she waited for the information, she drew back the curtain over the back window. The grille was still in place. The glass was cracked.

She could hear the others talking in the kitchen. How good of them to come to her assistance! A voice croaked in her ear. She listened. Oh well. It was no more than she'd expected.

She shut off the phone and went back to the kitchen. 'A couple of hundred pounds' worth was charged to my phone overnight; calls to Australia. Which means I can't use my phone because it must go to be fingerprinted.'

Hari said, 'We've got Leon's cards and phone, too. What do we do about them?'

'Let Zoe cope with those.' Bea rubbed her forehead. 'I despair. They're such amateurs. Oh, not all of them. The Admiral and his wife are…nasty. The trap they set for Leon was cleverly worked out, and if it hadn't been for that extra light fusing, I dread to think what might have happened. But one of them informed the media that Leon had been arrested for under-aged rape *before* it could possibly have happened. I wonder which of them made that mistake. The Admiral or his wife?

'Then the youngsters decided to take a hand in the game without thinking things through. Firing my house… that was probably done in the heat of the moment when they were high on drink, and thought it hilarious to throw a can of paraffin around and light it. Then someone, presumably Venetia, coolly makes use of my makeup. Ac-

cording to Rollo, it was Venetia who went off with my
watch on her wrist, too. And then, save the mark, they
all go off clubbing! Do they think they won't be called
to account for it?'

She answered her own question. 'They think they've
got enough on Leon to neutralize him. If he lives, they'll
be holding the DNA from his scratched cheek over him.
If he dies, he's out of the picture. And what with this and
that, they think they've knocked me out as well.'

Piers was stroking Winston, who was twisting his
head round to see if by any chance someone had left
a tasty morsel on his or her plate. Piers said, 'If you're
moving out, what happens to Winston?'

'I leave him here for the moment, with some more
food. The insurance people won't be round till tomorrow.
By that time I should have found somewhere else to live.'

Anna said, 'Bring him. Move in with me.'

Bea shook her head. 'Let me see if I can work something out first. Winston's best left in his own territory.
Everyone around here knows him, and he knows where
to go for extra food. My big problem is that I have to contact Carrie to tell her what's happened, but I've no landline and my brain has seized up and I can't remember her
phone number or even where she lives! Shock, I suppose.'

She slapped her forehead. 'Ah, I've just remembered. I
keep an old-fashioned address book in the top right-hand
drawer of my desk. If it's not been burned to a crisp, we
ought to be able to use that. Also, my old smartphone.
And, a sliver of light on the horizon, I've just remembered
that Carrie backs up to the Cloud last thing at night, so
even if our computers are out of action, we can retrieve
the data for the agency in due course.'

EIGHT

THERE WAS ONE more thing Bea had to do before abandoning the house. She steeled herself. This was not going to be pleasant. She took the stairs to the basement, treading with care, not touching the walls on either side. The stink was worse here, of course.

The main office was always dimly lit because the windows on the roadside looked on to a well, from where steps led up to the pavement. That part of the main office nearest the road seemed almost untouched. Carrie's jacket hung on the row of hooks by the stationery cupboard. There was a gritty feeling to the air and a layer of dirt and foam had settled on everything in sight. The floor…! She should have put some boots on. Her shoes were going to be ruined.

She set her teeth and stepped into the carpet, which went 'splodge, splodge'. The carpet was ruined. The flames hadn't reached far into this main office but a film of watery foam covered everything in sight. The desks were all there, the chairs, and the computers… also the telephones, and the metal filing cabinets which they still used for important documents. The cabinets would be fireproof, probably. Her staff left various keepsakes—mementoes of holidays, group photographs of leaving parties, the occasional stuffed toy—on a long shelf down one wall. All ruined by water. Someone had placed a pot of trailing ivy on her desk; the leaves were shrivelled, blackened. The pot plant was the property of a woman who had worked for Bea for five—or was it six—years? Married with a sick husband and a no-good daughter who sponged off her.

On the next desk over were some family photos. The girl who sat there was saving for her wedding. Next to her was a single mother whose child had learning difficulties. Her cardigan, dripping wet, hung over the back of her chair. Opposite was a woman in her fifties who had never married and who never would, but who saved every penny to go on a cruise once a year.

Bea took it all in; the schedules, the calendars on the walls, the private possessions, the odd pair of slippers: evidence of a dozen lives. Lives which were going to be changed for the worst when Bea abandoned the agency.

Desolation.

Bea walked through the disaster area, noting that the door to the small office which they used for interviews was firmly shut. She didn't bother to look inside, but went on to the doorway into her own office. Light came through here in plenty because the door between the two offices had disintegrated and what was left of it was hanging off its hinges. Everything inside her office had been reduced to a charred caricature of itself: desk and swivel chair; settee and upright chairs, visitors for the use of.

Remnants of the curtains drooped on either side of the vanished French windows, stirring now and then in the breeze. It was going to be another hot day. The grille—though charred—was still firmly locked in place. Hurrah for the grille.

Bea forced herself to approach her desk. Black as coal. Her computer had imploded. How extraordinary!

She had heard somewhere that stacks of paper don't burn easily because, where there's no air, there's nothing for the flames to feed on. The front of her right-hand drawer was charred but still complete. Her desk was not new: it had been Hamilton's, and before that had belonged to the senior of his two aunts, who had founded the agency way back in the old days. The desk had been built of oak, and had withstood the ravages of the fire better than the lightweight modern ones in the main office.

Bea prised the drawer open with a charred letter opener—she was going to have to wash again in a minute, wasn't she?—and rescued her office diary and address book. Also her old mobile phone and charger, hurray! And the office cash box.

All stank of the fire, but were still usable.

A swish of water. Hari and Anna, standing in the doorway, watching her. Hari was taking photographs of everything.

'Well?' Anna looked pale. 'Not a pretty sight. Are you ready to abandon ship?'

'I have to tell Carrie what's happened, and visit the hospital.'

'Yes, of course,' said Hari. 'But, after that?'

She shook her head. 'I just don't know.'

Sunday 10 a.m.

HOSPITALS ARE USUALLY quiet places on a Sunday morning. Bea enquired where Leon might be and was told that the Sleeping Beauty had been moved into the day room. She found him there, dressed in a hospital gown and reading a newspaper.

He was unshaven, but washed and clean and looked

completely in control of himself. Beside him was a black plastic bag, presumably containing his ruined clothes, some paperwork and, with a bit of luck, Sophie's black jacket, the borrowed kimono and flip-flops.

Bea felt herself grow weak at the knees in relief. She let herself down on to a chair next to him.

He didn't take his eyes off his paper.

'Morning,' she said, wanting to kiss him but feeling that for some reason he would not welcome an embrace. 'How are you?'

'I'm waiting for one of my fiancées to arrive with some clothes. And then I can leave.'

'Oh.' She relaxed, smiling. The hospital must have been receiving enquiries about Leon from three different fiancées—possibly four, if the reporters had been trying to find him—of whom she was only one. She said, 'Fiancée number one would be Anna, saying she was engaged to you so that she could get news of how you were doing. Fiancée number two must be Zoe, who I believe is bringing you some clothes. Fiancée number three must be me. If there's any more, they'll be reporters trying to find you.'

He made no reply, but turned over a page in the paper.

What was up with him?

He said, 'Fiancée number three left me to go off with an old friend. Or so I'm told.'

'Oh, you mean Piers? Yes, well, he came to collect me from the ward and—?'

'At the party. You abandoned me. You went off with an old friend, arms around one another.'

'What! No, but…' Talk about jumping to conclusions! The idiot! She suddenly realized that he was not at all calm. He was in control of himself, just. But he was a volcano, waiting to erupt. If he blew his top now, the hospital would explode into a million pieces. He was so angry, if you lit the touch paper you wouldn't just have to retire, you'd have to run for your life.

He said, 'Please don't bother to wait.' Ice cold.

Hot words rose in her head. She tamped them down. What good would it do to explode with hurt rage? Clearly, he didn't know what had happened.

The Sleeping Beauty had been woken by the kiss of a prince into a world different from the one she had known when she'd been growing up. Leon had slept through everything that had happened since he was drugged on Friday evening.

That in itself must be a source of embarrassment. No, of humiliation. He was a proud man, accustomed to being in charge of his life.

He turned over a page. To the adverts, which he was *not* reading. He was using the paper as a prop to hide behind. He shot her a disapproving glance. 'You don't look your usual self. Had an active night, did you?'

She wanted to laugh. Was he, could he really be jealous? She'd very much like to slap him from here to eternity, storm out and let him sink or swim...but, she wouldn't. No. 'I don't look my best, do I? Would you like the good news first, or the bad?'

'Not interested. I'm missing my shoes, my phone, my keys and my wallet. The nurse said I didn't bring any in with me, so I assume you took them last night for safekeeping. If you'll let me have them, there'll be no need for you to keep me company.'

She handed over the phone, keys and wallet. 'I should warn you: I've had to put a stop on *my* phone as it has

been used for calls to Australia without my permission.
You'd better ask Zoe to check on yours.'

He actually turned his head to look at her. 'Someone's
been using your phone? Who?'

She shook her head. 'Without proof, I'm not saying
anything. But I do suggest you get Zoe to check yours
as well.'

'They can't tamper with my phone. It's extra secure.
And my cards? I don't leave my PIN number carelessly
hanging around, even if you do.' He looked her over, from
head to toe. 'You aren't wearing your engagement ring.'

'I swapped it for...' She wanted to say she'd swapped
it for his life, but that sounded too pretentious. Even if it
were true. 'I swapped it for an ambulance.'

The muscles around his mouth indicated that he
wanted to laugh. *She'd swapped it for an ambulance?*
The stiffness began to leach out of his face. 'And thereby
hangs a tale...?'

'Yes.' She started to cry. How stupid! Why now? After
all that had happened, after all the dreadful hours of
anxiety, and the loss of her home...why now? Hadn't she
cried enough these last few days? She sought for a hankie and found a tissue.

Heels tap-tapped down the corridor. Zoe, bearing
shopping bags and a briefcase. Of course, many shops
were open on a Sunday and Zoe no doubt had access to
a platinum credit card for business purposes. Zoe did not
look pleased to see Bea, but what was new? It was her
normal expression. Bea hadn't seen the woman smile yet.

Zoe said, 'Good morning,' just as if she were accustomed to retrieving her boss from hospital every day.

Leon said, 'I suppose you're fiancée number two. Shall
we adjourn to a less draughty venue?'

THERE WAS A pleasant coffee shop at the main entrance to the hospital, and once Leon had changed into the clothes Zoe had brought him, the three of them gathered there. Leon wore a fine blue shirt, jeans and trainers. Zoe had also brought him a new smartphone. Good for Zoe. She said his cards didn't seem to have been used, nor his phone tampered with, but she'd brought him a new phone just in case.

In spite of the fact that this was a Sunday and therefore theoretically her day off, Zoe was in black-and-white business gear.

Bea felt she looked dowdy beside the two of them, and she knew she stank of fire.

'Now,' said Leon, taking charge. 'Will someone kindly tell me how I have ended up in hospital?'

Bea said, 'What do you remember?'

He frowned. 'We walked round to the Admiral's place. The Admiral handed me over to his granddaughter, who wanted to show me the indoor gym they'd set up in their basement, because she thought I might like something similar next door. Her cousins joined us. Two lively lads. They wanted to show off their equipment. They were quite amusing but after a while I said I mustn't neglect you. They said, didn't I know that you'd gone off with an old friend for some nookie? Then things became hazy. Nightmarish.

'I had an overwhelming urge to lie back down and sleep but I could smell gin, of all things. I hate gin. It makes me feel sick. I wanted to get away from the gin. I think I remember crawling up some steps, a lot of noise. Some woman asked me if I were ill and she helped me out through the side of the tent into the open air. I crawled into a hole somewhere…and that's it.'

Bea realized he must have been in one of the closed rooms off the corridor in the basement. So near to where she'd been! While she'd gone up the stairs to search for him, he'd crawled out into the party and fallen asleep in his own garden.

'Amateurs,' said Bea. 'They shouldn't have left you unguarded, not even for a minute.'

'But why?'

Bea told him why. 'It was a plan to discredit you. Zoe, tell him about the phone calls you had.'

Zoe was as precise as ever in her report, concluding, 'But of course no one would have believed it of you.'

Liar. People like to think the worst of anyone who has made a success of his life in terms of money or fame.

Leon looked anxious. 'What happened in the market place?'

Zoe said, 'Nothing, so far. The tale we concocted to explain your disappearance from the scene seems to have worked. Nobody who's got food poisoning would be thinking about having sex. So far that line of defence has held. But one of your directors has got hold of the story, I don't know how, and although I've tried to reassure him, you know what it's like, he'll pass the word on—'

'I'll need to speak to him. We need to make copies of the hospital notes which should confirm my story—'

'Ah-ha,' said Bea. 'Is the snake in the grass at work so soon? Where did this man get the rumour from? Is he the person who put the Admiral up to destroying you? Someone you know? Someone working behind the scenes, against you?'

Again Leon said, 'But *why?*'

'Perhaps he himself has been got at by someone? Is

there anyone who stands to gain more by upsetting the deal, than by letting it go through? The under-bidder for the Far Eastern contract, perhaps? If you ask around, I'm sure you'll find out.'

Leon rubbed his chin. 'One of the directors did want the contract to go to a different bidder, but to set up such a complex situation... I'm not sure that he'd be up for this.'

'He doesn't have to be,' said Bea. 'If someone with money says, "Who will rid me of this troublesome priest?" Or, in this case, "Who will wipe out my business rival?", there will always be someone to do his bidding. There may be three or even four people between the original money-bags and the actual doer of dirty deeds.'

Zoe didn't want to be left out. 'But would that person want to involve someone like the Admiral? That seems rather far-fetched to me.'

'Well,' said Bea, 'we saw for ourselves that Admiral Payne's house could do with some money being spent on it; and the wine—if you can dignify it by that term—that he served at the party was, to say the least of it, inferior. It shouldn't be too hard to find out if he's strapped for cash. And there's all those members of his family living there...! It may well be common knowledge in his circles that he's in trouble financially and the news has reached someone who has an urgent reason for discrediting you. The problem is, how can we prove it?'

Leon thought about that. 'I suppose I could start at the top and work down. Something's bothering me. Bea. What was that about your swapping your ring for an ambulance?'

Bea took his hand and put it to her cheek. 'I'd do it again.' She explained how she'd managed to get them away from the Paynes' house with the help of their waiting staff. 'I hope Sophy will bring the ring back some time. I said I'd give her five hundred pounds if she did so, but the ring is worth more than that, so maybe she won't.'

'So,' he said, with the glimmer of a smile, 'you didn't go off with Piers?'

'As if! Well, in a way, yes. I needed someone local whose phone number I knew by heart. I got hold of Piers, and asked him to contact Zoe…and then he got hold of Anna and Hari for me, and we all spent the night together. In different rooms, but—' another deep breath—'there's more bad news. My house is currently uninhabitable. Someone torched it. The firemen put the flames out but the electricity and the gas are off, and there's considerable damage, particularly in the basement. It's going to take a lot of sorting out.'

'*What?*'

Bea grimaced. 'Yes, the agency will have to close until I can find alternative premises. My office manageress had hysterics when I rang to tell her what had happened. It rather surprised me that she'd go to pieces like that. She went into weepy-waily mode. Not helpful. I had hoped she get on to some estate agents and find us an empty office that we might move into within the week, say, but I'm not sure she's going to be much help.'

'I see,' said Leon. 'Of course, you'll need some kind of rental agreement. Winston will be pleased, won't he?'

Zoe looked worried. 'You want me to find another house for Mrs Abbot to rent?'

'No, of course not,' said Leon. 'She'll move across our two back gardens and into my new house. The agency closes for a couple of weeks, say, then reopens there.'

Bea had half hoped he'd offer, but now that he had done so, she was uneasy. She acknowledged that the suggestion was reasonable, but somehow it didn't feel right. She said, 'That's a very generous offer, but I'm not sure that I... You see, there's one small snag. I don't think the police will let me use your house yet. They haven't finished digging up your garden. The tent's still there.'

Zoe shook her head. 'If they've discovered human bones, then the house itself will be treated as a crime scene. They'll have to have the floorboards up, and the drains, too.'

'A fat lot of good that will do them.' Leon was getting back to his usual decisive self. 'The builders have had to take everything back to the brickwork, rip out all the old plumbing and electrics. The floorboards have all been replaced. There's nothing original left for them to investigate. Zoe, get the architect and the project manager to explain it to the police so that Bea can move in when she wishes to do so.'

Bea said, 'No, I... What I really need is to borrow Hari for a bit. You see—'

Zoe's phone vibrated. She answered it, listened for a moment, switched her eyes to Leon, and said, 'I think you should take this.'

'Yes?' Leon stood up, resuming his persona as Captain of Industry. He started to pace up and down, listening, and then talking.

Zoe gathered herself together. 'He'll be wanting to take the next flight out.'

Oh. Really? Bea didn't like the sound of that. She tried not to show it, but she was unnerved by the idea that he could leave her while her house and business were in trouble. She swallowed something in her throat. Tried to joke. 'Doesn't he have a private plane yet?'

'He considers that an unnecessary expense.'

'Tokyo?'

'Zurich.' Zoe produced her own phone. 'I'll have his car round in half an hour. He keeps a bag already packed in his car for just such emergencies, and I have his passport with me.' She spoke into the phone, short and to the point. And cut off the call.

'Will you go with him?' Bea knew, a second after the words had left her mouth, that she ought not to have asked that question, for Zoe treated her to a look of contempt.

'If he needs me.'

'You have a young child?'

Yes, Zoe *had* resented that question. 'Boarding school. Any more intimate questions, Mrs Abbot?'

Bea tried the soft reply. 'I was a working single mother myself. It's not an easy life.'

'I am a widow. My husband died. I understand you were divorced.' Zoe's tone was one of distaste. And yes, she'd meant the comment as a put-down.

Bea thought of slapping Zoe, hard. But instead made a joke. 'Divorced, beheaded, died. Divorced, beheaded, survived. That's the memory verse for Henry the Eight's six wives. I never got beyond two husbands: one divorced and one died.'

'Oh, really?' Zoe was not going to allow herself to see the joke, was she? She was not an easy person to like but, Bea had to admit, she was efficient.

Leon came off one call long enough to say he needed to be in Zurich that evening, and would Zoe arrange… and then he was off on another call.

Bea tried to relax. She told herself she was redundant in this situation. Not wanted on board. Leon was going to fly off into the blue and confer with Heads of Industry in far-flung corners of the world, while Bea Abbot was relegated to a footnote in his life, to be wined and dined and possibly wedded when he had time to come back for her.

She felt bruised. No, wounded.

In need of hospital treatment? Well, no. Of course not.

She stiffened her shoulders. She would manage. She'd managed her life perfectly well without him all these years, and if she was now facing an unprecedented set of problems, well, she'd survive.

Zoe was on her phone. Again. She held up her hand to attract Leon's attention. 'Your car's outside.'

Leon continued with his phone call but laid hold of Bea's wrist and urged her to her feet, still talking. 'Yes, yes. We can discuss that when...'

Bea grabbed the bag of discarded clothing and his hospital notes while allowing herself to be towed to the exit. Zoe followed, also on her phone.

Leon's chauffeur-driven car was indeed outside in the car park, and drove up to collect them as they stepped into the open air. Bea wondered if Leon really meant to take her with him to the airport. He pushed her into the car ahead of him, took a seat and made room for Zoe to sit beside them. Still talking on his phone.

Bea didn't know whether to be amused or outraged. Was she being kidnapped? Did he really think she'd be prepared to fly off with him at a moment's notice, leaving her business and house in pieces, to hang around in a foreign city while he went to this meeting and that? She was no bimbo whose sole function in life was to soothe his fevered brow and provide him with exercise in the bedroom.

Besides which, she was not one to run away from a problem.

He clicked off his phone. Zoe had another call ready for him to take, but he waved her aside and turned to Bea. 'Zoe will bring you out a rental agreement for the house at a peppercorn rent. She'll put you in touch with the project manager and he'll ease your way in. You can come out to join me in a few days' time, when you've sorted out the insurance. Take this, my platinum card. PIN number: Winston Churchill's birthday. Get some cash on your way home. Get yourself a new phone, one with fingerprint access for security. I'll switch to a new phone, just in case the old one's been tampered with. Unlikely, but possible. I'll let you have the number. I'll drop you at the next tube station. I may be back this evening, or I may have to go on to Berlin. Whatever happens, I'll ring you tonight. All right?'

She wanted to say that she was perfectly capable of running her own life, thank you, but she didn't want to quarrel with him. Not then, anyway. She said, 'Throwing money at a problem doesn't always solve it.'

'Acknowledged. But it oils the wheels. This is a good opportunity for you to take a break. I'll buy you a ruby for an engagement ring, shall I?'

Rubies were not high on Bea's Must-Have list. She said, 'No, no.' She quoted, '"Diamonds are a girl's best friend",' and hoped he was listening.

While he took yet another phone call, she started to make a list. What was first on the agenda? A new phone. Some cash. And then, she had to decide what to do. If she decided not to abandon the agency to follow him abroad… No, ridiculous. Closing the agency was the only sensible thing to do.

On the other hand, she could well imagine the dismay her staff would be feeling if she had to close, even temporarily. They needed their jobs. Would her insurance cover their wages if she had to close for a couple of weeks? Even if it did, one or two of them would undoubtedly drift away. They couldn't afford to be unemployed. But if she stayed…what could she do?

Would Hari agree to help, because if so…? She would ring him as soon as she got hold of another phone. And some cash. And…she began to compose a list of phone calls to make.

Sunday lunch

ANNA OPENED THE door to Bea, saying, 'I'm just dishing up. We won't talk business till we've eaten, right?'

Bea said, 'I can't remember when I last ate a meal I hadn't cooked myself. I don't count takeaways.'

Anna said, 'A treat for us both. Peppered steak, a jacket potato and green salad, to be followed by Wensleydale cheese and biscuits. You haven't been here for a while, have you? So you may admire the improvements Hari has been making to the kitchen and bathroom while I dish up. I thought we'd eat by the French windows overlooking the garden, if it isn't too draughty for you.'

'Delightful,' said Bea, meaning it.

They ate. And it was good.

'And now we've done the polite bit,' said Anna, clearing away, 'we can get down to business. Coffee? Black?'

'Please.' Bea relaxed, closing her eyes while Anna bustled about her housewifely duties. Bea thought she'd always remember this respite. Time out, eating a good meal with a friend, overlooking a small but pretty garden. So peaceful. Perhaps one day Bea would have a pretty garden again. Without a mature tree in it. The sycamore had shielded her from the sun, which was fine in summer but had made the garden feel damp in cold weather. Perhaps she'd get a designer in, to show her what she could have in future?

When Anna placed the coffee before her, Bea said, 'This has been a lesson to me. I thought I was the strong one, who propped everyone else up when they were in trouble. I thought I could manage anything life threw at me. I was wrong! To my amazement, I find myself accepting help from all sorts of people.'

Anna smiled. 'It's payback time for your having been so good to me when I was in trouble. This morning I thought you were on the verge of giving up, perhaps of retiring and letting Leon take over—?'

'When he might find a moment to spare for me? Yes, I did think of giving up until I went down into the agency rooms and saw Carrie's jacket, and the pot plant another of my girls had brought in. Not that plants ever thrive down there. It started me thinking that if I gave up I'd put my staff out of work, too. I couldn't do that. Then I began to work out how I might keep the agency going—'

'Without moving it into Leon's house?'

Bea tried to look innocent. 'I didn't think Winston would approve.'

Anna laughed. 'I expect he would have made the best of it. Maybe I'll get a cat one day, when I retire. But not yet.'

'It wasn't my idea to have a cat, not at all. Winston adopted me, not I him. Perhaps it was the thought of what might have happened to him in the fire which got me so angry and made me want to fight back.'

'If you were a normal person with a due care for the preservation of your skin, I suppose you might go to a

hotel and let the police and the insurance people sort
things out, but—'

'The insurances! The hassle! The forms! The waiting
in for people to call, who don't come when they should!
Then getting three or more estimates for repair, and arguing with builders and electricians and…let us groan!'

Anna groaned in sympathy. 'I know. More coffee?
No? So, are you ready to resume battle?'

Bea stretched. 'You know me so well. Yes, I'm ready.'

'Hari said not to let you back till two o'clock and it's
about that now. So, shall we make a move?'

NINE

Sunday afternoon

As BEA AND Anna approached the house, they spotted two men carrying a large carton up the steps.

Bea quickened her pace. 'Is the new furniture being delivered already?' She ran up the steps and into the hall. The splintered wood of the door had been replaced, and new locks fitted. A repaint job was needed, but that could wait. There was a light film of dirt over everything in the hall. There was so much gunk in the air, the house would need cleaning every day for weeks.

Hari bobbed up from nowhere, shutting off his smartphone. 'Mrs A, you're back earlier than I expected. I know I said two o'clock, but I did hope to be further on before this. The insurance people took their time—'

'You managed to get the insurance people to come out on a Sunday morning?'

'By charm, and the threat of your having to close the business if they didn't visit today. I pointed out that if they didn't, it would cost them megabucks because you wouldn't be able to keep the business open, and they'd have to pay for lay-offs, et cetera. So they managed to send someone straight away. I recorded his findings as I took him around and I'll play it to you later.' Hari swivelled to one side to let a man holding a pane of glass pass by him through to the kitchen.

Then, 'Mind your back, missus!' An office chair swung past Bea into what had once been her living room but which, stripped of all her furniture and pictures, was so no longer.

She'd asked for it to happen. Nevertheless it was a shock. Only the mahogany dining table, out of all the original furniture, remained in place by the front window. She'd asked Hari to have the rest of her sitting-room furniture taken up to her bedroom for storage. She could only hope they'd left her a pathway to her bed.

She told herself to concentrate. How was she to create a workable office out of the chaos in front of her? It was a big room but it looked as if a bomb had hit it. Large men were attacking cardboard boxes, ripping up and folding cartons, piling up office units, chairs, computer systems…and a couple of large fire extinguishers.

Bea told herself she was delighted to see the fire extinguishers.

'Oh, Mrs Abbot!' Carrie, her office manageress. In tears. Carrie was wearing a yolk-yellow sleeveless top. She looked like a headless chicken, and squawked like one, too. 'What a terrible thing! I can't get over it! The shock!'

'Yes, indeed,' said Bea, who was still reeling from the shock herself. 'I'm so glad you could come in to help, Carrie.'

'It's all too much! I know you said I should ring round and tell the girls we'll be open as usual tomorrow, but I can't see how that can possibly happen, so I told them not to come in as the agency would have to close till further notice.'

'What!'

Someone appeared in the doorway to wave at her. 'Hi,

Bea! I'm upstairs if you need me!' And vanished. Piers?
Her ex-husband? Bea wondered what he was doing, and
then forgot about him.

'Now, Carrie, I don't think—'

'I said to them, we're all going to have to start looking for other jobs—'

'Carrie! Stop!'

Carrie wasn't listening. Her colour was high—too
high? She flapped her hands around. 'That man! Harry
whatever-his-name-is, ordered me…*ordered me!*…to go
into the girls' desks to retrieve their personal belongings!
I said to him, "How dare you!" and he said men were
coming to take them away, and I said to him, "Over my
dead body!" as if he had the right to…'

Bea met Anna's eyes. *Hysteria?*

Anna nodded. *Looks like.*

'There, there!' A youngish dark-haired woman, heavily pregnant, appeared from nowhere. She put her arm
round Carrie and bore her away to the kitchen, saying
over her shoulder, 'Hi, there, Bea! Everything's coming
on a treat, isn't it?'

Bea's mind reeled. What on earth was Leon's niece,
Dilys, doing here? She was supposed to be at home nurs-
ing her bump and cooking tasty meals for her IT genius
of a husband, Keith, who…

…rose from behind a mountain of boxes, hair and
beard curlier than ever, to shout out, 'Bea! Good news!
The hub for your Wi-Fi is in the hall so, with a bit of luck,
we can get everything back on line, though I can't say
exactly how long it will take!'

Keith had been one of the first people Bea had called,
once she'd decided to keep the agency working. Keith
was not only able to make IT systems dance to his tune,

but he was a good, dear man who'd made Dilys a very happy—and now very pregnant—wife.

'Mind your back, there!' Another desk arrived and was dumped just inside the doorway. 'Where you want this, eh?'

Bea tried to think. 'By the fireplace for the moment.'

'Coming through…!' Another desk.

'Excuse me, missus!' A large chair pushed Bea back to the wall. However many removal men were on the job?

Hari appeared in the doorway. 'Your old office furniture. Down below. Did I say? The insurance man said once it's been soaked in water and foam, it's no good. "Rip the lot up," he said. "Get in new stuff." I promised the removal men triple time, right? Bung it on the insurance bill. It's less expensive for them than your going out of business. I asked that useless…'

He was clearly going to call Carrie a 'cow' but just prevented himself in time. 'I asked your manageress to rescue any personal possessions and she had a hissy fit. I've got a couple of salvage men arriving in half an hour to start taking the old furniture out by the area stairs. Then we can start on…' He vanished again.

'He appears and disappears just like the Cheshire Cat.' Bea started to laugh, recognized hysteria in her own voice and made herself stop.

Anna said, 'Now, what can I do to help?'

'If I retrieve possessions, would you like to extract a list of the girls' phone numbers from Carrie and send her home in a cab? Then phone the girls to say we'll be open as usual tomorrow.'

Anna said, 'Can do,' and set off in search of Carrie.

Bea said, 'Where are you, Keith? Shall we put four girls round the big table, and have the other desks in a double line down the room? Does that work for you? I know we probably won't get the landlines working again straight away, but in an emergency in the past we've used our mobile phones and we can do so again. What's more, we always back up to the Cloud last thing on Fridays, so all our data is in storage, waiting to be accessed tomorrow. Right?'

'Crack on!' Keith disappeared into his boxes again as a typing chair staggered into the room over a pair of jean-clad legs…followed by a mountain of boxes, ditto. Bea rescued an empty carton from the pile on the floor. She darted into the kitchen to find some rubber gloves and some plastic bags…where she was pleased to see that Anna was already talking on her phone, and that Dilys was soothing a weeping Carrie.

Carrie had gone to pieces, and how! Bea had to admit she'd misjudged the woman. She'd thought her manageress had been aiming to take over the agency one day, an idea Bea hadn't much liked, though she hadn't been able to understand why. Had she felt, subconsciously, that Carrie was a fair-weather friend who would run for cover when stormy weather hit? Bea began to wonder whether or not Carrie might turn up on the morrow.

Bea descended the stairs to the twilight zone in the basement. No lights. Everything blackened by fire and foam. Bea took a deep breath and started to retrieve anything that could possibly be considered personal—or useful—or that belonged to the business.

Clothing first. Carrie's jacket had already been removed. Bea bagged up all the other items her staff had left: the odd mac, cardigan, sweatshirt, umbrella. Everything would need cleaning but should be wearable again.

Then personal items. She allocated a different plastic bag for each desk.

Anna came down the stairs, holding out her phone. 'Betty; wants to know if you'd like her to come in and help?'

Betty was a single-parent mum, quiet of voice and solid of presence. Bea said, 'Bless her. Yes, please!' and went back upstairs for another roll of plastic bags. Carrie was nowhere to be seen: good. Dilys was cleaning the kitchen and feeding Winston: also good.

Bea opened every drawer in every desk, removing anything she thought might be salvable, including the odd mobile phone and charger which had been superseded by the new generation of technological wonders, but which might still be usable under the circumstances. Perhaps she'd have to throw most of it away again later, but for now…*keep busy, keep busy, don't stop to think why…or that Leon has run away…well, not exactly run away, but…*

No, I'm being unreasonable. He had to attend to his own business.

To prove he'd been put out of action, he need only to have faxed the tox reports to the director who had heard the rumour of his misbehaviour. Leon had had no real need to see him in person. Had he?

Now, come on, Bea! He wasn't thinking straight. He'd been drugged, hospitalized, didn't know what was happening.

He ran away.

DON'T THINK ABOUT IT NOW!

It was also best not to think about going upstairs to see what had happened to her lovely, peaceful, sanctuary of a bedroom, because all her sitting-room furniture was now stored there.

She left the stationery cupboard alone. For now. It had always been Winston's refuge in times of trouble. He could claw the door open by himself, shut himself in, and bounce out when he felt better able to cope with the world. The cupboard was made of oak and was untouched by fire, though the doors were slimy with foam. It was firmly anchored to the wall, which meant she couldn't move it. It must have been there for fifty years or more. The carpet had been cut away around it. So…leave it for the time being.

The side office, used mostly for interviews, had suffered almost as much as Bea's own room, but there was nothing personal there, so she left it alone.

Her own office…charred chairs and desk. Ugh. She put her head down and got on with it, trying not to think. How fortunate it was that she had still been using Hamilton's old oak desk, because it had preserved everything inside it pretty well. She tried humming a nice, bright tune to herself. Office chequebook and address book. Both smelly but usable. Would the bank accept a singed cheque? It was all right, surely? Just charred around the edges. Where was her personal chequebook? Ah, in her big handbag in her bedroom, presumably.

Anna came down again, phone in hand. 'Betty's on her way. She says she'll bring in a flask of coffee and some bottled water. I just thought—have you rung your son, Max? If he hears about this from someone else…'

'You're right. I'll do that straight away.'

Anna disappeared.

Bea flexed her neck muscles. This was not going to be easy. She told herself that Max was a good boy, a hard-

working Member of Parliament with a pretty if prickly
wife and two delightful small children. But—and this
was a big 'but'—he always thought he knew best about
everything, and in Bea's opinion he was nearly always
wrong. Max would *not* want to hear that his mother was
in trouble, and he would find excuses *not* to help.

'Max, dear, how are you?… Yes, I'm quite all right, but
I thought you ought to know that there's been a problem
here. An arson attack. The agency rooms are unusable
and we haven't any electricity or gas for the time being.
However, friends are being wonderful and we intend to
keep calm and carry on.'

His response was predictable. 'I'm horrified! What do
the police say? They are on to the job, aren't they? You'll
be covered by insurance, of course…'

'Yes, of course.'

'What a thing! If only I were in London! But you know
we have to be up here in the constituency for a couple
of weeks more before we go off on holiday. If only I'd
known, I needn't have let our flat in London and you
could have moved in there, but I'm sure the insurance
will put you up in a hotel…as for the agency, well, it's
about time you retired, anyway, isn't it? You must keep
me informed. And if there's anything but anything that
I can do to help, you must let me know.'

'Thank you, dear. So kind of you. Yes, I'll keep in
touch.'

She knew that if, even if he'd been in London, and
she'd asked him to come and help shift ruined furniture
and set up new office desks, he'd have found an excuse
not to do so. That was just the way he was.

She dialled another number. Two people whom she
knew *would* help were youngsters she'd taken under her

wing and watched grow up, Maggie to run her own business, and Oliver to university and some sort of research post in a field Bea couldn't even begin to understand. Oliver was out of town at the moment and Maggie was heavily pregnant. They would still want to know what had happened.

Maggie first. She said straight away, 'That's awful. What do you need? Food? Hot water? I've got a couple of thermoses somewhere. I'm on my way!'

'Don't be daft. I forbid you even to think of it!'

'Forbid away, but I'll be over as soon as my dear husband has finished fiddling with something on the car... and if he doesn't get it done in double-quick time, I'll take a taxi, so there! Oh, and do you need anything else, specially? Ring me back if you do. Have you rung Oliver? Because he'll want to help. Last I heard, he was taking a couple of days off in the West Country learning how to surf. Daft creature! What a physicist—or whatever it is that he is—was doing, trying to surf...ridiculous! He'll probably knock himself out with his own board. But he can make it back to London in four hours or less. I'll get on to him straight away.'

Much heartened, Bea returned to her task of salvage. The little radio she kept in her desk was a misshapen lump of plastic. The flat shoes she kept in a bottom drawer were charcoal, as was the rug she kept for the occasional afternoon nap. Her favourite pen... Forget it. In fact, there was nothing else to save. Move on. Never look back.

She stood up, easing her neck and shoulders. If she knew anything about it, the basement was going to be out of action for days, if not weeks. Once the sclodgy film of water and foam on the floor had been drained away, they'd know more, but the carpet would have to go, and the floorboards would probably have to be replaced. The wallpaper was going to have to come off the walls, and maybe the plaster under it would need to be hacked off. Then there'd have to be new electrics, new plumbing…it might be months rather than weeks before the basement was usable again. She wondered if it were the aim of the arsonists to put her out of business?

'Missus, this lot ready to go?' The salvage men; good-tempered. Calm and practical. She nodded. 'Everything goes except for the built-in cupboard, right?'

They didn't try to take the desks out in one piece but wielded a sledgehammer till they'd reduced each one to a stack of planks, which they took out of the area door and up the steps to the pavement in front of the house.

Bea didn't watch, but turned her back on them to blow her nose and look out through the grille on to her wrecked garden. Someone—or perhaps two people?—had made a sort of pathway by the remains of the wall, crashing through and trampling down the branches, to get to the back of the house. The arsonists?

She despised people who gave way to self-pity. Weeping wouldn't do anyone any good. She used her hankie again. She thought that soon, very soon, Leon would ring and she could talk to him, and tell him how awful everything was. She mustn't put pressure on him. No. He had his own troubles to bear. But he would listen and sympathize.

'Mrs A, some good news!' Hari appeared behind her, still smiling, still full of energy. 'The generator has just arrived. I'd like to put it in the garden, if you don't mind, and feed cables up to give you power in the kitchen and your new office to begin with. Later, I'll take another cable up to your bedroom.'

Bea's voice cracked. 'Hari, you're a wonder-worker. How do you do it?'

'With a platinum credit card. Come away, now. I have to wrestle open that grille over the windows. The lock won't budge, so I may have to use brute force. Also, the salvage lads want to take the carpet up, and they're double-parked in the street, causing no end of a traffic jam. I don't suppose the neighbours will like the sound of the generator, either.'

'Oh dear, you're right. I'd better go round and apologize to everyone.' She peeled off her rubber gloves. Her shoes were ruined; there were smudges of dirt everywhere. Probably on her face as well? She hadn't time to change now, but she would wash her hands and face and call on the neighbours. They'd been inconvenienced enough.

She took one more look out of the window and realized that now the tree was down, she could see the spire of the church, even from here. An omen, perhaps?

She left the dim cavern of the basement as the salvage team started to tear up the carpet. 'Have this up in a tick, missus. And you'll be surprised how soon it will all dry out in this weather.'

At the top of the stairs she met Betty, the only member of the staff who'd volunteered to come in, with her twelve-year-old son at her back. They were halfway between 'OhmiGod!' and 'Isn't this a lark?'

'Oh, Mrs Abbot,' Betty cried, 'what a dreadful thing! But, what a miracle, the new office is almost ready to go!' She patted Bea's shoulder. 'Now, you find yourself a chair and put your feet up for a bit, while the lad and I see what we can do to help.'

'Bless you.' Bea managed a smile. Betty was a treasure, indeed.

The manic activity on this floor had slowed down. Keith was setting up new laptops on the dining-room table. Good. There was a double row of desks and chairs down the length of the room, and the pile of cardboard cartons had disappeared. The room did indeed look more like an office now. Anna was seated at the table in the window, talking on her mobile phone. She waved her hand at Bea but didn't seem to need help, hurray!

Dilys, Keith's pregnant wife, appeared from the kitchen, waving a dishcloth. 'Yoohoo! Hari says there'll be power back on in ten minutes, so I'll pop out to get some fresh milk, shall I? Oh, and some more biscuits.'

Bea washed her hands at the kitchen sink. Cold water. It would have to do. All their dishcloths looked grimy, and so did the hand towel. As for her dress…! Well, don't think about it now. She must call on her neighbours and explain.

On her way out of the hall, Hari intercepted her, holding up a bunch of keys. 'New keys for the front door. Two locks, top and bottom. I have more sets of keys which I'll give you later, when I've fixed something up for the back door.'

Bea opened the front door and stood there, drinking in the quiet scene. The removal and salvage lorries had gone. Traffic moved sluggishly along. The sun shone. Neighbours walked dogs. Teenagers congregated. A red bus crossed the end of the road. Sunday afternoon and all was well.

Well, mostly.

She looked down at herself. Smudged with dirt and dishevelled.

Get on with it. She turned to the right, mounted the steps to the front door and pressed the bottom of three bells. Ding dong. The house next door was occupied, as far as she knew, by business people she only ever encountered in passing.

The front door opened. A man in expensive casual dress stood there. Bea seemed to recall that he was something in the City. He was not pleased to see her on his doorstep. He said, 'You're the woman from next door, aren't you? You've got a nerve! Well, all I can say is, I'll see you in court!' He slammed the door in her face.

What!

Why...?

Perhaps he'd been woken from an after-lunch nap? She tried the house on the other side. This time the door was opened by a middle-aged woman who looked as if she'd had several facelifts. She didn't look very friendly, either. 'Oh. It's you. Well, you'd better come in, I suppose.'

A hallway like hers, but painted in dark red with white trim. A through living room like Bea's, but set up for a bridge party with four tables...waiting for guests to arrive?

A man—the woman's husband?—was sitting by the back window in an elderly person's high-backed chair, the sort for which you press a button and you get propelled to your feet. He was almost bald with a liver-spotted skin. A stout stick leaned against the chair. 'Who is it? Who is it?'

'The woman from next door, that's caused all the trouble.' Loudly.

'I came to apologize for the disruption,' said Bea, hoping they'd invite her to sit down. 'Apart from the problem of the wall, we had a fire next door. You must have seen it.'

'Who is it?' said the man. Alzheimer's? Deaf?

'We saw,' said the woman. 'And heard. I understand you set the fire to cover up the earlier damage, right?'

'What?' Bea was shocked. 'No!'

'We're sending the bill to you, right?'

'Who?' said the old man, cupping his hand round his ear.

They were sending the bill to her? For what? Bea wondered if she were going to fall down, or just faint or... perhaps she could just lie down on the floor and rest for a bit... 'Why should you think—?'

'The Admiral told us that's what we have to do. You're not getting away with it. Damages, as well. The shock to my husband's heart.'

'What is it you think I'm getting away with?'

'What?' said the old man.

'Don't pull that innocent face with me. It's your responsibility, and there's no way you can wriggle out of it. All bills to you, right?'

A grinding, coughing noise started up somewhere, drowning speech. The woman shouted, 'Oh, this is too much! Banging and crashing all day, and now...' She rushed to the window overlooking the back garden and slammed the French windows shut. The noise muted, decreasing to a purr...rose to a crunching howl...and back to a purr.

'Tree cutting,' said the old man, hearing that noise perfectly. 'I used to like using a chainsaw in the old days. I was a giant, if I say so myself.'

Bea ventured to look over the woman's shoulder down

into their garden, which was of similar size and shape to her own, though not as well looked after as hers had been. There was an untidy pile of bricks where the wall they'd shared with the Admiral had fallen at the end of their garden, and also where it had brought down part of the wall they shared with Bea.

A large man was in her own garden, attacking the fallen tree with a chainsaw, assisted by a twelve-year-old boy and his mother. All three were kitted out with safety glasses, and helmets.

Hari didn't do anything by halves, did he!

'How good of them,' said Bea. 'That's Zander, my sort-of-adopted daughter's husband. She said they'd be over to help, but I didn't realize they were going to start on the tree today.'

'Well, tell them to stop it!'

It was Bea's turn to say, 'What!'

The woman gesticulated. 'My bridge party. In half an hour I expect to have fifteen of my closest friends here for a charity bridge party, and I cannot have that racket going on. You must stop it, at once!'

The old man said, 'I used to cut up the logs when we had a wood-burning stove in the country at weekends. You remember that, Gayle?'

Gayle leaned towards Bea, until Bea could smell her hairspray. 'You will stop that noise, now, this minute!'

Bea looked steadily back at her. 'I understand that the noise is a nuisance, and I apologize for it. I hope it won't be too distressing for your guests, but I have to take advantage of my friends' help when they can give it. That tree has got to be cut up and removed as soon as possible. My friends and I have been working hard all day so that I can reopen the agency again tomorrow morning. I do realize this has caused you some inconvenience—the noise, the double parking—but if I'd done nothing, if I'd sat back and waited for builders and tree surgeons and the like, the noise and the disruption would have taken place over a much longer time, and put my staff out of work. This way it's going to be all over quickly, and my staff will still have a job to go to tomorrow morning. It won't be perfect, but it will be possible.'

The old man said, 'He's making a good job of it. Taking the logs out through the house, are you? Gayle, can we burn logs here?'

'No, we can't.' She turned back to Bea. 'For the last time, will you shut off that racket?'

Bea shook her head. 'I'm sorry. No, I can't.'

The man had his hands on the catch to the windows. 'Open up, Gayle! I want to go down and help him.'

Gayle turned on Bea. 'Now look what you've done! Let yourself out, will you? And remember what I said. If you don't shut off that racket, I'll put the damages on my bill!'

Bea left. She felt like having a good weep.

A woman was standing on her own doorstep. Forty-ish, slim, business-like. 'You the householder? I'm from *The Gazette*. Can you confirm that there was a fire here last night?'

'The local newspaper? That's quick.' Bea plodded up the steps. 'Yes, there was a fire.'

'Was there much damage? Would it be possible for me to take a picture or two?'

'I suppose so. Look, I'm dying for a cuppa. Why don't you come in and I'll tell you all about it.'

At this moment, big Zander—Maggie's husband—came up the steps from the basement with a load of chopped-up greenery, closely followed by a grinning twelve-year-old boy and his mother, Betty. All three of them were laughing. 'Hi, there, Mrs A!' said Zander. 'We'll stack the logs at the top of the steps here until we can get the truck round to collect it, right?'

'Bless you, all of you,' said Bea, moved almost to tears.

The journalist raised her hand, and flash, flash…pictures were taken.

Zander protested. 'Hang about! What's with the picture-taking?'

A glinting smile from the journalist. 'Your family? Son and grandson, is it?'

'No,' said Bea. 'Oh, this is getting complicated. Thanks, Zander; you're a real hero. And, Betty, I love the hard hats! Come on in, Ms…? And I'll try to explain.'

The woman followed Bea into the hall. There was still grime everywhere. 'Mind your clothes,' said Bea, leading the way to the kitchen. Where was Dilys? Hadn't she offered to make some tea? But a cable had snaked its way into the kitchen through the half-open door—the new door—so perhaps the kettle did work. And, hurray! There were thermos flasks and bottled water and packs of biscuits on the table.

Winston was already pawing at the biscuits. 'Shoo!' said Bea. And he shooed. Temporarily.

Suddenly, Bea realized how thirsty she was. She grabbed one of the bottles of water and glugged it down.

The journalist had only got as far as the sitting-room door. 'I thought your office was in the basement.'

'It was,' said Bea. She'd had enough water and craved tea. 'What did you say your name was?'

'June Jolly. And you are Mrs Abbot, the owner of an

agency which I understand you are running without planning permission?'

Bea gave her a straight look. 'Where did you get that from? Everything is legal. My husband's aunts founded the agency in the last century and the family have run it ever since.'

The woman bared white—very white, too white?—teeth in what was meant to be a smile. 'I understand that the matter is to be brought up in Council—'

Do I detect the fell hand of the Admiral? Could be. But best not to point the finger.

'Not that I'm aware.' Bea sought for and found a couple of fairly clean mugs and ran them under the tap to rinse them out, then switched on the kettle—no, it didn't respond. She popped some tea bags into the mugs and poured hot water from one of the thermoses, wondering whether or not she should take some aspirin for her headache now, or wait till she'd eaten something. It seemed a long time since lunch at Anna's house.

'I'd heard,' said June, 'that you were not doing too well financially, and haven't managed to maintain your property as you should.'

'What on earth do you mean? Oh, the fall of the wall? Well, you can see for yourself why it came down.' She waved her hand to the kitchen door. 'Have a look. It was ivy that brought it down. I don't like ivy, and always cut it back when it encroaches on my garden, as you can see from the remains of my walls. The gardens on either side are full of it. Someone pulled off the ivy from the other side of the wall at the end of my garden. There was a chain reaction which brought the lot down. My mother always used to say that ivy would take over the world, if not kept under control. Take what photos you like.'

She opened the fridge door. The fridge was working again, hurray. One empty milk carton, and two full. Dilys had said she'd get milk, hadn't she? Good for Dilys.

The woman looked. 'What's this tree that they're cutting up?'

'A mature sycamore which grew at the bottom of my garden. It was brought down by the wall falling on it. We have pictures, if you need them, and I suppose the insurance people took some, too. I'll give you the name of the insurance company, if you like. Sugar? A biscuit, if I can find some? I'm afraid we're all at sixes and sevens. Some of my friends have come in to help but we still don't have the power back on properly.'

June gave Bea a hard glance. 'Can you confirm that you had a fire here last night?' Her gaze swept round the room. She ran a finger across the top of the nearest unit and held it up for inspection. 'You must admit there was a fire.'

'Of course.' Bea had found the biscuit tin which was empty. In her experience, workmen could get through half a pack of biscuits each in five minutes or less. She emptied two packs of biscuits into the tin and hid the third at the back of the cupboard. She selected two chocolate digestive biscuits from the tin, placed them together, chocolate side in, and munched. Ah, that was good. She took a gulp of tea. Felt marginally better. The chainsaw started up again in the garden. Zander and Co. were having fun, weren't they?

Where was everyone else? Dilys? Hari and Anna? Was Keith still around?

June said, in a silky voice, 'I understand you have a cash-flow problem?'

'What?' Bea shook her head to clear it. 'I've been saying "What!" all day. I still don't understand why all this is happening. No, we don't have a cash-flow problem. Let me tell you what I know. Yesterday evening, while I was out and the house was empty, someone broke the window below which gives on to what used to be my office in the basement. They must somehow have got into my garden over the remains of the wall, which had fallen down the day before. Having broken the window into my office, they poured an accelerant into the room and set it alight. The firemen broke down the front door to get into the house, and put out the flames. Don't rely on my testimony. Ask them.'

Another hard, assessing stare.

Bea pushed the biscuit tin towards June. 'Help yourself. No, I don't have a cash-flow problem. In fact, we're doing rather well. Where on earth did you get that idea from?'

'We heard your house was up for sale.'

TEN

BEA INADVERTENTLY TOOK a step back. 'What! No! *No!* I cannot believe this. What is going on? Who said my house was up for sale?'

June pursed her lips. 'I'm afraid I'm not at liberty to say. So, you deny that your house is up for sale? You deny that you have a cash-flow problem, you deny that you set a fire for the insurance, and you deny that you are responsible for the destruction of a party wall?'

Bea bit back the urge to scream. 'Yes, I do. Where on earth did you get these wild stories?' It occurred to her that, if the newspaper printed a story accusing her of multiple offences, followed by a simple rebuttal from her *without giving any evidence to back it up*, readers would conclude that she was guilty.

Bea's thoughts flew across two gardens to Admiral Payne's house, wondering whether it were he or she… probably him?…who had been responsible for these allegations. He'd certainly primed her neighbours to accuse her of damaging their walls. But, if she pointed the finger at them without proof, they would retaliate by accusing Leon of child abuse.

She chose her words with care. 'I'm asking you to look at the evidence and to judge for yourself.'

June eyed Bea closely. 'We received an anonymous tip-off from a concerned neighbour.'

Bea shook her head. 'I don't think you'd go to all the

trouble of calling on me if it was just an anonymous tip-off. You must know who your informant was, and have enough respect for him or her to take what they said seriously. You asked me for a comment on your story and I have given you one. Now you have a choice. Go back and write the story you've been fed or look at the facts. But if you print false information, rest assured that I will sue the pants off you. Understood?'

June got to her feet. She went to the open door and would have stepped out on to the iron balcony if Bea hadn't stopped her.

'Don't go out there! The flames went up the side of the house. The staircase will have to be tested before we use it again.'

June looked out over the gardens. A nice sunny day. The happy growl of the chainsaw filled the air, accompanied by the merry shouts of the trio working to clear the tree away.

June said, 'Who are those people? How did you get contractors to work here on a Sunday?'

'They're not contractors. They're friends. Which reminds me! Hold on a mo, and then I'll show you around.' Bea skated back to the main room, which was now the office, and put her head through the door. 'Keith, are you there?'

Keith and Anna had their heads together over a laptop on the big table in the window. 'Yes...?' He held up his hand to hold her attention. 'Mrs A, we've got the data back down from the Cloud but—'

'Bless you, but I've just thought. We've no landlines yet, have we? No, I thought not. We ought to send out an email to all our customers and clients, and to our staff, saying that all telephone calls should go through my mobile phone—perhaps give two phone numbers?—until further notice?'

Anna said, 'Good thinking. Would Carrie come back to help us on this?'

'I have no idea. Possibly not.' Bea handed her own phone over. 'Use mine for a start, and I'll ask Betty if she'd like to help you. She's probably had enough of being a lumberjack by now.'

Keith said, 'Maggie's upstairs, too. Dunno what she's doing.'

So Maggie had come with Zander as she'd threatened to? Bless her cotton socks!

Back to basics. Bea called out to June to follow her, and took the stairs to the basement.

'Phew!' said June, encountering the damp, the dimness and the odour of fire in what had been the main office. The furniture had gone, as had the carpet. The floor still felt tacky, and the room was more like a smoke-lined dragon's cave than an office.

'Tell me about it!' said Bea. 'Through here…this is what used to be my office and—careful, Zander has had to break down the grille over the French windows to get into the garden!—and here's what used to be the garden.' She was surprised how much of the tree had already been removed. The boy was not—she was pleased to see— being allowed to operate a chainsaw himself, but was taking cut lengths of wood over to his mother, who was stacking them in neat piles.

Bea raised her voice. 'Betty, can you take a break? We need to update our customer and staff address book, and give everyone a couple of mobile phone numbers to use for the time being. We can use mine for a start. Also, I found a couple of mobiles in the desks when I cleared them. Perhaps one of them is still usable? If not, perhaps we could use yours for an hour or two, all expenses paid?'

With some thankfulness, Betty abandoned her task. 'I'll come straight away.'

Her son was not happy. 'Aw, Mum! I don't have to stop, do I?'

Hari swung his chainsaw in the air. 'I'll look after him, missus.'

June was taking pictures. 'I see you have quite a few bird feeders out here and a birdbath, too. And were those stone planters filled with flowers? And shrubs around the walls?'

'I am trying not to think about how it used to look,' said Bea, distractedly. She was sure she'd forgotten to do something desperately important, to talk to someone, go somewhere…but she couldn't think what it was. First off, she must deal with this importunate journalist. 'If you need pictures for comparison, we took some snaps a couple of weeks ago when we had a barbecue party here for Dilys's birthday, and I could get them out for you—if I can get them off my computer. Oh. My computer's imploded. But if we can get the stuff back down from the Cloud…'

'Who is Dilys?'

Dilys: that's who she'd forgotten. Dilys was heavily pregnant. In fact, both she and Maggie were, but Maggie could take care of herself while Dilys was such a silly little twit in some ways she'd probably not tell anyone even if her waters had broken. So where was she? Upstairs? Bea turned back into the house, explaining to the journalist, 'Dilys is Sir Leon Holland's niece, who is married to Keith, our wonderful IT man. If we're back on line tomorrow, it will entirely be due to him. I'm worried about her. I'd better go and check. She may be with Maggie—'

'Who is Maggie?'

'My sort of adopted daughter. She was one of my lodgers, and is now married to Zander, the man who's perched on the top of the tree at the moment. She's a magnificent project manager but also heavily pregnant. I don't know which of them is due first, Dilys or Maggie, but I think I'd better find them, wherever they are, and tell them to stop whatever they're doing.'

June stopped and gestured to the garden. 'Do you mind if I take a few pictures here?'

'Be my guest.' Bea was desperate to check on the two girls. The quickest way would be up the iron spiral staircase to the first floor, but she'd just told June not to use it and she mustn't do so, either. Suppose it were to collapse while she was on her way up!

Back through the dank space that used to be their office she went, and up the inside stairs, with Betty at her heels. Betty said she'd just wash her hands and then she'd see what she could do with the spare phones…

…which made Bea worry about the water situation. Was the water still on? Was the cable from the generator connected to the water heater so that they could wash in hot water and where, oh where were Maggie and Dilys, and what were they up to? Neither girl was anywhere to be seen on the ground floor.

Prompt on cue, down the stairs came Magnificent Maggie, a scarlet ribbon in her dark hair, wearing a billowing, matching scarlet kaftan. Maggie looked terrific, and ready to pop at any minute. She was waving a tablet and a pad of paper, and talking on the phone. Maggie had always been able to multitask. 'So when I say tomorrow, you're not going to tell me you can't do anything for a week, are you…?' She caught Bea up in a hug, and propelled her into the kitchen, still talking. 'No, that is not acceptable. My client needs… Yes, that's more like it. Tomorrow morning, before noon. I'll be here to let you in.'

Bea said, 'Maggie…?'

Maggie shut off her phone, said, 'Just a mo,' tapped away on her tablet and made some notes on the pad of paper, too. Then, with an enormous sigh, she shifted herself on to a stool and smiled widely. 'I love you for needing me. This is so much more fun than sitting at home looking at the telly.'

'You're supposed to be taking it easy—'

'Taking it easy drives me mad. And then I drive Zander mad. The babe isn't due for another week, and you're not going to refuse the services of the best project manager in town, are you?' She shoved the pad of paper at Bea. 'Priority: electricity, telephone and security. Right? They've all promised to attend tomorrow. And yes, I did check with Hari that I was using the right people.'

Bea was astounded, and then told herself that she ought not to have been surprised. Maggie could pull rabbits out of a hat quicker than anyone else she knew. Bravo, Maggie. Bea switched the kettle on and, wonder of wonders!, it responded. It seemed that boiling a kettle was the appropriate thing to do, though goodness knows there were a dozen other things that she suspected she ought to be doing at that very moment, but couldn't think what they were. 'Security? You mean the alarm system?'

'That as well, but lower down the list. No, I'm having metal—'

Betty erupted into the kitchen, holding out Bea's

phone. 'I said you were tied up and they asked to speak to Carrie, but…' A shrug.

Bea took the call, from a customer who was distraught to think that all her arrangements for a silver wedding party might be at risk because of the fire. Bea soothed, explained and handed the phone back to Betty. And then thought, *How had the woman known about the fire?*

Maggie, meanwhile, had been on the phone again. 'So what you're saying is that if we get some heaters in to dry the place out…?'

The kettle boiled. Bea made tea and located the biscuit tin, which was not where she'd left it. Surprise, surprise! Only one biscuit left. Luckily she'd had the forethought to hide one packet away. She retrieved it from the cupboard and emptied it into the tin.

Betty brought the phone back in. 'Sorry, Mrs Abbot. It's Carrie this time. She says she's gone down with flu.' Bea and Betty exchanged glances which conveyed a lot more than irritation and concern. On Betty's part there was grim anger that Carrie should let them down when they needed her so badly. On Bea's part there was irritation and—faintly—a light at the end of the tunnel as she considered a future without Carrie.

Bea took the phone, listened to excuses. 'Of course, Carrie. Take as much time as you need. Betty can take your place till you get back.' She shut off the call, and handed the phone back to Betty with raised eyebrows. 'Do you want her job, temporary or otherwise?'

Betty hesitated. 'She might really be ill.'

'Sure. But if she doesn't come back, the job is yours. If you want it.'

'I haven't worked here for very long and—'

'You've been here long enough to know who does

what, why and when. You don't lose your head in an emergency, you don't mind what you're asked to do, and you have a nice little boy who probably ought to be hauled away from the chain gang and put under the shower to clean him up. That is, if we have any hot water, which we may not. So, do you want the job, temporarily, until we see which way Carrie jumps?'

'Can do.' Betty started for the stairs. 'As for the boy, he's like his father. Never did know his limits.'

Maggie shut off her phone, made more notes and said, 'Security. I got Hari to measure up. You need at least eight—probably nine—metal mesh 'gate panels' to enclose the bottom of your garden. Three metres high. With padlocks. Delivery by noon tomorrow.'

Bea closed her eyes for a moment and put out a hand to steady herself. 'That's…a relief.' She propelled herself to the fridge. No time to faint. Tea all round. There was only one carton of milk left. As Mummy Bear might have said, 'Who's been drinking *my* milk?'

She made Maggie a mug of tea and pushed it towards her.

Now, if the power was back on in the kitchen, was the fridge working again and what about the freezer? And, what had Anna done with the food she'd taken out of it?

Maggie sipped tea, and eased her back. Was she having a contraction?

Betty put her head round the door, eyebrows raised, mobile in hand.

'No,' said Bea. 'You deal with it. You're the office manageress for the time being, aren't you? Is the boy all right?'

'I can't prise him off the stack of logs he's building. He's a bit OCD, wants everything perfectly aligned.

Thinks you should install a wood-burning stove…' And off she went, talking into the phone.

Bea said, blankly, 'Probably the most useful thing I can do is to go out for some more milk and biscuits, and then organize a takeaway.'

Maggie caught her sleeve. 'Before you go anywhere, you'd better cast your eye over this schedule.' Her phone rang, and she answered it. 'Oh, Oliver? You deserted us to go surfing, and look what happens! You're on your way back from Cornwall? When are you due in? Can you make your own way back from the station? Right, see you when we see you.'

Bea picked up Maggie's discarded cup of tea and drank it. Slowly, with enjoyment.

'So, Oliver's coming back. Good. He can sleep in his old room. I think I made the bed up with clean sheets after his last visit.'

'What about your current lodger? The one with the orange jeans. He's away for the weekend?'

'Abroad on a job. He's been sleeping in what was your room. I'd better ring him and ask if he can commute from the family pile for the time being. He won't want to put up with cold water in the shower. Which reminds me. Where is Dilys? I haven't seen her for ages. She's just silly enough to start in labour and think she shouldn't tell anyone because we're all busy.'

'It's all right, I put her in with Piers and told her to tell him if she got so much as a tiny twinge.'

'Piers? What's he doing here?' Bea had forgotten about her first husband.

'Painting. Not to be interrupted. Hari asked him to take some stuff to the lab this morning. On the way he picked up some painting materials, brought them back here and started work in the top flat. He said he wanted you to give him an hour before the light goes, but I've forgotten to tell you, and I think you should forget about it, too. As for Dilys, surely she'd have the sense to say if her waters broke?'

They looked at one another in sudden alarm. 'Or would she?' Bea started for the hall. 'If Piers is painting, he wouldn't notice if someone threw a grenade into the room…'

Maggie came after her, but more slowly. 'Go ahead, Mrs A. You can climb the stairs quicker than I at the moment.'

Bea was panting by the time she reached the top of the house. She stood still, hand on throat, thinking she was getting too old for this lark.

The door to the bedroom that used to be Maggie's, and which was now used by her latest lodger, was open. She could see Piers's back. He was working at an easel and didn't even hear her.

Dilys drifted into the doorway, saying, 'Anything I can do? I've had a lovely rest and Baby's not too active, and it's only the Something Hicks that's contracting—'

'Braxton Hicks, false contractions.'

'Yes, that's right. So, shall I see about putting some supper together?'

Bea wanted to say, brutally, 'With what, you stupid girl!' For the fridge and freezer were bare, weren't they? And, incidentally, where had all that food gone? She'd last seen Anna stacking it into cool boxes…

Well, never mind that now. She managed a smile. 'Thank you, Dilys, but I think we'll have to order a takeaway. I also think you should take Keith home and give him—'

Piers seized hold of Bea's arm and swung her into

the room. 'Stand just there. No, looking back over your shoulder to me…and don't move!' He seized a stick of charcoal and approached his easel, saying, 'I asked Dilys to stand in for you, but… Don't Move!'

'Piers, I can't sit for you at the—'

'DON'T MOVE! I need to—'

Maggie appeared in the doorway, holding on to her bump. 'Piers, you may not have noticed, but the light is going.'

'Two minutes more!'

Bea held her breath. Piers worked on his canvas with a sort of contained fury, and then threw his charcoal on to the floor and wiped his hands on a rag. 'There!'

Bea looked down at the charcoal stick. So did Dilys and Maggie. Who was going to pick it up? It wouldn't occur to Piers to do so.

Dilys said, 'I don't think I can get down there at the moment.'

'Of course you can't,' said Bea. She bent down to pick it up herself.

Maggie was amused. 'I hate men…!'

Piers reddened. 'What was that?' but he didn't apologize.

Bea looked around. Piers's painting materials covered every surface in sight. 'Maggie, remind me to get hold of my lodger with the orange jeans to make sure he's not coming back tonight.'

Piers said, 'Don't bother. I can put everything in the sitting room next door, ready to start again tomorrow morning.' He clapped his hands together. 'And now… I'm hungry. Shall I go and fetch something for us to eat? Is the electricity back on yet? How's Hari coping?' Without waiting for a reply, he swung off down the stairs.

Dilys made as if to pick up some of his equipment, until Bea stopped her. 'Leave it. He's got to learn. You have a husband downstairs who's been working his socks off all day and performed miracles. He needs to be told that you are perfectly all right—which I can see you are—but he should now be taken home and told how wonderful he is and how lucky you are to have him. Right?'

'Oh, but he *is* wonderful,' said Dilys, following Piers down the stairs but at a slower pace.

Bea tried to shift Piers's easel, and failed.

Maggie said, 'You leave that be!'

At which Bea abandoned the attempt and they both laughed. Bea said, 'May I ask if *you* are all right?'

'No, you may not. I've got Zander trained, too. We do *not* ask how I am feeling every half-hour of the day. We have an agreement, the babe and I, that while we are both out enjoying ourselves and not sitting at home moping with nothing to do, we will make the most of it. Babe likes me to be busy. She's going to be like that, herself. When this is all over and not before, she'll make her appearance. And you'd better use my phone to ring your lodger and tell him not to come home tonight, right?'

Late afternoon

Time for a break. They were all ready for it.

Anna had replaced the contents of the fridge and freezer, which seemed not much the worse for wear, though it would probably be wise to finish everything off as soon as possible. There was electricity into the kitchen for lighting and for four electrical appliances—which included the microwave—but no hot water. There were new locks on the front and back doors, but no alarm system and no landline. Hari had fixed up a car battery on every floor so that side lights could be used to steer those who were staying to their beds.

Betty had returned Bea's phone after switching it over to voicemail, and had taken her son off home, vowing to be back next morning, early. The boy had begged to be let off school so that he could come too, but she'd told him, 'No', even though he'd said he could always swing it by saying he had a serious dental appointment.

The garden was almost clear. Hari and Zander had sawn up practically all of the old tree. Hari reported that the roots had shown signs of rot, and this might have been a factor in the tree's fall. Two great stacks of wood had been carried through the 'tomb'—as the boy had christened the old office rooms—and disposed of by lorry, but another two piles remained to be dealt with on the morrow.

Hari and Zander had acquired a bale of barbed wire from somewhere and strung it across the bottom of the garden to deter intruders.

The mess in the garden was still enough to make Bea weep, if she'd had the time and energy to do so. Cherished plants had been broken off at the roots and mashed to pieces, the stone planters were in fragments, trellises dangled off walls, and bird feeders had been tossed hither and yon. Even the pigeons had deserted their usual habitat. The garden shed was a pile of debris no more than a foot high, and it didn't seem likely that any of the furniture or the tools within would be usable again.

It really was best to think about something else.

Keith—after having connected up and tested almost all the new laptops—had been taken home by Dilys, both worrying that the other had been overdoing it. Both said they'd be back early tomorrow.

Zander had taken Maggie off, too. He'd said he'd try to get leave of absence from his job on the morrow, but Bea knew that he had a responsible job at a charity in the City and had told him not to bother. Maggie had said she'd be there come hell or high water, and nobody mentioned the fact that she looked as if she ought to be heading straight to the maternity ward.

The journalist had disappeared at some point without saying goodbye. Bea tried not to think about what she might see fit to write.

Why hadn't Leon rung? He'd promised to do so. She ached to hear his voice and be able to tell him what had been happening.

Now and then Bea tried to contact her orange-jeans lodger, but his phone was either engaged or had switched off. Annoying!

Everyone who was left gathered round the kitchen table to forage for something, anything, to keep them going. They switched their phones to voicemail and told Winston to get off! Which he did for all of sixty seconds.

Bea had a bet with herself as to which of them Winston would try to charm into giving him some food. She was right. He went for Hari, who most people would have put down as the hard man of the party. Well, he was exactly that in many ways, but he was creamy fudge in the hands of an experienced practitioner like Winston.

Bea dished out bread and ham and cheese to all, with mugs of tea.

Hari was like a machine, *perpetuum mobile*. Never still. Even while he was eating, he was looking over copies of the schedules Maggie had left for him. 'Electrical contractors, first thing tomorrow. Good people. I know them. They'll do. Water...mm.'

Anna said, 'I've got appointments throughout the day tomorrow. I'm wondering if I could cancel the morning interviews and—'

'Don't think of it,' said Bea. 'What you've done for me today is beyond praise.'

'I'm staying overnight,' said Hari, still occupied with paperwork. 'I can doss down anywhere. A settee if you've got one but the floor if necessary. By the way, I think Maggie's right; if we can get some heaters into the basement to dry it out quickly, we may not need to have the plaster off the walls, or to take the floorboards up.'

Piers said, 'I'll stay, too. Of course. Then I can get an early start on the painting in the morning.'

Bea had to smile. 'Piers, Hari has ears like a bat but, from what I remember, you sleep so soundly you wouldn't hear if a burglar banged into your bed.'

Piers said, 'You think we're going to be burgled?' He sounded so comical that everyone laughed, though the situation was far from amusing.

Bea tried to think straight. She didn't actually *know* anything, but she was beginning to think that if she didn't take precautions, yes, something else would occur to deprive her of her home. Hari obviously thought so, too, or he wouldn't have said he'd stay the night.

So, what else could go wrong? Perhaps the water would be cut off? Or, another fire? She'd been able to put her suspicions of the Admiral and his family out of her mind almost completely while she was busy, but now she had a growing conviction that that had been a mistake. Why had they attacked her and Leon? And what were they planning to do next?

Bea's phone registered another incoming call. She looked at it, saw who it was from and decided not to answer it till she'd finished eating.

Anna said, 'I think moving the agency up a floor is a brilliant idea. You'll be back on line straight away. The agency is saved, and so are all the jobs of your staff.'

Anna did *not* say that she wondered how Bea was going to cope with having her own bedroom turned into a bedsit, and Bea didn't mention it. In fact, she didn't dare think about it. Too distressing.

'On the other hand,' said Anna, 'there's going to be considerable disruption here for some time, and Leon's house is standing empty in the next street. I haven't observed any police presence in his garden today. Even their tent has gone. You could move in there while this house is being restored to its former glory.'

No one said anything. No one met Bea's eye. She thought about it. Lovely, big empty rooms. No furniture... but furniture could be hired, or her own taken round there. There was power and Wi-Fi already laid on. She could move straight in. So, why not? There was a lot to be said for shifting across the way.

She couldn't understand why she didn't jump at the offer. She would talk it through with Leon when he rang.

ELEVEN

Sunday evening

BEA WENT TO the back door and looked out. Hari had replaced the door and window frames, and the glass within them. The new door stood open, giving on to the iron staircase—which couldn't be used yet.

She looked down into the garden below. Without the tree, the garden would get a lot more sun. Perhaps she should plan a completely new layout?

She looked across the barbed-wire barrier into Leon's garden. As Anna had said, the police tent had gone. The scaffolding still cladding the exterior couldn't mask the fact that the house was a perfect example of its kind. Bea could move over there tomorrow with all mod cons laid on.

His garden was an eyesore. Nothing had been done to it for years. The builders had left some odd planks and bags of rubble behind, plus a metal drum or two, which didn't improve things. There were mounds of earth here and there, from which bones—human and otherwise—had been excavated.

The human bones had probably been there for longer than anyone currently living in these houses. In any case, they had nothing to do with Bea.

She switched her eyes across the tumble of bricks into the Admiral's garden. Their shed still stood, in a manner of speaking, leaning to the left and covered with ivy. The back of their house, by contrast with the gleaming new paint that coated Leon's house, looked shabby. There were lights on in the basement flat, and the flicker of television on two of the other floors.

They were not nice neighbours to have, but you couldn't choose your neighbours, could you?

'I'm not moving,' said Bea. 'They want to drive me out of my house, to destroy my living and my credit, and I'm not going. I know restoration will be difficult and time-consuming and drive me to distraction. I shall probably regret staying many times before the house is back to normal. But I'm not moving.'

'Good,' said Anna. 'I was playing devil's advocate. I'm glad you're not giving in. Do you have the slightest idea why you've been targeted?'

'At first I thought everything that happened—the invitation to the party, the drugs, the "evidence" collected against us—was directed at discrediting Leon and upsetting this important sale he's masterminding in the Far East. I thought the Admiral must have a financial interest in the sale not going through, because it looks as though he could do with an injection of cash. His house has been neglected and he seems to be the head of a large family. Greed is a powerful motive. I'm sure that that is partly what it is about, but it doesn't explain why I and my house should have been targeted, too.'

Anna wasn't sure, either. 'To isolate Leon from his support group?'

'Y-yes. There is that. I can also go along with the youngsters stealing my watch, misusing my phone and my makeup out of sheer deviltry. I know that some rich young things think they're entitled to have fun at other people's expense. They aren't, of course. But they think they are. But why torch my house? Because they want me to be in so much trouble that they can blame me for the fall of the wall as well? No. No insurance investigator is going to stick me for responsibility for the wall once he's seen the evidence. I think that the wall was pure accident, or pure stupidity…not sure which. I lean towards stupidity. Someone who didn't know what they were doing had a go at the ivy and brought the lot down. The tree falling was collateral damage. Neither was intentional. But, torching my house *was* intentional. Why?'

'The youngsters heard that the adults were out to get you, so thought it would be fun to make you suffer?'

'Why didn't they target Leon's house, then? The party wall was down. There was no reason why they shouldn't have thrown paraffin in that direction, too.'

Piers said, 'Ah yes, but that fire might have spread to their own house, and they wouldn't risk that.'

Hari said, 'Where did they get the paraffin? Do *you* normally keep a can of paraffin around the house? I do because I use it when I'm painting. I buy it at a hardware store, and keep it in a locked container well away from my living quarters. But why did *they* have some?'

Bea opened her mouth to say she'd seen something, somewhere, which was relevant, but closed it again because she couldn't bring it to mind.

Shrugs all round.

Piers leaned back in his chair, long legs stretched out in front of him. He quirked his eyebrows. 'In my opinion, they thought you were the easier target. They thought that if they got you on the run, Leon wouldn't have time to pursue the problems at his end. Only, Leon decided to attend to his business and left you to cope on your own.'

Anna and Hari froze. They'd been thinking the same thing? It mirrored what Bea had been thinking, of course. Leon had run away and left her to deal with a terrible mess. Yes, he had his own war to fight on another front, but… No, she must not be judgmental. She looked at her watch. He'd promised to ring her that evening. Perhaps he'd tried and she'd been on the phone. But he could have left a message, couldn't he? That's what she'd done when she'd rung his number and it had been engaged.

Meanwhile, she had to get on with her life.

Piers looked up at the ceiling. 'I don't know exactly how you're fixed, Bea, but if a sub would help…?'

She was so touched she wanted to cry. Instead, she managed a smile. 'Thank you, but the insurance should cover everything and the agency really is doing well at the moment.'

Anna pushed her empty plate away. There were empty plates and dirty mugs everywhere.

Is the dishwasher working? If not, how am I going to wash up with cold water? I suppose I have to boil kettles. Ugh.

Anna said, 'I'm trying to think what I'd do next if I wanted to upset you. You've lost your landline telephone, the electricity and the gas, but that's collateral damage from the fire. The baddies—whoever they are, and I suppose we mustn't name them without proof—didn't target those things directly.'

Bea's phone pinged once more. She'd turned it over to voicemail during supper, which had probably been a mistake. She might have missed Leon's call. But it wasn't Leon's voice on the phone.

It was Zoe's voice, icy cold. 'So there you are! I've been ringing and ringing. Every time I've tried, you're engaged or you're switched off. Didn't you realize I'd be waiting to talk to you about moving into Sir Leon's house?'

'Sorry. Problems. He said he'd give me his new phone number.'

'Yes, of course. Have you pen and paper?' An exasperated sigh indicating that she didn't think Bea was organized well enough to find some. Actually, at that moment, Zoe was right.

Bea hooked the calendar off the wall and scrabbled for a pen in the mug where they kept the odd screwdriver, some biros and a bottle opener. 'Go ahead.'

Zoe dictated the number. 'You won't catch him yet. He's in a meeting and not to be interrupted. However, I've been in touch with the police and they don't want anyone to move into his house till they've decided whether they need a forensic search in there or not.'

Bea started to speak, 'But—'

'Please don't interrupt. I have only a limited time in which to speak to you. Because his house will not be available for a while, Sir Leon is leaving Switzerland for Brussels later this evening, and he'd like you to join him there. From Brussels he intends to leave for Dubai in two days' time. He suggests you travel light as you can obtain whatever clothes and cosmetics you require in the hotel. I am arranging to courier your tickets to—'

'Stop!' What was this? Was Leon trying to carry her off round the world as a sort of adjunct to him? As a companion or as a mistress? Without discussing this with her, or asking her opinion?

Bea repeated, 'Stop. I can't leave. I'm staying put. I have work to do at this end. I will be happy to talk to him about it when he has a minute to spare. Perhaps you can ask him to ring me when he has a moment?'

Heavy breathing from the other end. 'You don't wish to accept his very generous offer?' Incredulous. Offended? Yes, both.

Bea said, 'It is a kind and generous offer but I have responsibilities here which I can't ignore.'

'I don't understand you.' Hard and judgmental. 'Sir Leon is the most generous and kindly of men and he is anxious to help you out of your present difficulties. He will pay for you to take a well-earned break from the agency, which means he can have the pleasure of your company while he deals with the fall-out from his own financial crisis. Am I to inform him that you consider your affairs more important than his?'

A trick question. Whichever way it was answered, Bea would be in trouble. She could say, 'Give him my love,' and leave it at that. However, as of that very moment, she didn't want to send him her love. She wanted to hit him over the head with something large and lethal. And to do the same to Zoe. Bea controlled her temper with an effort. 'I'm sure you already have a plan B.'

A short silence. Then, 'Please don't trouble yourself to ring back as Sir Leon needs me at his side.' End of conversation.

Of course. If Bea declined to play games, then Zoe would step into the breach.

Bea found she was shaking. She checked her voice-mail, noting there were other messages to deal with.

Piers watched her, his expression guarded. Anna and Hari flicked a glance at one another.

Anna owed her career to Leon's generosity. Hari was a freelance who often worked for Leon as a security problem-solver and, occasionally, bodyguard. Neither of them would wish to upset Leon.

All three of them knew that Leon and Bea had talked of marriage.

Piers, however, had no particular reason to wish Leon well. In fact, Piers was now hiding a grin. Horrid boy!

Someone—probably Dilys, who thought such touches were important—had rescued a single red geranium from the shattered planters down in the garden, and placed it in a wine glass on the table top. The breeze from the open kitchen door stirred its petals. There was still dirt and grime in the air, but the flower spoke of revival. It seemed to say that the fall of the wall hadn't destroyed everything good, and that a plant, though crushed, would bloom again. Perhaps Dilys had the right idea.

Anna flicked a glance at her own phone, lying on the table. Doubtless there were also messages there, awaiting her attention.

Hari's phone buzzed. He looked down at it, and killed the call.

Bea tried to sound positive. 'My dears, you have all been beyond wonderful today. I don't know what I would have done without you. But really, I am quite all right now, and you must start thinking of yourselves. Anna, you have to be at work tomorrow bright and early, and so, I'm sure, has Hari. Piers, before you go, if you could tidy up your painting materials and stack them in the sitting room upstairs? My lodger will be back soon.'

'And you?' said Hari.

She managed a smile of sorts. 'I'm going to change out of these filthy clothes and call on the Admiral and his lady. I want to claim my watch back, and I want to stir the pot till the scum floats to the surface.'

'You're not going alone,' said Anna. 'Hari?'

'No need to bother Hari. I'll come with you,' said Piers. 'I want another look at that painting of theirs which is supposed to be a Lenkiewicz and isn't. Also, I think I spotted a pseudo-Sargent hanging in the hall. I'll bet my bottom dollar it's another fake.'

'Hari, how about you?' Anna repeated.

Hari twitched her a grin. 'You know what I'm going to do. You go home and get ready for tomorrow. I'm staying put.'

Everyone looked at Hari's phone.

Bea said, 'You have had a summons on your phone from Leon asking you to take on another job? Perhaps to follow him to Brussels?'

A smooth reply. 'I've recommended someone else.'

Anna worried at her bottom lip. 'He does pay you well to—'

'I'm freelance. He pays me by the job. I am unable to help him this time as I have a prior engagement to Mrs A. You'd do the same if you were in my shoes, wouldn't you, Anna?' He fixed his eyes on her face. Perhaps he wasn't entirely sure which way she'd jump?

She nodded. 'Yes, I would. Leon has been generous to me; he's helped me forward my career. But Bea is my friend.'

The rather hard lines of Hari's face relaxed. He nodded. Anna had come through, as he'd hoped she would.

Piers did a double-take. 'Blow me! Hari, do you mean he's already been on to you, asking you to abandon Bea and fly out to guard his back?'

'Leon's frightened,' said Bea, excusing him, 'but unwilling to admit it, even to himself.'

Hari said, 'The danger's here, not there.'

Everyone nodded.

Anna said, 'I agree. But why?'

Bea sighed. 'I don't know. The only thing I can think of is that the Admiral believes I shouldn't be running an agency in what is predominantly a residential district, even to the point that he's raising the matter at a Council Meeting. But I really can't see why he should bother. In the first place, my dear Hamilton's aunts started the agency long before he or I was born and, so far as I know, nobody has raised an objection since. In the second place, the woman who sold Leon that house ran a charity there for years, which is one of the reasons he wanted the place for himself. I'm not sure how far negotiations have advanced, but he was negotiating to take on the directorship of a well-established charity which had rather lost its way recently, and he went through all the right channels to make sure he could run it at his new house before he closed the deal. So why is the Admiral complaining about the agency now?'

'Then it must be something to do with the walls falling down?'

'I can't see why? Can anyone else think of a reason why I should be targeted?'

No one could.

'Well, Mrs A,' said Hari, 'if you want to walk into the lions' den, we should take precautions. It won't be dark for a couple of hours, and everyone at the Admiral's house is still up and moving about, which means I can't get into the house through the basement as I did before. Piers, if you take her over there, I'll shadow you both from Leon's garden. Keep your phone charged up and my phone number on dial. Then all you have to do to get me is to press the call button. Right? Mrs A, the same?'

Anna was indecisive. 'Bea, I don't like to leave you, but it's true I do have a report to write for tomorrow. While you get changed, I'll listen to the messages on your phone and either return them, or write you a note so that you can deal with them later. Then—you are right—I must go home. Hari, I shan't go to bed tonight till I know you've got Bea safely back here and that nothing further has happened. Promise to ring me?'

'Promise,' said Hari, and the warmth in his eyes promised more than a pledge to keep her informed.

Bea braced herself to face the chaos upstairs. Hopefully she'd be able to get into her en suite though it was probably filthy with soot. Then her walk-in dressing room had a window overlooking the garden…if the window there had been broken, she could imagine the state her clothes would be in. But, fix on a smile and up we go! Pretend we don't mind that there won't be any quiet place to retire to tonight. She toiled her way up the stairs.

Piers called after her, 'You're sleeping in the spare room, right?'

Bea opened the door into what had been her bedroom, and gasped. Her bed had been dismantled and the parts set against the back wall while all the furniture from her sitting room below had been brought up and arranged in their usual positions. Even the pictures—even that wonderful portrait of Hamilton, her beloved husband—had been re-hung on the walls. The settees and the big chairs faced one another across the big television set, just as they had done down below; the lamps with their heavy china bases were in their usual places on the side tables; the card table was in the back window, with its own chair, placed so that she might play patience in the evenings and look down over the garden and up to the church spire.

Her very own quiet place. Her refuge from the world. Tears welled up. She brushed them away.

Piers could be a right pain in the whatsit, but she recognized his hand here. He'd used his gifts to provide her with a replica of what she'd lost. It wasn't perfect; the telly wouldn't work as the power was off, and he hadn't tried to move the big mirror over the fireplace or replicate the embrasures on either side of the fireplace, either... Well, there was no fireplace in this room... But she could sit here in comfort in the evenings. She could even entertain in a small way. It was good.

So she was sleeping in the spare room? Yes. Again, it wasn't perfect. She would have to sleep on a different mattress, and there were two dressing tables crammed in side by side. But she could get at her cosmetics, and use the shower room and...she'd better get a move on!

First, a shower. The water was cold, but that didn't matter. Much. Now, what should she wear for this important call on the Admiral and his lady? She settled on a soft willow-green top over a darker green skirt. Matching shoes.

A sparing hand with the makeup. It wouldn't do to keep Piers waiting. He was the impatient sort and, anyway, she had to keep going, because if she once stopped and thought about taking a rest, she'd fall on to her bed and never get up again.

Her full-length mirror had been wedged into the space behind the door to the en suite, but she managed to squirm round to check that her skirt hung straight. Handbag. New keys. When would young Oliver arrive from Cornwall? He'd only have keys to the old lock... well, she'd deal with that later.

A squirt of perfume. She didn't usually bother, but

she needed all the help she could get this evening. Would Leon try to ring her while she was out? She wouldn't want to take his call while she was across the way. Oh dear. Well, it couldn't be helped.

On with the play.

PIERS RANG THE bell at the Admiral's house. The street lay basking in pleasure at the warmth of the evening sun. Next door Leon's house gleamed expensively in its coat of fresh paint. The panes of old glass had been cleaned, within and without. The ground-floor windows had been fitted with roller blinds which had been pulled down to keep out the heat of the sun.

Bea remembered that it was a Sunday. Here in the street, some families were leaving after a weekend break spent in Town, piling into cars with their luggage, stowing away fractious children, kissing relatives goodbye with injunctions to 'drive safely'. Others were returning to the city from a few days away in the country; younger professionals hauling tote bags along, bearing bags of goodies bought from farmers' markets, rosily tanned, calling to one another with sharp voices, some on their phones even as they put their keys in the door of their houses.

The door to the Admiral's house creaked open.

'Have you forgotten your keys again?' Lady Payne, in a red silk top over black jeans; very stylish. Who had she been expecting? Not Bea. 'What, you again!' She fell back, looking wildly over her shoulder…for reinforcements? From the back of the house—the kitchen?—came the sounds of someone cooking. That wouldn't be the Admiral though, would it?

Piers brushed past Bea into the hall. 'Good evening, Lady Payne. Yes, it's us again.'

Bea was all smiles. 'Sorry if it's an inconvenient time but—'

'I thought you'd moved away!'

Bea said, 'I came to collect my watch. It was my mother's, you know. Sentimental value.'

Piers was taking a picture of the pseudo-Sargent on his phone. 'I say, where did you get this?'

'Who, what?' Lady Payne turned from one to the other. Definitely knocked off balance.

Someone rang a sharp 'ting!' on the doorbell behind Bea, and pushed the door open to enter. The three youngsters. When they saw Bea they rocked back on their heels. The sharp-eyed blonde, Venetia, was in the lead, followed closely by two lads in their late teens or early twenties whom Bea recognized from the party. They bore all the signs of a day spent in the sun; reddened skins, grass-stained jeans, jackets draped over shoulders and tousled hair. Had they been to Henley to watch the boat racing? Or been punting on the Isis at Oxford?

The girl was wearing Bea's watch.

'Whoa!' said the older of the boys, car keys in one hand, a six-pack of beer dangling from the other. He stood close to Venetia, who didn't seem to resent his invasion of her space. He looked Bea up and down, and clearly knew who she was. With a grin which conveyed the message, *I know something you don't!* he said, 'To what do we owe the pleasure?'

'I'm Mrs Abbot,' said Bea, refusing to rise to his mockery. 'From across the way. And you are...?'

'Venetia,' said the girl, dropping her bags and jacket on the floor. 'And he's Sir Gideon. A Bart, in case you don't know about such things.' Insolent, very. Making it clear that she didn't think Bea was educated enough to know what a baronet might be.

'And I'm your neighbour from across the wall,' said Bea, deciding not to notice the slur, and switching to a slightly-silly-little-woman mode. 'I became ill after your party, and have just come out of hospital—they say not food poisoning, and I'm sure you weren't to blame, though I suppose they'll find out what it was when they've completed all their tests and so on. I am just about to fly away for a few days, but first I wanted to pick up my watch, which I see Venetia has kindly managed to find for me. So good of you, dear. May I?' And she held out her hand for her watch.

Venetia glanced at Gideon. A subtle smile. Bea watched her decide to play to the gallery.

'So sorry,' Venetia said, in a creamy tone. She didn't sound sorry. She sounded as if she were choking back laughter. 'But it isn't yours. It's mine. Given me by my grandmother.'

Bea countered that. 'Being an old-fashioned wind-up watch, it tends to lose or gain at least five minutes a day. Which is it? Gain or lose?'

A shrug. 'I don't worry my head about things like that.'

'I have photographs and insurance cover on that watch.'

'So what? Finders keepers. It's mine now.'

TWELVE

IT WAS TIME for Bea to bring up the heavy guns. 'You know I managed to retrieve my phone and powder compact, which I also "mislaid" the other night? All three appear to have been used by someone without my permission. I've sent them to the lab for fingerprint identification. Perhaps you'd like to give me your fingerprints for comparison purposes?'

An indrawn breath from someone in the group. Who? Lady Payne?

The lad Gideon frowned and looked to Venetia for a lead. Venetia grimaced, understanding that her bluff had been called.

Lady Payne said, 'You're not thinking of going to the police?'

'That depends,' said Bea, smiling.

Lady Payne frowned. 'You're trying to blackmail me?'

'Such an emotive word. And double-edged, don't you think?' In other words, both sides held some good cards in this poker game.

'You won't dare go to the police!' Venetia, laughing. Knowing exactly what cards each side held.

'Venetia, give her the watch!' Lady Payne, warning the girl not to rock this particular boat?

Sulkily, Venetia undid the clasp on the watch, held it out at arm's length...and let it drop on to the floor.

Bea nearly screamed. If the girl had broken the

watch…! Bea noticed that Piers was standing well back from the group. He had his camera out. Bea hoped he'd managed to record the moment when Venetia deliberately dropped the watch.

Gideon laughed, open-mouthed. He was slightly buck-toothed but he had a title, so Bea supposed that would make up for it in the eyes of the girls. The other boy—slightly younger than the other two?—was hanging back, also laughing. Venetia looked pleased with herself. Lady Payne looked grim.

Piers picked the watch up off the floor, held it to his ear, smiled and handed it to Bea with a bow. 'It's still going. You can always bill Venetia if it needs attention.'

'So I can,' said Bea, trying not to let her voice wobble. 'The young have to take responsibility for their actions. I assume Venetia is over eighteen? She certainly looks it.'

Venetia shrugged. She said, 'When's supper? We're going out, after.' Presumably there was someone in the kitchen, preparing a meal for the family? Without waiting for a reply, she disappeared in that direction, saying, '*Bon voyage*, Mrs Abbot.'

All Bea wanted was to get out of there. She turned to go, only to find Gideon looking at her with narrowed eyes, swinging a six-pack of beer in a plastic bag to and fro. Presumably the beer was meant for the evening meal? He wasn't proposing to hit her with it, was he? Er, yes. Possibly. She told herself to shift, and found herself stuck to the floor.

Click! Piers had caught the lad in the act.

'Gideon!' Lady Payne, warning him.

Gideon roared with laughter, but stopped swinging the six-pack. With his eyes still on Bea, he echoed Venetia. 'Yes, what *is* for supper? I could eat a horse.'

The youngest of the trio, a thin-faced lad who looked like a smudged copy of Gideon, muttered, 'Excuse me,' and slid round Bea to disappear down the hall.

Bea unstuck herself and turned to Lady Payne, enthusing, 'Thank you so much. And yes, of course I'll bill you for the damage to the watch. So kind. I do hope that nobody else had food poisoning after the party. So awkward for you. And now, we really must be going.'

'One minute. Where are you living now? You've moved out of your house?'

'Oh, locally. You know? Friends have been so good.'

Stony-faced, Lady Payne shut the door behind them.

Bea descended into the street slowly, with care. Piers spoke into his phone. 'Hari? All's well. We're on our way back.'

They walked along, in step with one another.

Bea said, 'Venetia's the leader of the gang. It will be her fingerprints on my phone and powder compact. She's older than the other two, I think. Certainly not under-age.'

Piers nodded, checking the shots he'd taken on his phone. 'The frame on the painting in the hall states that the portrait is by Sargent. It isn't. There's a small Cotman by the stairs. That's genuine. I think someone's been selling off the family jewels and substituting copies in an attempt to fool the general populace.'

They turned the corner into the main road. Traffic, loud.

Bea said, 'Gideon was the arsonist, at Venetia's bidding. The Admiral and his lady may have started on this persecution of me, but the youngsters have enthusiastically taken it over. Can their elders still control them? Doubtful.'

'Is Venetia a psychopath, do you think?'

'My guess is that she and Gideon are sleeping together. Cousins, do you suppose?'

He nodded. 'Looks like it.'

Suddenly she felt it was all too much. She reached out and caught hold of the railing nearby, and stood there, head hanging…for a count of five.

Piers said, 'Come on, then,' and put his arm round her, holding her up and close to him.

She said, 'I'm sorry…' She was close to tears. She despised herself for it.

'It's all right. I'm here.'

She tried to relax against him. Was too wound up to do so.

He rested his head against the top of hers. 'I know I've let you down in the past. Many times. I can't promise I'll do any better in the future. You know what I'm like. But I'm here for you now.'

She nodded, managed to get herself upright and, with his arm round her, made it to her house.

Hari had given her some new keys? Yes, she had them…but the door opened at her approach.

'Mrs A! I turn my back for five minutes!' Oliver, her beloved sort-of-adopted son, of mixed race, brighter than any button she'd ever seen and a total blessing. He picked her up bodily and carried her into the kitchen.

'Oliver! Put me down, at once!' She protested, laughing, but not too much. Once upon a time she had been able to pick *him* up and give him a cuddle, but that was a long time ago when he was just a stripling, and not someone important in the physics world, or wherever it was that he flourished. He'd shot up in height and put on weight since the time she'd taken him in, hadn't he? He was even, she noticed with amusement, growing a beard.

Oliver deposited her on a stool and handed her the box of tissues—gritty, but still usable. Winston, who was sitting on the table where he ought not to be, nosed her gently, understanding that she was not quite herself, but still enquiring whether or not she was able to feed him, now!

Bea said, banging tissues on her eyes. 'I am an idiot! Oh, Oliver, I am so glad to see you! And Hari, and Piers, too. Of course. Forgive me, I must be growing old.'

'Nothing to do with fighting off a powerful drug, of course,' said Hari, switching off his phone and smiling at her. 'You should try to take it easy for a while. Everything's under control. Anna's back home, wants to know if you need anything putting through her washing machine tonight.'

Bea shook her head. She couldn't think about that now.

Oliver put the kettle on. What a sensible person he was! Strong, hot tea was just what she needed. He said, 'Maggie's been on the phone, updating me. I am well able to take some time off, so consider me at your service.'

Winston nosed her arm again. He did, occasionally, show her some affection. She wasn't fooled. This was cupboard love. She was his servant, the source of his food and provider of a comfortable home. However, he did understand that this was a two-way contract, and he was prepared to allow himself to be cuddled and stroked— for a limited period of time, of course. And only by those he trusted.

Bea picked him up and cuddled him. 'You great, fluffy...ugh! You smell of fish! Where have you been today, eh?'

He didn't reply, but stretched himself out in her arms, making himself comfortable, blinking at her with great yellow eyes.

Piers was bringing the others up to date. 'So we got out without loss of face, and they understand we have enough to go to the police. As I see it, they can't use the DNA against Leon while we have their fingerprints on Bea's phone and cosmetics. Bea also made it clear that they can't just raid us to collect and destroy the evidence against them, because she's already sent it to the lab. Checkmate.'

Bea stirred herself. 'Has my other lodger turned up yet? I've tried and tried to phone him, to tell him not to come, but couldn't get through.'

'Orange trousers, green hair?' That was Hari. 'He turned up, accompanied by a long lad covered with tattoos and wearing ripped jeans and T-shirt ditto. I explained what had happened, stressing that we had no hot water or lighting. He communed with his friend and decided to move out till things get sorted. I let him upstairs to pack a few things. He was predictably horrified by all Piers's stuff in his bedroom, which prompted him to say that he'd come back for the rest of his things tomorrow. I didn't think you'd object.'

'No,' said Bea. 'It was never meant to be anything but a temporary arrangement.' And she didn't really need his rent money. Correction; with all the expenses she was incurring, she probably *did* need his rent money. Well, she'd think about that tomorrow.

Hari continued, 'To give him his due, orange jeans did ask if there was anything he could do to help and I said not really, so he said he'd ring you tomorrow to see how you were getting on.'

Good of him. He wasn't quite as self-centred as she'd expected him to be.

'Splendid,' said Oliver, 'because I'm moving back in for the duration.'

He can't stay that long. He's got his own career to think of.

Piers was trying to be helpful, too. 'Bea, you can't do anything else tonight. Why don't you rest for a while? Now that Oliver's here, he and Hari and I can take it in turns to keep watch.'

Bea struggled to her feet, dislodging Winston, much to his annoyance. She could see the cat thinking—hadn't he suffered enough this weekend? He'd been thrown out of his refuge in the tree, been forced to hide in the stationery cupboard, been groomed by a stranger, and—what with all the banging and thumping that had been going on—couldn't they see he needed a stable, warm lap to sit on for a while?

Bea pushed Winston to the floor. 'I think I can make it upstairs. Call me if there's a problem.'

She got as far as the door before turning to say, 'The youngsters. They're the danger now. They're out of control, don't know when to stop. Acting as a group, they'll take more risks than individuals, right?'

Hari said, softly, 'What do you know, Bea?'

'I don't *know* anything.' Irritably. 'But they'll think of something. They're having a meal and tanking up on beer at this moment, making plans. I don't think they've got jobs…perhaps they're at university, college, whatever? They don't look like responsible, wage-earning people to me. I wonder, will they attack Leon's house? No. They didn't before and I don't think they'll try it now…and don't ask me to back up that statement with proof, because I can't. They might attack my car. It's parked in the street. I haven't used it for a couple of days. But would they know which car it was? No. So it's water. The water company can turn off our supply from the meter in the pavement outside. If the youngsters turned off our water, we couldn't remain in the house, could we? Oh, I don't know. I'm probably imagining things.'

Oliver said, 'Right, we'll give that some thought.' He collected a mug of tea with a lid on it with one hand, slung Winston over his shoulder, and urged Bea up the stairs. 'Come on. Let's see you settled on the settee, with a rug over your feet.'

Up they went into her new sitting room. It was quiet and peaceful there, with the evening sun streaming through the window. The settee was in its usual place. She let herself down on to it, and Oliver deposited Winston in her lap. That great fluffy creature started to purr. She could see him thinking that this was more like it. His servant was lying down so that he could make himself comfortable on her. Good. He licked her hand to show his appreciation…which reminded him that his fur could do with a good clean.

Bea knew Winston wouldn't settle till he had finished his toilet, but she accepted the mug of tea from Oliver, and sipped it. Oliver moved a small table to her side.

She smiled at him, remembering the homeless waif she'd taken in so long ago, and thinking that his adopting parents would never recognize him now. Growing a beard suited him. She wondered if he'd ever tried to find his birth mother. He'd always said he didn't need to do that, but… Soon he'd be bringing a girl back home. Bea didn't think he was sleeping around. She might be wrong about that. But she wouldn't ask him.

'Settle down,' he said, taking the empty mug off her. She wouldn't sleep. She knew she wouldn't. Winston was steadily working his tongue over his whole body. 'Leon is supposed to be ringing.'

'Give me your phone. If he does, I'll come and wake you.'

She closed her eyes…

…and opened them, thinking that something was wrong. Winston was fast asleep, stretched out lengthways between her and the back of the settee. A rug was over her legs. She was warm and felt rested, but… She yawned.

Was the light fading? She must have slept for quite a while.

Oliver came into the room, carrying a tray. Some tinned soup, with bread and cheese.

She sat up with care, so as not to disturb Winston. 'Everything's all right?'

'So far. Piers has disappeared upstairs to paint. Hari's mooching around, doing something with a camera and some trip wire. There's nothing happening in any of the gardens. I've dealt with all the messages that have been piling up on your phones. There's nothing there that jumped out at me. I've tried to contact Leon. So far he's not accepting calls.' He put the tray on her lap. 'Eat up. And then, could you bear to talk me through everything that's happened? I want to make a recording, so don't miss anything out.'

He placed a miniature recorder on the table. 'By the way, Hari thinks you're right about their targeting our water supply, so he's taking precautions. Who have you been upsetting, Mrs A?'

'I wish I knew. Apart from the Payne family, that is. But, even there, I can't see why they should have it in for me. Even if they could pin the fall of the wall on me, what they've done doesn't make any sense.' The soup was good. So was the bread and cheese.

When she'd finished, he said, 'Now, start from the beginning, with the fall of the wall. I want the facts, yes, but I'd also like you to give me every suspicion or conclusion or stray thought that might have crossed your mind. I want names and dates as far as you know them. I want catty comments about these people, the way they dress and act, the way they furnish their house. I want to know who their friends are. I want masses of speculation, preferably libellous. I want you to give it to me off the top of your head, with wild surmises thrown in. You have a brilliant memory for detail and you understand people. So start. We have plenty of time.'

It did take time. When she'd finished, he said, 'You've forgotten something. What's all this about finding some human bones in Leon's garden?'

'I know very little about them. The builders turned up some bones, thought they were from the dogs that had been buried there over the years. It was a pets' cemetery, with headstones for Fido, aged eighteen, at one time. I never went into the house or the garden, so I didn't see them myself. The bones were old, but the builders thought they might be human and called in the police, who dug up all the bottom of the garden. Their tent was there for a while, but it's gone now. Someone said that if the police were interested, they would want to dig up the drains and take up the floorboards at Leon's house, but I can't see that they'd bother since he's had everything renewed. That's all I know.'

She thought back. 'Leon asked me to find out something about the people who'd lived there years ago. Lady Payne did mention them. Something about her neighbour

having had a husband who died at sea and that she'd then
set up a charity in his memory. It did cross my mind to
wonder if he hadn't been lost at sea, and that it might be
his bones in the garden, but I can't see why she'd have
buried him there. Isn't there some sort of law about pre-
venting proper burial? Anyway, dear Edith said the old
lady has gone doolally, so there won't be much point in
questioning her about it. The police have all that in hand.
It's nothing to do with me.'

'What was her name?'

Bea shrugged. 'I don't think she said.'

'Do you know if your own particular contact in the
police is involved in this?'

'I haven't heard from him for a while. He got over-
worked and took a long leave of absence. When he came
back he applied for some kind of desk job, I don't know
what exactly. I haven't seen him for a while. And no, I
can't talk to him about this. And I can't go to the police
because, if I do, it'll come out that Leon was supposed
to have abused Venetia…at least, I suppose it was Venetia. We're hamstrung. Can't move.'

'Let me think over what you've said. Maybe I can
come up with an idea or two.'

'Leon,' she said. 'Hasn't he rung yet?'

He handed her over her phone. 'No. You want to try
him now?'

Bea tried his new number and it went to voicemail.
Again. So Leon was still busy. She left a short message
for him to ring her when he was free.

She relaxed, sliding down into the embrace of the settee. Leon, who had seemed so close to her, so much a part
of her life, now seemed to have receded into the distance.
He had his priorities and she had hers, and never the

twain shall meet. She'd hoped they could bridge the gulf, but it seemed less and less likely as time went on. It was painful to accept this, but not as painful as she'd thought it would be. Perhaps she was just numb and couldn't feel anything much any longer.

She was startled when her phone rang. It wasn't Leon, though. It was Zoe, his PA. 'You rang, Mrs Abbot?'

'I'm sorry to trouble you, Zoe. I was trying to reach Sir Leon.'

'He's been asking after you. Where are you now?'

'At home. Complications.' How could she explain in two words?

'Are you not coming out to join him? He's expecting you.'

'I have to get the agency back to work—'

'Can't you get someone else to see to it for you?'

'Not really, no. Where is he now? Did he manage to find out what the link was between the Admiral and his business affairs?'

'What? Oh. No. I think that was just last-minute jitters, someone starting a rumour without foundation. I don't think the Admiral's involved at all. It was just bad luck that Sir Leon fell sick with food poisoning at their party. No great harm done.'

'But the hospital results showed that we were drugged, and didn't you say that some reporter or other was on your track—'

'Clearly, it was nothing. The sale's going through, and Sir Leon is expecting you to be at his side when it does. So, how soon can you come?'

'It's tempting to think I can abandon everything here, but there's the agency to consider.'

'Yes, yes. He says you always think of others before

yourself, but let's put things into proportion, shall we? He understands that the agency is your pet baby, and has provided you with a living of sorts, but isn't it time you thought of retiring? Or selling it? He suggested that he might buy it off you. You'll have to close for a couple of months anyway, till you can get it up and running again, so why not take the opportunity to have a holiday while you're at it?'

'I can't do that. I have a responsibility to my girls—'

'And he has a responsibility for the jobs of thousands of people around the globe. You can't compare the two.'

That was a blow below the belt. Leon thought that his job was far more important than hers; that she should recognize their relative importance in life, and behave accordingly. It was a shock. And yet, she realized she ought to have seen it coming.

'No,' said Bea, slowly, reluctantly, knowing that her words would change their relationship for good. 'I can't throw away everything I've achieved, everything I've worked for, just because I could do with a holiday. That would be irresponsible of me.'

'But Mrs Abbot—!'

'Have fun. I'll catch up with him when he gets back to London.' She ended the call and dropped the phone. She felt dull and empty. She was going to regret refusing to fly out to him, wasn't she? Yes, she would regret it, but she knew she'd regret it even more if she turned her back on everything that had made her what she was.

'Good,' said Oliver. 'Now, I'll get started, shall I?'

'On what?'

'Finding out the connection between Admiral Payne and Leon.'

She didn't say that was an impossible task. Oliver

was a bright lad, and if he thought he could do it, then that was exactly what he would do. She shook off her rug and stood up.

'I've thought of something that *I* can do. I'm going to check back over all the phone calls that have been coming in for the agency, to see if there's anything I've missed. I particularly want to find out who's been spreading the word that the agency has gone kaput. Hopefully, that'll lead us back to the Admiral or to Lady Payne.'

THIRTEEN

Sunday evening

FIRST, BEA MADE a list of all the phone calls that had come in since that morning. Some were from her staff. Anna and Betty had replied to all these, but Bea worked her way systematically down the list, checking that everyone knew exactly what was happening and that they would turn up on time tomorrow. She warned them that the main telephone line was still out of action, but confirmed that she'd reimburse anyone who used her mobile for work.

Only Carrie seemed unsure about returning, citing a bad cold. Or flu. Or a failure of nerve?

The other girls were excited and horrified by what had happened, but were anxious to keep their jobs and promised to be there on the dot. Two of them even offered to bring in food and bottled drinks! Bea told them she'd rescued some personal items and hoped they'd be all right, but that if they'd got damaged they must claim against her insurance...without going overboard to claim for a gold fountain pen when they'd only lost a cheap biro! Cue laughter from the girls.

Then Bea started on the calls from customers and clients. There were ten of them. Again she worked her way down the list, reassuring everyone that the agency would be open again on the morrow, and that nothing would change in the way the agency would be operating. At the end of each call, she asked how they heard about the fire…and found two names cropping up time and again. Both had been on the phone to the agency's customers, spreading the word that Bea was finished.

And yes, Lady Payne was one. The other was Bea's next-door neighbour, the one who'd been about to host a bridge party, and whose husband had wanted to go down and help Zander cut up the tree. *I was a giant in those days.* And that woman had said the Admiral had told her to send all her bills to Bea. And so the story had gone full circle.

The question remained: how had Lady Payne discovered the names of Bea's customers? Ah. Of course. There were testimonials to good service on the agency website!

Bea took the list to the back window.

The daylight was definitely fading, even though the sky was still bright. Her garden was full of shadows, softening the wreckage caused by wall and tree. No birds sang. Nothing moved below.

Across the ruined wall, Leon's house stood stiff and silent, its windows blank. There were lights on in the Admiral's house. No blinds had been lowered there, no curtains drawn. Television lights flickered. The youngsters passed in front of the windows on the top floor, drinking from cans. Beer? Probably. They didn't seem to be going out…?

What about the youngster—what was his name? Rollo?—who they'd said was too young to go clubbing with them? No, there he was, crossing one of the other bedroom windows. There was a flicker from a television set in his room, too.

Bea lowered her gaze to the next floor down. That's where the Admiral and his wife slept…and presumably their son and daughter-in-law on occasion? Two people who had the right to leave cosmetics and clothes in those rooms, anyway.

The rooms on that floor were apparently unoccupied. The Paynes had either gone out, or were downstairs in the big sitting room, watching the telly, perhaps. Yes, the reception rooms on the ground floor were brightly lit, and yes, a telly light flickered there.

Down in the basement there was also an overhead light and a telly on. Now, who was it who lived there? Lady Payne had said something about…her sister? An elderly relative? Bea didn't know her name.

Bea raised her eyes to the sky. No longer did the tree impede her view of the church spire, which was lit to burnished gold in the rays of the gradually sinking sun. A sign of hope?

A few clouds hovered, way up high, touched with pink and gold. The wind had dropped.

Dear Lord, such a beautiful evening. What a pity it is that we mortals spend our time fighting one another instead of enjoying the beauty of the world you made for us to live in.

I stand here with my life in fragments around me but, looking at that sky, I am filled with wonder at your goodness to me. I cried to you for help, and you sent friends to stand by my side.

From the bottom of my heart, I thank you.

She heard her name called from the kitchen, and went down to find Hari tacking some dark material over the back door and window. A bright bulb in a wire holder—powered by the generator?—illuminated the central unit and left the rest of the room in shadow.

Oliver was crouched over his laptop, stroking his

newly grown beard and looking pleased with himself. 'Mrs A, I've found the Admiral. He sits on the board of a large number of companies, including one of the Holland Holdings companies. It's not an international one, but some of his fellow board members also sit on the board of Holland Holdings International in the Far East. It would give him contact with people who might want to upset the sale for some reason. I'm going to dig a bit more, see if I can get the minutes of the last meetings…'

Hari said, 'I've suggested that Piers go home. He refuses. Does he always get into such a frenzy when he's painting?'

What a nuisance Piers could be! 'So that's why he wouldn't move his stuff out of the lodger's room! But surely the light's fading for him now?'

'He says he's painting a door, which doesn't make sense to me, but there…what do I know about painting? Do you want me to turf him out?'

'I'll have a word with him in a minute.'

Hari tacked the last nail into place. 'I've covered over the windows in your new office already so no one can see in. I'll do your bedroom in a minute, and then the top of the house. The enemy will think the house empty if no lights show. I've fixed up a camera in the window of the front room focused on the water meter on the pavement outside, and another which will operate if anyone interferes with the wire I've strung across the back of the garden. I'll sleep in here on the floor.'

Bea knew better than to argue that he indulge himself by sleeping on a settee or in a bed. 'You think they'll try something else tonight?'

'I trust you'll get a good night's sleep.' As bland as milk chocolate.

Meanwhile, a name and a face had slid into Bea's head. Tippi van Dekker. Divorcée, remarried. Well connected. A gossip. She was one of the people who'd rung the agency in a state about a forthcoming party because Lady Payne had told her the agency had folded. Bea had glimpsed Tippi at the Admiral's party on Friday night. Tippi might well have some gossip to relate. Tippi's current husband was something in one of the ministries, wasn't he? And lived not far away?

Bea picked up her phone, and was fortunate enough to find Tippi at home. 'Mrs van Dekker, it's Bea Abbot here from the agency. I'm sorry to interrupt on a Sunday evening. But could you spare me a minute? Oh, no. Nothing to do with the arrangements for your party next month. That's perfectly in order. I noticed you were at the Paynes' party the other night and I wondered if I might ask you about them. You see, we'd never been invited before but…'

A high, sweet voice with the very slightest rolling of 'r's and 'l's. 'This is the perfect time to ring as I've been at home alone all day, feeling neglected. I am the archetypal golf widow. Hugo Payne put my husband up for this club, which is oh-so exclusive, and entered him for a tournament which has a big pot on the table, or wherever it is that they keep their pots. I tell myself it's better being a golf widow than being dunned for gambling debts, which my last husband but one used to do, and I must say that this one never blenches at my credit card bills.'

'Hugo Payne?' said Bea, her heartbeat going into overdrive. 'Lady Payne's son?'

'Got it in one. He's secretary of a prestigious golf club somewhere in the Home Counties. I only went once. Everyone either looked at me as if I'd two heads, or tried to peer down my cleavage. I don't know which is worse. You'll hardly believe it, but they don't allow women into the clubhouse until after eight or something equally ante-diluvian, although I gather there's a number of members who are revolting—too, too amusing. But Hugo says he's been fighting a rear-guard action to keep the women out. So, how do you know the Paynes?'

'We're neighbours. Our garden walls adjoin, and my friend Sir Leon Holland has bought the house next door to them.'

'Ah, so that's it. I must confess I was the teeniest bit surprised to see you there with the Big Bad Bear—' *did she mean Leon?*—'though I must say I think he's rather dishy, and we won't talk about who's sleeping in whose bed like Goldilocks, will we? You'll bring him to my little party, won't you?'

Had Bea received an invitation? No. But she was going to be given one, so that she could take Leon along? Bea crossed her fingers. 'So kind. At the moment we're all at sixes and sevens, but—'

'Yes, Edith said. As I told you earlier, she rang me to say you'd gone out of business. But you really haven't, have you?'

'Certainly not. Now, I'm not very well acquainted with all the members of the Payne family. Could you bear to sort them out for me? First there's Edith, Lady Payne. She rules the roost, doesn't she?'

'Known her for ever. Our people come from the same village—squirearchy and all that. We even went to school together. Well, she was Head Girl in the sixth form when I started in the reception class. She got married while I was still at school. I remember going to her wedding. She had six bridesmaids and we all thought he was *so* hand-

some; well, it's the uniform that does it, isn't it? I don't
know whether you know it or not, but he's only a Rear
Admiral. He got made up for counting lifebelts or something equally banal. Born at the wrong time, never saw
any real action at sea. Mind you, if you listened to Edith,
you'd think he'd won every sea battle since Trafalgar. In
my view, he's a lightweight with a pretty moustache and
beard. Oh, and a bottom-pincher. Retired long since. In
naval terms, he's a dinghy and she's a battleship.'

Bea spurted into laughter. 'I like that. What about
their son, Hugo? You say he's the secretary of an exclusive golf club?'

'That's the beginning and end of him, my dear. A
prestigious job that he can boast about but which doesn't
bring in much money. His wife is a wishy-washy creature, manages a dress shop which she'd like to pretend
she owns, but doesn't. They live in a pretty little town
in Surrey, the sort that has a market every Friday which
sells cheap clothes and plastic toys. Private school fees
practically wiped them out and they'd been going to put
the kids into state schools till the family came to the
rescue. I would feel sorry for them if they didn't put on
such airs and graces. You should hear them boasting
about their "town" house and their "little country cottage". You'd think they owned the house in Kensington
whereas they're only allowed to stay there for the occasional night, and their "country cottage"—which is
their main residence, by the way—is a hideous Victo-
rian building that used to be a rectory conveniently situ-
ated halfway between the church—which has long fallen
into disuse and been converted to flats—and the gates
to the golf club.'

'They were here for the party?'

'No, I don't think so. Fridays and Saturdays, all week-ends, he has to be at the golf club, and she'd never miss a Saturday in the shop because that's when they do their best trade.'

'So they did manage to educate their children privately?'

'Yes, well; I do feel sorry for the boy, because he was a bit of an afterthought, and so much younger than Venetia. Did I hear there was a miscarriage between the two of them? That might explain it. It's quite an age gap, isn't it? Edith talks about getting the girl a Season. I doubt they can afford it, and anyway…' The lilting voice trailed away.

'Yes,' said Bea. 'Venetia takes after her grandmother, doesn't she?'

A sigh. Then silence. Tippi didn't normally 'do' silence.

Bea said, gently, 'Would you agree that Venetia could be…impulsive?'

'She's very young!' Sharply.

'And thinks the world owes her a place in the sun?'

Another pause. 'I can't talk about it.'

So there was something to talk about?

Tippi said, in an artificially jolly voice, 'Lots of young-sters nowadays think they're entitled to the best. That's what they've been brought up to think, isn't it?' Light laughter, intended to hide unease.

How tempting it would be to accuse the girl of steal-ing and using Bea's phone and cosmetics, not to men-tion her watch! But, until they could tie the fingerprints to Venetia and thus checkmate what Lady Payne had on Leon, it would not be a good idea to do so.

'I understand you don't wish to talk about her, but you might perhaps point me in the direction of someone who *is* prepared to do so? Is she at university?'

'She dropped out, but lots of people do that, don't they? I believe she's gainfully employed nowadays—or, rather, that she's got an internship working for some big firm in the City. She's certainly personable enough.'

'Internships don't pay anything, do they?'

'I believe not.' With restraint. A spurt of words. 'Don't say I told you, but the girl is a wild child, likes smashing things—cars, mainly. Not hers. Borrowed ones.'

'"Borrowed" as in "borrowed without permission"?'

'I don't think she has a licence any more. Rumour has it that it's cost the family a pretty penny this last year, in order to keep her out of court. And her cousin doesn't seem to be... No, I shouldn't have said that.'

'Gideon? He's through university, isn't he?'

'Sent down. That's the way they put it when they've been found out doing something they can't cover up. Edith says he's on a gap year, whatever that may mean. He doesn't have a paying job, so far as I know. Edith did ask me if my husband knew of anything for the lad but my dearly beloved said he wasn't such a fool as to risk taking him on.'

A guess. 'He's a gambler?'

'I really couldn't say.'

Which meant that he probably was. So, one cousin gambled while the other smashed up other people's cars? 'What about Gideon's brother? Still at university?'

'Mm. When he feels like it. I've heard him say that, myself. "When I feel like it." All three of them seem to think the world owes them a living.'

'I met a young lad at some point. Is he another brother?'

'That will be Venetia's much younger brother, Rollo. Doesn't take after her. Still at the awkward stage. What is he now...fifteen, sixteen? Moves in jerks, as if he were a marionette. A difficult period for a boy. He's still at school, but it's the summer holidays, isn't it? Edith's never had any time for him, and neither have Hugo and his wife, so I suppose that's why he's hanging out with Mona. There's nothing for him to do at home in the country. I believe he has an ambition to play in a band with some friends.' A snort of derision.

'There's a title somewhere in the background? Venetia made a point of informing me about it, as if a mere serf like me ought to understand how much more important her cousins are than I.'

'Oh well, yes. That's the Barwell side of the family. Edith's elder sister, Mona, married Viscount, Lord Barwell, from a distinguished old family who had fallen on hard times. He went AWOL years ago. Some kind of scandal. Fraud? Something like that. I heard he went to live in Miami or someplace where it's warm winter or summer.'

'I don't think I've met Mona. Is she the one who lives in the basement?'

'That's her. Not at all like Edith. Shy and retiring as a field mouse; doesn't use the title. I suppose I've met her half a dozen times over the years but, as Edith says, Mona's not one for socializing. It was a second marriage for both of them and she never had any children, but she brought up Malcolm, who was Lord Barwell's son by his first wife, and did a good job by all accounts. Malcolm isn't around anymore. He dropped the title, married an Australian and went off to live in Auckland. No, that can't be right, because Auckland's in New Zealand, isn't it? Another city in Australia beginning with 'A'? Antwerp's in Holland, isn't it? Anyway, Malcolm had two boys, both Honourables who like to flash their titles around as if it makes them special. Malcolm sends them back here for their education, and Mona looks after them in the holidays.'

'Two Honourables, then? Gideon and...?'

'How time flies. I remember them when they were so high and playing cricket in that garden of theirs at the back and then there was a party one summer when the elder boy was twenty-one but that was held somewhere in Soho, I think, and it was just for the youngsters and we didn't go. Edith doesn't hold many parties nowadays. In fact, I was slightly surprised when she rang to invite me the other day, such short notice, but one doesn't want to disoblige old friends. I remember their cricket party because that was when I caught my number two playing around with a part-time model, and it was Edith who pointed me in the direction of the excellent solicitors who have looked after me ever since. I saw the young ones the other night, enjoying themselves at Edith's. They weren't there very long, were they? Did you meet them then? I suppose they got bored and went off clubbing somewhere. I wonder if they have more chance of getting summer jobs here than back in Australia?'

'The elder boy is sleeping with Venetia.' That was a guess.

'I really can't comment.' Silence. 'What makes you think that?' Cautiously.

'Their body language. And she's the boss.'

A sigh. 'Yes, I had heard something, but... I don't take any notice of rumours.'

'No, of course not.' *Venetia has been the subject of rumours? It would be good to know what the gossips were saying about her.*

'Must go,' said Tippi. 'Lovely to talk to you. Don't

forget my little party. Bring Sir Leon, won't you? I can promise you there'll be some reasonable booze, better than at Edith's, anyway.'

Click. Off went Tippi.

Bea had been conscious for some time of Hari answering the front door and letting someone into the house.

And there was Sophy, the waitress from the party, with sullen-faced Miguel at her back. They weren't wearing their black outfits today. Sophy was in jeans and a sweatshirt, and so was Miguel.

Sophy was looking around her with horror. 'Oh, Mrs Abbot! This is awful. Did the fire do so much damage? Someone said you'd been put out of business, like, but I phoned the hospital and they said you'd been discharged, so I thought it can't have been too bad, like, and I would have come round here to give you back your ring this morning, but we had a job for a lunch out Marlow way, like, and I didn't wear your ring, not once, but put it on a string round my neck so that I could get it back to you soonest.'

'Oh, Sophy!' Tears. Bea despised herself for crying. She hugged Sophy, hard. Miguel shifted from one foot to the other, embarrassed.

'I was so worried about you,' said Sophy. 'Wasn't I, Miguel? You don't look so good even now, Mrs Abbot, but the other night you looked so awful I was really worried, and Mr Leon, too. I thought Mr Leon was going to die, like, but Miguel said he was tougher than that, and he is going to be all right, isn't he? Have you got him out of hospital, yet? I said to Miguel that you were sure to bounce back, like, because you always do, don't you? I remember when your husband died, God be good to him, and you looked like a ghost and wore his ring all the time, but then you pulled your socks up, like, and took over the agency. I know how much his ring meant to you, and I don't want a reward, honest!'

Here Miguel nudged her, clearly not entirely in agreement with her disclaimer. She pushed his shoulder back. 'Oh, you. No, I don't, Miguel, and you shut your mouth because this is my decision, like, not yours.' And to Bea, 'Miguel wanted to know what I thought was going on last night at the Paynes', like, and I told him you helped the police sometimes with stuff, and I said it was probably something like that, and we didn't need to know, like, what it was exactly. I said the Paynes were a nasty lot and you were probably investigating them and got found out and they were taking it out of you, like. Am I right?'

'Something like that,' said Bea, drying her eyes for the umpteenth time that day. 'Sir Leon is all right and has taken himself off abroad for a while. I am so, so grateful to you. I dread to think what would have happened if you hadn't got us out of there.'

'See!' Sophy was triumphant. She untied a string from around her neck and fished Bea's ring out from between her breasts. 'And there you are, safe and sound, like!'

Bea pushed the ring on to her finger. 'Bless you a thousand times. I'll write you out a cheque straight away, and add something for your mobile phone and the money you gave me. As for your jacket, I'll have that cleaned and return it to you.'

Sophy gave a little bounce. 'Oh, you don't really have to…but if you want to, like, I suppose Miguel will tell me I ought to accept something from you.'

'Now, where's my chequebook? Not the office one but my personal one. In my handbag. Now, where has that got to? Come upstairs with me, Sophy, will you, and help me find it? Everything's been moved around. I *think* I know where it might be…'

Hari was signalling to her. 'Yes, Hari?'

'Have you got a tame electrician on tap, Mrs Abbot? I thought I had one nailed down, but he's slid out from under. I've tried two more, but there's nothing doing to-night. The thing is, there's different circuits for lighting and for power on each floor. If we can isolate the ones for the basement, we might be able to get power and light back on upstairs.'

Miguel's face lit up. This was man's work! 'Let's have a look. I've stuck around lots of times while my uncle fiddles with that stuff.'

Bea and Sophy exchanged glances and left the men to it. As they climbed the stairs, Bea explained to Sophy how they'd rearranged the house so that the agency could still open in the morning. 'Look out for a brown leather handbag. It's a Mulberry. I may have left it, well, anywhere, before I went off to the party. The men have moved all my sitting-room furniture up one floor into what was my bedroom, but my clothes are here, there and everywhere…ah!' She spotted the handbag under a chair and retrieved her chequebook. 'Would six hundred be about right, Sophy?'

Hari hadn't yet got round to blacking out the window, and Sophy was able to look out over the ruined garden. 'What a view! And you can see right into the Paynes' house, like. You know they short-changed us on Friday? Said we had agreed to four waiters, and we did, but they said Miguel didn't count, and then they added up the empty bottles and the leftovers and said we'd kept one for ourselves, which we hadn't. And no tip, not a penny.'

Bea took the chequebook to the table in the win-

dow and looked out over Sophy's shoulder. 'You hadn't
worked for them before, had you?'

'And won't again. They got us through Mrs van
Dekker, who'd told the Paynes she always used us
through you, but Lady Muck said she couldn't afford to
go through an agency, like, and got straight through to
Miguel, saying it was an emergency, and he didn't realize
what a skinflint she was, seeing that the recommendation
had come through the Dekkers. Never again.'

'Are you doing the van Dekker party? I was talking
to her earlier. She's invited me and Sir Leon.'

Sophy pulled a face. 'I keep forgetting he's a "sir"
nowadays. He doesn't mind, does he? We've done his
parties before, out at the college for Mrs Anna, and all.
Proper food and drink and no messing, with good tips.'

Bea signed the cheque and tore it out of the book.
'Have you ever worked for the people in the house next
door, the one that's just been painted? Sir Leon has
bought it but hasn't moved in yet.' She handed the cheque
to Sophy. 'This all right?'

A brief glance, and a nod. Sophy put it in her bra. No
pockets, of course. Sophy looked across at Leon's house.
'Sure. I used to do her bridge parties. The Duchess, they
used to call her, though she wasn't. She went around looking like Queen Mary, like, that's the one before the one
that's Queen now. Or before her, maybe. We learned her
at school, din't we? Long blue coat and a blue hat perched
on her curls. With a diamond brooch and strings of pearls
tight round her neck.'

'I've heard the woman who used to live there was a
bit doolally.'

A shrug. 'I'll give you she was a bit odd, like, dressing
as she did, and running some kind of charity that I don't

think made any money, but the diamonds were real. You can tell, can't you? And rings, like! She had two rings on each of her fingers, and long chains, and she smelt of old talcum powder and maybe something else. I don't reckon her plumbing had been investigated for years, if you see what I mean.'

Bea saw, but didn't pursue the matter. 'I was told she'd gone a bit strange and had been forced to sell so that she could go and live in a home.'

Another shrug. 'She was all right up to Christmas, when I last saw her. There was a group of them playing bridge at one another's houses, like, though not at the Duchess's, come to think of it. She seemed bright enough, then. Alzheimer's, you think? What a shame.'

'Her charity: was it something to do with her husband being lost at sea?'

'His name was spelled funny, like. I know because she used to take a little collecting box around with her, and we all had to put something in it, even if it was only fifty pence at a time. I thought it was rather sweet of her, really. It was the Renard Trust for those Lost at Sea. She said it was something to do with foxes. Is that the fox, Renard? I never met him, her husband. He had a title, too, but I can't remember exactly what. He was lost in some accident at sea. Always went sailing at weekends—sometimes with the Admiral, sometimes by himself, like—and then one time there was a storm and he didn't come back.'

'I understand she's moved into a home somewhere?'

A shrug. 'Dunno. We thought, Miguel and I, that you were working on something for the police last night, only something went wrong, like. Can you say what really happened, or is it all hush-hush?'

Bea tried to work out what to say. 'Yes, it certainly

did go wrong. I am so grateful that you spotted the
flames and rang the fire brigade. Did you see how the
fire started?'

FOURTEEN

SOPHY SHOOK HER HEAD. 'We was that busy, like. The youngsters knocked into me on their way out the marquee and didn't bother to say "sorry", but that lot don't never apologize, do they? They was high as kites, prob'bly on something, like, laughing fit to bust; never mind they'd jogged the tray out of my hands and two glasses fell and got broke. We kept the boxes for glasses out the back of the marquee, so I got the dustpan and brush and was taking the bits outside when, blow me! They nearly tumbled me over again as they come back in. I went on out with the broken glasses and that's when I saw the flames and called Miguel to come see, and then I called the fire brigade.'

Bea kept a tight hold on herself. 'Two young men? Would you know them again?'

A nod. 'The two young lads that belonged to the house. Hair all over their eyes, good clothes, no manners. Students? More money than sense, like. Think they've the right to grab your boobs and fumble up your skirt. That sort.'

'There wasn't a girl with them?'

'I didn't see no girl.'

Venetia must have remained indoors to try out Bea's cosmetics and use her phone. Or was it the boys who'd used the phone, to ring home to Australia? Now, there's a thought. If their parents were in Australia, the boys might have grabbed the chance for a free call after the party was over and before they went out clubbing.

Bea pulled her thoughts back to the arson attack. 'You think it was the boys who set the fire, but you didn't actually see them do it?'

'I didn't see no one else come in from outside. When they come back, one of them was carrying something bulky, like, a white container of some sort? Dunno what they did with it.'

That made sense. So the two boys had set the fire using a container of paraffin—where had they got that from? Then they'd put the can out at the front of the house to be taken away with the rubbish. And Hari had found it.

'After that,' said Sophy, 'it was better nor Saturday night on the telly! Guests popping out to see the fire, and rolling up the canvas sides so that they could see better, and the Admiral bleating that there wasn't nothing to see but nobody took no notice, like, did they? The fire died down and they all started to drift off, and you come along, and in such a state!'

Bea reckoned she'd had a lucky escape. When the fuse had blown, Lady Payne had ordered the boys to search for a replacement, but they were in possession of Bea's keys and must have thought it would be a lot more fun to set her house alight than to bother with a small domestic problem like replacing a fuse. It had probably only taken them five minutes—perhaps less—to find the paraffin, set the fire and return. After that Lady Payne had kept them busy searching the house for the two escapees... who'd been under their noses all the time.

Sophy eyed Bea speculatively. 'So what were you up to, then?'

'I'll tell you in a minute. Did the police not turn up at the Admiral's house eventually?'

'It was all over by then. Everyone but us had left when

they come knocking, and asking if we'd seen anything. Lady Payne told the coppers everyone had seen the blaze but no one had seen who'd set it. She said, and I heard her with my own ears,' here Sophy imitated a high, upper-class voice, '"It must be some vandals from one of the other gardens who took advantage of our walls having fallen down!" and, "Wasn't it all too, too dreadful?" Horrible old cow. They took her word for it, like, which they hadn't oughter, had they? The police took our names and said they might get back to us and we didn't say nothing, not with her looking at us, like. She's scary!'

'I don't know what else you could have done. Sophy, have a seat, and I'll tell you exactly what happened…'

And she did. In detail, starting from the moment the wall had come down, recounting the Admiral's calls to their neighbours to lay the blame on her, progressing to the invitation to the party, their separation into different rooms, their being drugged, the scraping of Leon's cheek and their blundering escape into the garden.

Sophy's eyes and mouth grew wide. 'You mean…' She waved her arms about. Turning to look out over the gardens, she said, 'That's evil! But…why!'

'That,' said Bea, 'is what I'd like to know. There's a number of theories going around. First, it's something to do with Sir Leon's selling his overseas assets. The Admiral has shares in a lot of companies and he's short of money—'

'The skinflint!'

'Yes. So he might easily be persuaded to take part in a plot to discredit Leon and interfere with the markets for monetary gain.'

'But why target this house?'

Bea pressed both hands to her head. 'I've been trying not to think that way, but yes, as you say, why should anyone want to wipe out me and my agency?'

Sophy hesitated. 'Those youngsters, they're way out of line. The way they were acting, off their heads laughing, not caring who saw them—'

'I'm with you. I think that Admiral and Lady Payne hatched a plot to discredit Sir Leon and me but that, when the youngsters took a hand, it passed out of the control of the senior members of the family. I think the youngsters fired my house for kicks! But, there were no witnesses to the arson, and I can't go to the police with what I know till I can ensure Sir Leon's safety.'

'But you won't let them get away with it.'

'No, Sophy, I won't. But I must confess I feel as if I'm continuously being hit like a punchbag. No sooner do I try to rebound from one thing than the next blow descends. Hari thinks they'll try to cut off the water supply tonight and possibly try another attack through the garden. And I haven't had time to sit down and work out why this is happening.'

'It doesn't make sense.' Sophy looked out of the window over the devastation below. Bea joined her.

A ginger cat appeared at the top of what remained of a neighbour's wall. A good place to sit and groom himself.

Nothing moved in Leon's back garden. The rays of the setting sun were reflecting light from the newly cleaned windows of his house.

There was a stir in Bea's garden below. Winston, balanced on a pile of logs, eyed the distance from where he was crouched to the remaining part of the right-hand wall. He made the leap, and disappeared down into the next garden. Business as usual. Bea wondered how the neighbour's bridge party had got on that afternoon.

The dumpy figure of an elderly woman came out of the basement flat into the Admiral's garden. Bea checked with Sophy. 'That's not Lady Payne. Is it her elder sister, the one who lives in the basement?'

'Her? She come out to ask us if we'd like a cuppa when we arrived to set up for the party. Said she always goes to see an old friend on Friday evenings, but that we could use her toilet if we needed, sooner than go up into the house. She was nice. We thought she was the house-keeper. She don't look much like Lady Payne. You sure they're sisters?'

Agreed, they didn't look much like one another. Bea watched as the woman—Mona, was that her name?—picked her way across the garden to the tumbledown shed in the corner and knocked on the door. The young lad—Rollo?—pushed his head out. She said something to him, upon which he returned to the house with her.

'That's the youngest member of the family,' said Bea. 'Is she saying there's a phone call for him?'

Sophy said, '"Supper's ready?" I didn't see him at the party. What's he doing in the shed? Having a quick fag?'

Bea wondered, 'Do you think Mona might be worth talking to?'

'How would you get past Her-that-rules-the-roost, like?'

Bea wanted to say, 'I'll get the police to ask her some questions,' and realized she couldn't talk to the police. Not yet. Which meant it was up to her to get at the truth.

And from one second to the next, she was paralysed with fear.

She had to force herself to breathe in and out. In and out.

Panic!

She could not—could not!—*could not!*—enter that house again.

Too much had happened to her there.

She'd been drugged, tossed around like a rag doll, been searched, her property had been stolen...

No, she *could not*... She winced away from the thought. It was too much! She couldn't be expected to... the humiliation, the way she'd been forced to hide and... to have to bribe her way out of the situation! No, no, *no!*

Let someone else do it.

Oh? Who?

Anyone else. The police.

You know that if you hand this over to the police, Leon will be pilloried for something he didn't do.

Am I my brother's keeper? Well, yes, I suppose I am. True, he ran away, and left me to deal with the problem, but does that mean I'm the right person to deal with it?

You've always known you were stronger than him.

What! What was that?

You've always known you were stronger than him.

No. No!

Face facts. You're stronger than him.

Oh. Yes. Perhaps.

She closed her eyes. Dear Lord, I can't...not even with you backing me up... I'm too tired... You can't ask this of me.

I am always with you. Remember that I am already there...before you...behind you...around you... I am in the light. I am the Light. But, I am also in the dark.

She opened her eyes. 'I suppose I'd better go over there and have a word with her.'

Now it was Sophy's turn to be uneasy. 'You won't go alone?'

'I'll wait till she's by herself, and no: I won't go alone.'

Miguel and Sophy departed with renewed admonitions to Bea to take care of herself. She tidied up in the kitchen, and boiled kettles to wash the dishes. Miguel hadn't managed to isolate the circuit in the basement but, courtesy of the generator, they now had a light—from a table lamp—in the blacked-out kitchen, and could run the kettle, the fridge, the freezer and the microwave.

Oliver remained bent over his laptop, now and then making notes on a pad of paper. Hari swooped up and down the stairs, carrying cables and tools. The generator muttered away to itself in the garden.

The early evening faded slowly, imperceptibly, to dusk.

Bea had another try at getting through to Leon, and ended up in voicemail again. Ah well. Better than nothing. He needed to know what was going on; how helpful so many people had been; how they'd propped her up when she'd felt low. She tried to keep her report as short as she could. Leon had enough to worry about where he was, without her going into details about insurance claims and reporters. Nevertheless, it was good to be able to share her worries with someone, if only by voicemail. Perhaps he'd ring back tomorrow.

Feeling slightly refreshed, Bea went to find Hari, who was doing something complicated with wiring in the new office. 'Hari, I want to have a quiet word with an old lady, name of Mona Barwell, who lives in the basement at the Admiral's house, but I don't particularly want to bring the rest of that crew down on me.'

Hari said, 'Let's have a look-see.' He shut off the table lamp he'd been working by, led the way to the window, and lifted the blackout curtain. 'Why do you want to talk to her? She's their cook-cum-housekeeper, isn't she? Look, she's in the big kitchen on the ground floor now, cooking a meal, while the young lad is setting the table for her. How many is she expecting to feed? Six, seven? The Admiral and his wife are watching television in their sitting room next door. They're not lifting a finger to help, are they? I can't see the lad's parents.'

'My informant said they have to work at weekends. By the way, what do you fancy for supper yourself?' She peered over his shoulder. 'Are the youngsters still around? Ah, I see them.'

The three of them were in one of the bedrooms at the top of the house. Venetia was rolling around on the bed with the older boy, while his younger brother recorded the event on his phone.

There was an indrawn breath from Hari as the younger brother took his turn with Venetia.

It surprised Bea that Hari would be shocked. Surely he must have come across promiscuous youngsters before? Yes, it had shocked her, but she'd thought him un-shockable. It was rather endearing. She said, 'A pizza do you for supper?'

Hari said, 'Don't that lot ever draw their curtains?'

Bea switched her eyes back down to the Admiral's kitchen. 'Do you think the youngsters will condescend to eat the food their elderly relative has prepared, or will they go straight out drinking? There are seven people in the house at the moment. Not good odds. And I'd rather not come across the youngsters. They're unpredictable.'

'What about the schoolboy?'

She shrugged. 'He did return some of our stolen prop-erty, which argues he isn't involved in what the others are up to.'

'One of the advantages for us of their switching on the lights inside but never drawing the curtains, is that they can't see what's happening outside. Especially when it gets darker. Ah…'

Bea looked where he was pointing. The youngsters were changing clothes. One was towelling himself down after taking a shower. Were they preparing to go out for the evening? Were they going to join the grown-ups for supper?

If the young lad had laid the table for six or seven, it looked as if they were all going to eat in. So, Bea would get her household something to eat, too. She couldn't go visiting till things calmed down. 'Supper, then?'

Hari said, 'I'll finish blacking out your windows after supper. If we're not showing any lights, they'll assume we've deserted the place and that'll give them confidence to try something else…that is, if they're still intent on mayhem.'

The three of them ate in the kitchen office, not talking much. Now and then Hari leaped up the stairs to peer out of the 'new' office window to keep track of what was happening as the Admiral and his family moved around their brightly lit house.

The youngsters joined the seniors for supper in the big kitchen. Afterwards, Admiral and Lady Payne retired to their ground-floor sitting room and turned the telly back on.

Mona and the young lad, Rollo, filled the dishwasher and set it going. Rollo slipped out into the garden, put a padlock on the door of the rickety shed and smoked a fag.

Mona turned off the lights in the family kitchen and retired to the basement. On went some side lights there, and then came the flicker of her television. Rollo finished his cigarette and joined Mona in the basement, slumping into a chair beside her. She made them mugs of tea or coffee. He commandeered the remote and flicked through programmes on the telly. She tapped his wrist and took the remote off him. He shrugged, and settled down to watch whatever it was she wanted to see.

He was a misfit in that house, wasn't he? Neither fish, flesh, nor fowl. But at least Mona was looking after him.

The youngsters hung around for a bit in their rooms at the top of the house, changing clothes yet again. They were going out for the evening? To the pub? It looked like it. They disappeared from the top floor, reappeared briefly in the sitting room downstairs to have a word with their grandparents, and vanished from view. They had left all the lights on at the top of the house. Typical. They didn't have to pay the electricity bill, did they?

Hari said, 'Two in the basement, two on the ground floor. Give them all a while to settle down before you sneak across to have a word with the old lady. Take care not to turn an ankle as you go. Perhaps take a walking stick to negotiate the barbed wire and the rubble of the wall? I'll come with you and hover in the shadows when you go into the house. It will be like a stage set. I shall be able to see everything that happens inside, but they won't be able to see me, in the audience. One peep out of them, one word from you and I'll be right there with you.' He gave her the once-over. 'You'll be all right.'

She didn't feel all right.

She felt wobbly and fearful and there were so many thoughts running across her head that she couldn't disentangle any single one of them, except for the voice shouting at the back of her head that she *did not want to go over there!*

Hari had no doubts.

She had far too many.

She began to pace.

Just give me the facts, ma'am.

There was a shortage of facts. A lot of information—too much information?—but a shortage of facts.

Think Cluedo. Who did what to whom, in the library? Or, in this case, in the garden of Leon's house, which hadn't been his at the time, but which had belonged to a gaga elderly lady who dressed like the late Queen Mary and carried a charity box around with her. Said charity: for those lost at sea. Because, her husband had been lost at sea. And then, she'd got Alzheimer's and was now living in a home somewhere.

Question: what happens to the property of someone who's not capable of looking after their own interests? Doesn't the law provide a guardian of some kind?

Who signed the bill of sale for the house?

Leon hadn't mentioned any problem in that direction. Presumably, therefore, there hadn't been a problem.

Bea beat one hand on the palm of the other. 'This is irrelevant.'

And went on pacing.

Sophy said the Queen Mary lookalike had been around and playing bridge with her friends until recently.

Well, OK, Alzheimer's could strike at any time and its progress varied from one person to the other. Her house had been sold, Leon had put in his builders and...

Had the previous owner told Leon about the dog cemetery in her garden?

Bea stopped pacing. She spoke aloud. 'Yes, she did. Leon told me so. He said he was going to have the garden landscaped when he'd finished with the house. He'd wanted to have an outside tap and, yes, a fountain. He'd planned to cut a door through the wall into my garden. All of which meant…'

She noticed that Hari and Oliver had suspended whatever they were doing to listen to her. She shrugged, tried to smile. Told herself to keep her mouth shut.

Now, suppose Queen Mary's husband had not been lost at sea, but for some reason had been buried in his own garden?

Mm. Let's follow this line of enquiry. Is it possible that Queen Mary went on living there, grieving, setting up a charity in his memory and playing bridge…which is not a game for the mentally handicapped? Would she do that, if she'd buried him in the garden? No, she wouldn't. If she'd killed and buried him, she wouldn't have wanted to draw attention to the fact by perpetuating his memory in a charity for those lost at sea. Could she have done so out of guilt? But then…to sell the house, knowing that Leon planned to dig up the garden? No, it wasn't feasible.

Conclusion: Queen Mary didn't know about those bones!

Of course, they might have been there a hundred years or more. These houses were old enough. The bones wouldn't have been from a plague victim. No. Too early. These houses were only just being built when the plague last hit London. In any case, for reasons of hygiene, plague victims were buried away from the houses, usually in special pits. They were not interred in someone's back garden.

So, the bones belonged to a recent victim of crime?

Or, of course, Queen Mary might just be so far round the twist that she'd killed her husband and remained in denial about it ever after.

This is irrelevant! What have those bones to do with Leon…or with the Paynes?

Sometimes, if you're doing a jigsaw puzzle and can't see where the pieces fit, you turn it round and look at it the other way up. So, suppose you did that. It would mean that the bones meant something to Bea. Which was nonsense.

It also meant that the focus of investigation passed from Queen Mary to the Paynes. Now that did make sense in a way.

It meant that one husband going missing was sheer carelessness, but that two husbands going AWOL was…! Ah. Another husband had gone missing, hadn't he? Went off to Australia, according to Lady Payne. Went to Miami, according to Tippi.

Lady Payne is a liar, of course. Lady Payne had said that Queen Mary had Alzheimer's. That single fact could be checked.

Bea found her mobile and tried to get through to Leon. He wasn't picking up. Bother! But it wasn't going through to voicemail, either.

The dulcet tones of his annoying PA came through. 'Mrs Abbot? I observe that you are trying to communicate with Sir Leon—' infuriating chit!—'but he has instructed me that he cannot take any calls for the moment. May I take a message?'

'I'm sure you can give me the information I need. When Sir Leon bought his house, did he deal direct with the owner? I've been told a rather strange tale: that she has Alzheimer's and therefore wasn't responsible for—'

'What nonsense!' A snort. 'I was with him when the papers were signed and we all had lunch together afterwards. The seller was moving into a flat nearby. I can assure you she was perfectly *compos mentis*.'

One strike against Lady Payne, who'd said the QM had gone gaga. 'I'm sure she was. She told you about the dogs which had been buried in her back garden?'

'Most unsanitary. They do things differently nowadays. Two Labradors and a retriever of her husband's, which he himself buried in their garden years ago. Sir Leon said would she mind if he had the remains removed and cremated. She agreed, of course. He was also toying with the idea of installing a fountain and he wanted to cut a doorway through the end wall into your garden. He didn't *need* to ask her permission, but he wanted her to feel comfortable about what he planned to do. Naturally, she understood that once she'd sold, he might do as he wished. But she made no objection, I assure you.'

'Was there ever any proof that her husband was lost at sea?'

A sharp note entered Zoe's voice. 'Whatever are you on about now? Certainly he was lost at sea, and she obtained official notification of his death when he'd been gone for nine years. Believe me, Sir Leon wouldn't have bought the house if the title hadn't been clear in her name.'

'I have never been round the house or into the garden, but I believe you may have done so, when supervising the builders. Is that correct?'

'Yes. But—'

'As you say, Leon was thinking of cutting a door in the wall between his garden and mine. I suppose that has sometimes happened before between neighbours who are on good terms. Was there ever a door between Leon's garden and the Admiral's house next door?'

'Certainly not. It had been bricked up years ago.'

'But there had once been such a door? You saw the archway, and a difference in the brickwork?'

'I believe so. Now, if you don't mind—'

'One last question. Was the purchase made through one of Leon's companies? Was his interest in the house kept secret as long as possible?'

'Naturally. We didn't want the price being hiked because he was known to be a wealthy man. And now, if you please...' Zoe clicked off.

Bea discovered that Oliver and Hari were both looking at her. She said, 'We've been looking for the wrong man. Ten to one, those bones belong to the Admiral's family, and not to that of Queen Mary.'

DRESSED IN A high-necked black sweater, jeans and trainers, Bea followed in Hari's footsteps as he led the way down her garden, delicately avoiding the worst of the rubble. She waited while he cut the barbed wire along the line of the original wall, and let her through into the Admiral's plot.

She looked to the left into Leon's garden, to the trench from which a body had been removed, and the pits where the dogs had once lain.

She looked ahead and to the right, and found herself staring over the low balustrade at the ceiling of Mona's sitting room. As she moved stealthily forward, she could see more and more of it.

A standard lamp of the old-fashioned variety was the only illumination, apart from the bluish light of the television screen. It wasn't a large flat screen, but it was at least new enough to show a picture in colour. Some murder mystery, perhaps?

Hari signed to her to proceed and she did so, carefully stepping in her trainers across the garden which had harboured the marquee only two nights ago. She came to the low wall which prevented people from falling down the steps into the basement area. Facing her on her left was a blank, unlighted window...possibly giving on to the indoor gym to which Leon had been taken? Then came a door with a transom window above it, which would lead into the corridor bisecting the basement area. To the right lay the French windows which gave access on to Mona's sitting room.

The evening was warm and the French windows had been left open a crack. The sound of a gunshot drifted out, echoed by one from above Bea's head.

Bea looked up. One floor up, a window had been left open and the sound came from there. The Admiral and his wife were watching the same cops and robbers programme as Mona.

Hari nodded to Bea.

She knocked on the French windows, opened them wide, and entered the room.

FIFTEEN

'GOOD EVENING,' SAID BEA. 'I'm your neighbour, Mrs Abbot. I thought it would be a good idea to make your acquaintance... Mrs...? Lady...? I'm afraid we haven't been introduced and I'm not sure of your title.'

Identical looks of astonishment from Rollo, slumped in an armchair with his feet up on a coffee table, and from the comfortable-looking, grey-haired woman sitting beside him.

Mona Barlow didn't bother about dieting or makeup, bought her clothes from Marks & Spencer and washed her hair in the shower. She hadn't had Botox and her ankles had swollen in the heat. If she'd presented herself to the Abbot Agency in search of a job, she'd have been snapped up immediately as one of those capable women who dealt with difficult family situations without fuss. She was a Treasure, a Super Nanny. Her dress identified her as a poor relation, but she hadn't the apologetic air of one who expected to be overlooked.

Struggling out of her seat, Mona said, 'Mrs Abbot? Do come in. How nice of you to call. Yes, I'm Mona Barwell. Rollo, turn off the telly. If you want to watch that programme, you can go upstairs. Do sit down, Mrs Abbot. I understand you were taken ill at the party the other night? Is that right? I'm afraid I was out, but I heard something...'

She indicated a comfortable chair and, as Rollo was

being slow to obey, twitched her finger at him. 'Now, Rollo! Mrs Abbot, a cup of tea?'

Rollo, chewing his lip, turned off the telly. Rollo's eyes were sliding all over the place. Their hostess, however, seemed oblivious to his unease. Perhaps he was never at ease in society?

Bea summed up Mona Barwell as a genuine person, and innocent of wrongdoing. No, she couldn't be! Surely she must know what had been going on? It wasn't possible that she had no idea! Was it?

'Your sister, Lady Payne, kindly brought me down here on Friday and made me a cold drink. Unfortunately it disagreed with me, and I passed out. Rollo managed to find and return some of the property I mislaid at that time. I am truly grateful to you, Rollo.'

Rollo mumbled, "S'all right!'

Mona might not care about her appearance, but she was no fool. Her eyes were robin-bright. 'I understood there was a problem, but that all's well that ends well?' Yet there was a slight frown between her eyes. Either she had entertained some doubts about what had happened, or was concealing guilty knowledge? Which?

Bea said, 'I must apologize. I borrowed one of your young relation's kimono and flip-flops to get to the hospital. I'll have them cleaned and returned to you.'

Mona sat upright. 'Hospital? I hadn't heard about that. Rollo?'

'I wasn't here. I d-don't know anything. I f-found some of their stuff upstairs when the others had gone off c-clubbing, and I gave it back to Mrs Abbot. That's all.'

Mona's frown intensified. '*Their* stuff? Whose stuff?' She didn't take her eyes off Rollo. Bea could feel the message sent from one grey head to the youngster… *Just you wait till I get you alone!*

Bea said, 'Sir Leon Holland's shoes are still missing. I understand you'd gone out for the evening, Mrs….? Lady…?'

Rollo's head twitched. 'She's g-got a title but she d-doesn't use it. Drives Dad mad.'

'That's right. I'm Mrs Barlow,' said Mona. 'Come to think of it, I found a pair of men's shoes when I was cleaning the gym earlier today. I'll get them for you.' She disappeared. Rollo said something inarticulate, switched the telly on, shot a frightened look at Bea, changed his mind and switched it off again.

Bea let her eyes wander around the room. There was an old-fashioned dresser with an array of mismatched blue and white plates on it; rather charming in its way. Also charming was the heavy, old-fashioned crystal vase containing fresh flowers on the coffee table.

Mona reappeared, holding up a pair of shoes. 'I'll put them into a bag for you, shall I?' She went into the kitchen next door, found a clean plastic bag, put Leon's shoes into it, and handed it over. 'Is that everything, Mrs Abbot?'

Bea asked, 'Mrs Barlow, how much do you know of what's going on?'

Rollo squirmed in his chair. 'Honest, they never tell her anything. She's not the one who… Anyway, it was me that pulled the ivy off the wall!'

'I know,' said Bea. 'I saw you. You climbed a ladder and started pulling off the ivy, without realizing that the roots had locked into the bricks and worked their way under the footings.'

Rollo said, 'They were all on at me for b-being useless and I thought if I c-could clear the ivy from the wall and rebuild the shed, they'd let me have it to practise my g-guitar in. I didn't mean any harm.'

'No, I don't suppose you did,' said Bea, thinking that a lack of good judgement was probably the theme running through Rollo's life. 'You aren't a gardener. A gardener would have known that the best way was to cut the ivy off at the root and then let the plants die so that they'd release their hold on the mortar between the bricks. Then, in time, the ivy could have been picked off without tearing the wall down. But, as Rollo pulled it away, the roots took out all the mortar and there was nothing to hold the bricks together.'

'It wasn't my fault!'

'I'm afraid it was. Your weight on the ladder ensured that the wall fell away from you, and that's why it fell on the tree in my garden and brought that down, too. But the insurance people will deal with all that.'

Mona patted Rollo's shoulder. 'Worse things happen at sea.'

'They certainly do,' said Bea. 'Death came to your neighbour's husband at sea, didn't it?'

'Yes, poor Penelope. That dreadful storm, I'll never forget it. I sat up with her all that night, waiting for news. His body was never found. It happens, sometimes.'

'Indeed it does. How did your own husband die?'

'Knocking around in the Caribbean, car accident.'

A tingle went up the back of Bea's spine. 'You have proof?'

A frown. 'What is this? Of course we did. My brother-in-law got the details. We'd been divorced for ever so there didn't seem any rush to... What is this? Why are you asking?'

'I'm wondering whose bones have been dug up next door.'

Mona produced a strained smile. 'Well, obviously not my ex-husband's.' But there was some thought in her eyes which cleared the smile away. She shifted in her chair. 'I suppose it will be some vagrant or…a hundred-year-old skeleton, I expect. Someone who passed away when they lived in that house years ago. Long before Penelope was born. It was her family's home, you know. She was an only child, and her parents lived to a ripe old age. It can't be anything to do with them.'

Bea waited.

Mona shook her head at whatever she'd been thinking. No smile, now. She looked straight at Bea, 'I think you should explain yourself. Why are you here, and what makes you think you have the right to ask us questions?'

'I'm here because your family has involved me in your problems. In the past, you and your family lived on one side of the wall, and I on the other. Then your friend Penelope set off a chain reaction by selling her house. When did she tell you who had bought the house and what he planned to do with it?'

'She swore me to secrecy, and of course I understood why. Sir Leon didn't want everyone to know till the sale had gone through.'

'Neither you personally, nor Penelope, were worried about the garden next door being dug up?'

Mona told her lips to smile, but couldn't quite make it. She was going to lie. 'Well, of course there were the dogs' bones, and it wasn't really nice to think of them being dug up. Penelope did ask him to respect them, and he said he would try and it depended where they were, but that he did need to put a water pipe in for a fountain and to cut a door in the end wall. Naturally, Penelope had no say in the matter, once she'd sold.'

'Am I right in thinking there was once a door between your garden and Penelope's?'

'Yes, but we had it bricked up.'

'Your sister covered up for you?'

'Covered up what?' Mona reddened and her fingers pleated the skirt of her dress. 'The accidental death of your husband? Or was it murder?'

Mona laughed. A good attempt, but not convincing. 'I'm sorry, but… No! Why on earth would I…? No, really!'

Bea said, 'You didn't kill him to protect your family? To profit from his estate? No, I can see you didn't. Could you bear to tell me about it?'

Mona said, 'I have nothing to hide.' But her eyes betrayed a dawning horror. She was beginning to question…to wonder…to surmise!

'Tell me,' said Bea, in her softest voice. 'What was his name?'

'But… No, you've got it all wrong. I was married twice, you know. The first time was when I was very young, to a business partner of my father's. He was such a lovely man, much older than me, but we were very happy. We weren't able to have any children, a great sorrow, but then he had a heart attack and died, leaving me this house and a good income. I wasn't trained to work—in those days we girls weren't, you know—and I had nothing to do. I was so lonely, you can't imagine. It was then that I met Penelope and we became good friends.

'Then along came Magnus. He had a title and plenty of charm, but no money. What he did have was a lost and bewildered little son who needed mothering. I suppose I fell in love with the boy, rather than the father. Magnus's first wife had left him, you see. Penelope warned me he wasn't good husband material, but I didn't listen. When his divorce came through, we got married, and Malcolm stopped having nightmares and began to laugh again.'

Mona was explaining far too much. What she said had the ring of truth, but perhaps not the whole truth?

'It was about that time that a door was cut in the wall between your two houses?'

'That's right. It was convenient because Penelope's husband, Renard, had these dogs but couldn't take them sailing, so Penelope and I used to walk them twice a day. When she went sailing with him—which wasn't often but it did happen—then I would go in to feed them, and take them out for walkies. Malcolm was afraid of the dogs at first, but he got used to them in the end, and he and Hugo—that's my sister's little boy who often used to stay with us in the holidays, too, because they—my sister and brother-in-law—were stationed all round the world... Anyway, the boys were in and out of the two gardens all the time. Eventually they grew up and the dogs died, as did Penelope's husband. But I still went through the door to have tea with my friend every Friday afternoon, and sometimes more often.'

Oh. Bea winced. She'd been utterly, horribly wrong. This woman was a genuine do-gooder. 'So what happened to Magnus, your second husband?'

'I got him a job through a friend of my first husband's. The boys—Malcolm and Hugo, my sister's child—went away to school and came to us in the holidays. They got into the usual sorts of mischief but nothing to keep me awake at night, the young limbs.' And here she smiled, remembering. 'I soon learned that Magnus wasn't much good at managing his money and that he needed constant top-ups. He'd suggested we have a joint account at the bank but he was overdrawn so often that I soon stopped that, and I kept the house in my name only. It was second time round for both of us, and we…adjusted.'

'Was he faithful?' A stab in the dark.

Mona shook her head. 'He liked to spread his charms around, but I'd married him for better or worse, and little Malcolm was the light of my life, so we jogged along all right, with me turning a blind eye if Magnus came home a little the worse for drink now and then, or smelling of perfume. It didn't seem very important.'

Definitely too much information. She's talking too fast, giving too much detail.

Mona said, 'Then it all came crashing down. Magnus was arrested for fraud. He wanted me to bail him out, but it would have meant selling the house and, well, everything. I was putting Malcolm through university at the time. Hugo, too, because it wasn't fair that I should spend money on a child who was none of my kin, while Hugo was my very own nephew. So money was tight. I talked it over with my solicitor and Penelope, and I decided that, however painful it was, I couldn't let the rest of the family suffer for what Magnus had done.

'So, he went to prison…' a sigh '…and I divorced him. Malcolm was desperately upset. Well, we all were. But poor Malcolm…he couldn't bear to finish his degree. He went off on a gap year around the world, ended up in Australia and married a girl out there. Like his father, he had a title but no money. Unlike his father, he knew how to put in a good day's work. He dropped the title and started up his own business. I only had to help him for a couple of years and he's really made good now. I'm so proud of him. We still keep in touch, of course, and I look after his sons in the holidays because they're both in universities here. How time flies.'

Rollo's head was sunk between his shoulders. He muttered, speaking to his shoes, 'They treat her like a c-cash c-cow. They get her to p-pay for everything—their schooling and university fees. If they're ever short, they come to her for a hand-out. When G-Gideon and Venetia got into trouble she bailed them out, using the money she'd planned to spend on the house, and were they grateful? No. They still treated her like dirt.'

'Now, now.' Mona tapped Rollo's knee. 'It's what I'm here for, isn't it? What would I do with all that money in this great big house, if I hadn't got my family to look after? And I know it's some time ahead, but maybe I will be able to help you with your music when you grow up.'

Bea tried to get back to basics.

'So what happened to Magnus? How long was he in prison?'

'Nine years and seven months. I'd almost forgotten about him, so much was going on, because my sister and her husband made this house their base when they were in the UK, and then Hugo got married, too. Suddenly the house was filled with growing children again. I got such a shock one day when I opened the door and saw Magnus standing there. He hadn't written to me at all. I hadn't had any idea he was being let out early. He said he'd missed me and wanted me to take him back, but I suspected—hard-hearted creature that I am—that what he was really after was money. Fortunately, my sister was staying with me at the time. She called out to ask who it was, and then she came, and...what a scolding she gave him! Told him to keep away, or else! Then my brother-in-law joined in. He was on shore leave—he wasn't an Admiral then, of course—he was stationed somewhere, so many places around the globe.

'So Magnus left. But he phoned me, after, and asked me to meet him, saying…promising… Oh, of course I knew it was all lies. He'd have promised anything to get me to take him back but I didn't really want to, because I remembered the times he came home after dining some floozy or other, pretending it was nothing. Edith was furious with him. She didn't want me to meet him. She said he'd done enough damage, hadn't he, and that she couldn't trust me not to take him back, which I wouldn't have, honestly I wouldn't. But she thought I might. And I suppose…'

A long sigh. 'Anyway, she insisted that if he rang again, she'd speak to him and she'd arrange for him to go abroad if I agreed to pay him an allowance, which I did, although it went against the grain because I was helping to put Edith's grandchildren through boarding school at the time. I never saw Magnus again. He went off to the Caribbean, and my brother-in-law set up a direct-debit scheme to pay an intermediary to make sure Magnus got the money every month. Everything settled down again, with the grandchildren growing up and keeping me young. It's been a good life.'

'You got proof that your husband died abroad?'

'That's right. My brother-in-law got word that Magnus had died out there. Penniless, of course. I paid for the funeral. St Lucia, or St Kitts, or somewhere. A drunken argument; he was run off the road and died. The details didn't really matter because we'd been divorced for ever, but it tidied things up.'

'When was the door bricked up between you and Penelope?'

'Oh, years ago. No matter what I said, the children would go next door to play silly games, try to shoot the neighbouring cats, chase one another, out of my sight. One of the boys got hurt jumping off the wall, and Penelope didn't like the way they treated her very last dog, Rover—such a lovely dog, but nervy. Venetia—' a reminiscent smile—'was quite a tomboy, too. Penelope and I both had words with them, but it was no good. They didn't take any notice. Both gardens were pretty wild then. Edith got worried that they would stray further, try climbing walls into other people's gardens; you know what youngsters are, daring one another to do silly things. So she said we ought to brick up the door, and of course she was right. After that I used to go round to Penelope's front door instead of through the garden.'

Rollo was almost horizontal in his chair. He put his hands round the back of his head with his elbows hiding most of his face. 'They make her live down here in the basement, which is cold and damp in the winter, while they take over all the best rooms.'

'Don't be silly, dear,' said Mona, tapping him on his knee again. 'It's cosy down here and much easier for me than climbing all those stairs. And, I'm so old-fashioned, I like my own bits and pieces around me.'

He mumbled, 'I wouldn't mind if they didn't treat you like dirt.'

She shook her head at him. 'Now, now, Rollo. You're giving Mrs Abbot entirely the wrong impression of us.'

Rollo lowered one elbow to stare at Bea. 'I realize that it was my fault that the wall fell down. My father said I was only a child and not responsible, and that he wasn't responsible either because it was all your fault for not maintaining the wall properly. He told the insurance people that none of us were anywhere near the wall when it fell down, and he forbade me to speak to them myself, but that's not right.' He was on the verge of tears. 'I said to him that it wasn't right to put the blame on you, but he...' Rollo swallowed.

Bea tried to fill in the missing words. 'He hit you?'

Mona was distressed. 'Oh, no! He didn't, did he, Rollo?'

Rollo swiped at his eyes. 'I deserved it, didn't I? And then grandfather came down and said the wall wasn't ours but yours, anyway.'

Mona jerked upright. 'But of course it's ours! I should know, shouldn't I? He had no right to... I suppose he thought that...' The habit of looking after her family was asserting itself over the need to be truthful. She tapped Rollo's arm. 'Rollo, you are *not* to get into a state about this. You are a minor, and your family is responsible for what you do. I am properly insured. I may not have had enough money to pay for redecorating and rewiring, but I assure you that I have always kept the insurances up to date.'

'Really?' Rollo fumbled to catch his granny's hand. 'You know what? You're a star. I know that Gideon and Venetia have cost you a lot this last year...'

'Hush,' said Mona. 'Hush. Mrs Abbot doesn't need to know about that.'

'...and Dad's new car, not to mention—'

'Yes, yes,' said Mona. 'You're a good lad. The best of the bunch. We'll manage, somehow.'

Bea said, 'Investments don't retain their value nowadays, do they? The value of the houses go up, but so do living costs. Is that why Penelope decided to sell?'

'She had planned to live out her life here, but yes, her

income was shrinking, and she didn't really fancy taking in lodgers as some people have in this road, and it was getting harder and harder for her to run her little charity, especially after the friend retired who used to help her with it. Then she and I got these letters from an estate agent on behalf of Sir Leon, only we didn't know it was him at the time. We're always getting letters asking if we'd like to sell, but in this case it was for cash, and they arrived just after Penelope had had a nasty fall and was beginning to see that she needed to move into a flat somewhere. I went with her to look at some places, and we found one overlooking the park; two big bedrooms and a huge sitting room and everything so attractively fitted out and big enough to take her favourite pieces of furniture. So she decided that she would follow up the estate agent's offer. The estate agent said the buyer was only interested in this house and the next, and was prepared to pay over the odds for it.'

Bea nodded. Leon had wanted to buy a house whose garden wall intersected with hers. 'You told your family about the sale next door?'

'Well, yes, I suppose so. Just in passing. They've never been particularly interested in Penelope and her doings. I helped Penelope move, and the builders came in and took the house next door apart. I suppose we all grumbled about the noise and the dust, but the children were mostly away at university, and the spring is when my sister and her family fly off to the Caribbean for a holiday in the sun, so, well…it didn't seem important.'

'Until…?'

Mona's hands plucked at her skirt. She stilled them with what seemed to be an effort. She was trying to pretend she didn't know where this interview was going, but she knew all right. 'Well, when my sister and brother-in-law came back, they got in a terrible state, saying that Penelope had no right to sell her house, which was ridiculous and she's so much happier now she's in her new place. Then Penelope told me who it was who'd bought the place—it was done through some sort of holding company so she hadn't known the name before—and that they were going to go ahead and dig up the dogs' bones...'

'And they found the body of a man.'

Mona frowned. 'I thought at first—God forgive me—'

'You thought it might be Penelope's husband, who was supposed to have been lost at sea. You thought that he must have turned up years later and maybe had had a heart attack and died. You thought that she might have been too embarrassed to tell anyone, and so had buried him in her garden. You'd known her all those years. You knew she was as sharp as a tack, but that was the thought that first crossed your mind.'

Mona reddened. 'That was nonsense, of course. But yes, it did occur to me.'

'And then you worked out whose body it was, and you didn't know what to do about it.'

Rollo said, 'Aunt Mona?' Horrified. He was catching on, too.

Mona threw back her shoulders. 'I told myself it wasn't possible. It must be a tramp who'd crawled in there and died when Penelope wasn't looking. Or, it was somebody who died years before I was born.'

'Neither of those explanations satisfied you. You realized exactly what had happened. You knew the police were going to be able to tell how long the body had been in the ground, and that they might also be able to tell how he'd died. You knew it was a matter of time till the whole sordid story came out, and that some day soon they were going to come knocking on your door, asking for DNA samples from Gideon and his younger brother.'

'Aunt Mona!' Rollo, in anguish. 'What does she mean? She can't mean…! Tell her it's not true!'

Mona said, very quietly, 'Now, Rollo. No need to panic. I'm hoping it's not true. Praying it's not true. But if it is…'

'You *know* that it's Magnus,' said Bea. 'Because Edith's reaction when you told her the police had discovered the bones was extreme. It confirmed your worst fears. For a start I'd guess that Edith was furious with Penelope for allowing her buyer to dig up the garden.'

'I told her that getting angry with Penelope wouldn't help. That Sir Leon had every right to dig up his own garden if he wished to do so.'

'And then—what did Edith say?'

Mona shook her head. 'She's my sister. It's up to her how she responds when the police come calling. I said that I was happy to leave it in the hands of the police, and that if they wanted to talk to me, I'd cooperate.'

'She asked you not to go to the police with your suspicions, and you agreed.'

A nod.

'Aunt Mona!' Rollo, working himself up into a state. 'You mean it's the remittance man out there? Your husband? Gideon and Grey's grandfather? But…it can't be! He went to the Caribbean and—'

'I don't know what happened,' said Mona. 'I'm trying not to think about it.' She got up from her chair with an obvious effort, and switched on another side lamp. 'Would anyone like a cup of tea now?'

A sharp voice broke in. 'That's your remedy for everything, isn't it, sister mine? A nice cup of tea, arsenic included. Well, I don't think the police will be fooled by it. Rollo, it's rude to sit when your elders are standing. Stand up and let me have your chair. Mrs Abbot, I suppose you've worked out how and why my sister murdered her husband all those years ago?'

SIXTEEN

ROLLO SPRANG UP, face red, anxiety flaring. 'No, Gran. No! She wouldn't murder anyone! She c-couldn't!'

'Of course she could,' said Lady Edith, settling herself in Rollo's chair. She was perfectly coiffed and made up, wearing a wraparound pink silk top over silk and mohair trousers. Designer, strappy shoes. The contrast with dumpy and poorly dressed Mona was painful.

But Bea knew now where the money had come from in that family, and who spent it. She also liked and respected Mona Barwell, while she neither liked nor respected Edith Payne. Which did not, of course, preclude the fact that either of them—or both—might be lying.

Edith said, 'Mrs Abbot, if you have come to complain about your wall falling down…?'

'I haven't.'

'That was my f-fault,' said Rollo.

Lady Payne ordered. 'Shut your mouth. You don't know what you're saying. It was nothing whatever to do with you.'

Bea said, 'I didn't come about that.'

'Then, you must have come, uninvited, to ask if we might be so kind as to let you have another piece of your personal property that your friend left here the other evening, after you had both disgraced yourselves.'

Ah-ha, here it came! Leon's DNA, collected when Venetia scratched him!

Mona looked confused. 'What do you mean, Edith? I've given her back the shoes I found in the gym.'

Edith was smiling, not nicely. 'Mrs Abbot knows what I mean. That's why she's here. Sir Leon left something valuable behind when he crept out after the party...'

So Edith didn't know exactly how she and Leon had managed to escape? Good, that meant Edith wouldn't go after Sophy and Miguel.

'Something valuable? What?' Mona didn't like the way the conversation was going. 'Rollo, you were try-ing to tell me something—?'

Rollo shuffled his feet, looked agonized. 'I d-don't *know* anything. I overheard the others s-saying some-thing, but they wouldn't let me in on whatever it was, and what they said didn't make s-sense.'

'Of course it didn't make sense,' said Edith. 'And no-body's going to take any notice of what a little runt like you has to say. An amusing little game got slightly out of hand, that's all. But it left me with a joker in hand.'

'A game?' Mona fumbled towards the truth. 'Do you mean the fire at Mrs Abbot's place?' She looked at Bea. 'I saw that your house had been in a fire but it happened when I was out. I don't like big parties. I didn't think I'd know anyone there and Edith said I'd only be in the way, which was quite true, so I went round to Penelope's, as usual.' Her voice tailed away. 'Rollo, tell me you weren't involved in setting the fire. Did you take the paraffin for my heater out of the shed, and... No, Rollo! Tell me you weren't involved!'

'No, I w-wasn't, honest! You know what they're like, the others w-won't let me join in with anything they do, though I knew they were up to something and I tried to f-find out what it was. Gideon gave me a t-twenty and told me to go and get him some f-fags, which I told him they wouldn't sell me because I'm under-age, but it was a g-good excuse to get out, because I hate that sort of party, too. So I hung around in the High Street and had some C-Coca-Cola and some chips, and didn't come back till I thought it would be all over. I hoped Gideon would f-forget about the money, but he didn't, and he gave me a right c-cuffing because I'd spent some of it but not got him any fags. Then they threw me out while they were talking and laughing about the evening, and I c-couldn't hear properly. Only, when they went out c-clubbing, I found all that stuff on Venetia's bed and I brought it down and gave it to Mrs Abbot.'

'So you did,' said Bea, 'for which I was very grateful.'

Edith's eyes narrowed. 'Rollo, there was an envelope that I gave Venetia. Rather important. You didn't give that to Mrs Abbot, did you? No! I'd have noticed.'

He shook his head. 'No, it was under the bed, on the floor. I d-didn't see it till later and—'

Edith's nostrils flared. 'Go and get it! Now!'

'Hold on a mo,' said Bea. 'Rollo, do you know what's in that envelope?'

'Yes, I—'

Edith rose and swiped at him. 'Get it, this minute!'

Rollo's mouth tried to smile. 'I flushed it down the toilet!'

A lie?

Edith shrieked and set about the boy, kicking and pummelling him. 'You couldn't have been so stupid! Oh, if... you've ruined everything! How could you be so dumb!'

'Stop it! Edith! Control yourself!' Mona tried to get herself between her sister and the boy, and was backhanded away.

Bea didn't know what to do. She glanced at the window to see if Hari would now come in, but didn't spot any movement out there. Night had covered the garden with shadow.

Edith had the boy on the ground. She kicked him. 'I always said you ought to have been aborted...!'

'Edith! Please!' Mona helped the boy up, guiding him to a chair, keeping her own body between him and Edith. 'It's all right, Rollo. You did the right thing.'

Edith yelled, 'It's very far from all right! That idiot has ruined everything!'

Mona said, 'Suppose you tell me what he's supposed to have done.'

When thieves fall out, good men come into their own.

Bea made herself small in her chair, hoping she'd now learn exactly what had been going on, and who had been involved.

Edith was breathing hard, fists clenched, eyes sparking anger. 'We set it all up so carefully: the party, the invitations! Everything had to be arranged in haste, but we managed it and got them both here and we got the evidence which would have secured our future! And then the fuse blew!' She turned on her sister. 'If you'd only rewired the house as you were supposed to do!'

Rollo was rubbing his ribs. 'And whose f-fault was it she had to spend the money she'd saved for the electrician, in order to bail Venetia out...!'

Edith backhanded him. He ducked, but she connected, all right. Edith tore the table lamp out of its socket, and threw it against a picture on the far wall. The glass shattered and showered fragments around, but Edith was not to be stopped. 'And then they escaped, and how they did it I don't know! You weren't around or I might have thought it was you helping them, but they got out before we could take the photographs! But all wasn't lost because we had the evidence to put Leon away. We were going to be safe, even if my husband's stupid plan to scupper the sale didn't work. Words fail me!' She threw herself back into her chair and stared into space, her fingers tap-tapping on the arms.

Explosive. Approach with care.

Mona helped Rollo into her own chair, and looked him over. 'No great harm done.' She looked over at Bea. 'Do you know what my sister is talking about, Mrs Abbot?'

Bea said, 'As far as I understand it, Lady Payne panicked when she realized that the wealthy man who had bought the house next door intended to cut a doorway through the wall into my garden. She panicked because she knew that, apart from the dogs, a man's body had been buried under the party wall and its protective shroud of ivy. She must have prayed that he would miss the human bones. But when the wall fell, it disturbed the pillared supports which had been put in to strengthen it and, as they shifted in the ground, the bones were brought to the surface.

'At that point she was confronted by a problem, which was how to stave off recognition of the body. And, if that failed, how to ensure the continuance of her comfortable lifestyle? Only recently you, Mona, had sacrificed some necessary work on the house in order to bail the family out of trouble. The house was beginning to look shabby. The Admiral was retired and should have a decent pension, but I suspect he may be as much of a spendthrift as his brother-in-law, Magnus Barwell, had been. Perhaps the Admiral gambles, as his great-nephew Gideon does? Or crashes other people's cars, like his granddaughter?'

Lady Payne was silent. Somewhere along the line, Bea had guessed correctly.

Bea went on, 'Lady Payne hoped against hope that the identity of the corpse might never come to light but, if it did, she needed a scapegoat—and as you have just observed, she has decided to lay the blame at your door. With regard to her own future, she devised a plan to entrap Leon and hold his reputation hostage. He would pay well, she thought, to keep his good name untarnished. But yet another minor problem arose. Lady Payne discovered that I, Mrs Abbot, was not only Sir Leon's very good friend, but that I had a reputation for unravelling mysteries. She sought to enlarge her original plan to include me… Which, if I may say so, was a major mistake.'

Bea continued, 'Lady Payne, I must give you credit for quick thinking. You arranged a drinks party on the cheap and at short notice. You involved your husband, who had his own scheme running to destroy Leon's reputation. He got someone to inform the press that Leon had attacked an under-age girl. This rumour was supposed to wreck an important deal in the Far East, for which he would claim a reward through his contacts in the world of finance. But the report was phoned in *before we arrived at the party*, and Leon managed to rescue the deal.'

'I don't know what you mean!'

'Oh, I think you do. At this very moment there's an expert at work tracing the Admiral's contacts and they reveal an interesting background to his attempts at extortion and blackmail.'

Lady Payne blustered, 'My husband didn't do anything, and you can't prove that he did.'

'No, I can't. But my friend Oliver has uncovered the link between him and another director, who favoured the underbidder for the Far Eastern contract. Who will, presumably, not be best pleased that your husband's little scam has failed. To return to the party. You, Mona, were encouraged to be out that evening. Sir Leon and myself were invited. Lady Payne's scheme was to entrap, compromise and thereupon neutralize us. For this scheme she needed the services of a pretty young girl and some hefty young men—and there were the youngsters, delighted to be involved, especially if money were to be channelled their way. Sir Leon and I were given knockout drugs in our drinks, and arranged in compromising positions in order to be photographed. Venetia scratched Leon's cheek to get his DNA under her fingernails. When she'd done that, she cut her fingernails short, and placed the evidence in an envelope. And that, Lady Payne, you thought would be sufficient to stop Leon ever moving against you; would stop me becoming involved, and would force Leon to pay you a pension to ensure a more than comfortable retirement.'

'No!' Mona, wide-eyed.

Bea continued, 'Chance intervened. While I was lying in that chair over there, aware that I'd been drugged and that gin had been thrown all over me, with my skirts up and my legs sprawling, I could still hear what was going on, though I couldn't move. The lights blew. A fuse. The circuit had been overloaded. Probably if less had been spent on the family and more on the house, the fuse wouldn't have blown, and the scheme wouldn't have failed. But fail it did.

'Lady Payne tried to get the youngsters to help her search for a replacement fuse, but this was where they took the initiative. The young men had possession of my house keys, which gave them the idea of doing me an extra bit of no good. They set my house on fire. It didn't take them long. But, by the time they'd returned to help Lady Payne, both Leon and I had managed to escape and eventually we got ourselves to hospital. Fortunately the drug used was not fatal. I recovered more quickly than Sir Leon and returned to retrieve those belongings of ours which had been misappropriated. Rollo did return some of our belongings, but that all-important envelope remained here.'

'Now do you understand what you've done!' cried Lady Payne, aiming another kick at Rollo. 'If we'd still got that envelope, we could have got Leon to pay through the nose for its return! Words fail me.'

'I wish they did,' said Bea. 'Unfortunately, you've got one more card to play, and it's an exceedingly nasty one. Your sister has kept you and your expensive family afloat for years, and how do you repay her? You accuse her of murder.'

'Yes, that's right,' said Edith, pulling herself together. 'It hurts me to say so, but it's true. Mona killed her husband. She told me all about it, after it happened; how he turned up again one weekend when we were all away and, well, I'm sure she didn't mean to kill him, but there was a tussle, he fell and hit the back of his head and died. She panicked. She was too scared of the police to admit what had happened. She couldn't bury him in our garden here because the children were all over it all the time. So it was easy enough for her to put her husband's body into a wheelbarrow, take him through the gate in the wall into Penelope's garden and bury him under the ivy. Then she trumped up the story about it being too dangerous for the children to go next door, and had the door bricked up.

'Mona confessed it all to me when we got back to

London. I couldn't bear the thought of my sister going to jail. It was very wrong of me, I know, but I allowed her to persuade me not to go to the police. She begged me to help her cover up what she'd done by getting my husband to set up a remittance for Magnus, who'd supposedly gone to live in the Caribbean.'

'Which remittance you cashed yourself?'

'Naturally. After a few years we decided it was best to let him die abroad, because we had friends who were going there on holiday and they were talking about looking the man up for old times' sake. And that's it, really.'

Bea studied Edith and then looked at Mona, who was staring ahead, motionless. Mona had known this was coming.

Rollo, however, hadn't known. 'That's mean, Gran! And I d-don't believe any of it!'

Lady Payne spat at him. 'Shut up, you! If it hadn't been for you…but, as it is, I don't suppose Mona will get more than a few years for manslaughter. They don't hang murderers nowadays and she's old and frail. We'll take care of this house and her money while she's inside, so it shouldn't make any difference to our lives.'

Rollo put his hand on Mona's arm. 'It's not true, is it? Tell me it's not true.'

Mona looked straight at him. She was smiling. 'If the police believe her, what will you do?'

Rollo blinked. 'I don't understand.'

Bea did. Mona was playing for Rollo's soul. Would she win, or would the boy fall into line under his grandmother's spell? Would she let Mona go to jail in order to ensure that his comfortable life continued as before?

His features convulsed. Was he going to cry? He took his hand off his great-aunt and rubbed his forehead. Looked down at the floor. Yes, he was definitely going to cry.

'That's my boy,' said Lady Payne, contempt in her voice. 'You know which side your bread's buttered, don't you?'

Rollo's face straightened out. Some of his immaturity leached away, leaving him looking older and, strangely, more like his grandmother. He got to his feet, his limbs stiff, but obeying him. 'Auntie Mona, I don't believe you did it. You couldn't. It's against everything you've taught me. I think,' he gulped, 'that yes, perhaps there was an accident, and he died. But I don't think you'd have covered it up. You're so brave, always trying to do the right thing. So,' another gulp, 'if it wasn't you, then it was someone else.'

'Listen to him!' said Edith, contempt in every line of her. 'That's what a good education does for you! It teaches you to reason!'

'Yes, it does, Granny,' said Rollo, trying to stand straight and not slouch. 'It tells me to remember all the nasty things you've ever said and done. You've never thought me of any use; you've slagged me off whenever you've seen me; you've said a hundred times you only let me stay with you for the holidays because my dad and my mum had to work. I've tried to keep out of your way, and in return… No, I'm not making excuses. I spied on you.'

He clenched his fists and stood tall. 'I knew I was being sneaky, looking at stuff which was none of my business and listening to your phone calls, and I knew it was wrong not to tell. I ought to have blown the whistle, but I didn't because I knew how much trouble I'd be in, with you, if I did. You've cheated Auntie Mona hundreds of times over the years. Yes, she paid the face value of the bills for your holidays and your cars, and subscriptions to this and that, but you'd always negotiated yourself a commission, hadn't you? You even managed to get a commission for paying off Gideon's gambling debts by inflating the total. As for Venetia, you knew very well she was drunk as a skunk when she borrowed those cars and smashed them, not once but twice! And you encouraged her to sleep with—'

Edith slapped him, hard.

He put his hand halfway to his face, then took it down again. Bea could see he was shaking, but it didn't stop him talking. 'Hit me all you like. This is the truth. My "good education" makes me remember all the kindnesses and self-sacrifices that Auntie Mona has made for us. How she's taught me to respect the truth, and to respect her. She didn't kill that man; you did. I hope it was an accident, but whatever happened, covering it up would be just your line. And getting Auntie Mona to fork out for a remittance for him after he was dead, and even paying for his funeral? That was just all going into your own bank account, wasn't it?'

Bea risked a glance at Mona, who seemed to be smiling. Was Mona encouraging the only other member of her family who had the guts to stand up to Edith?

Rollo told Mona. 'If Granny arranges things so that you have to go to prison instead of her, I think you should sell this house and put the money in a trust or something so that none of us can get at it. I'll go to a state school. If I work hard enough, I can get a bursary to university, or get an apprenticeship or whatever. I'll come to see you whenever they let me and… I want to say how sorry I am that I didn't come clean before. I just wasn't brave enough to say anything. Forgive me?'

'Yes, Rollo. Of course I do.' Mona looked at her watch, and sighed. 'Well, it seems a pity to have to drag the police out on a Sunday night, but we'd best get it over with. Edith, all bets are off. I knew you used to inflate the bills. I understood it, in a way, because your husband was never going to be a good provider, was he? But after we had a little talk about it, you did promise me you'd stop and I believed you…which was foolish of me, wasn't it? I hoped against hope that if I kept the family together, the children would grow up to be decent members of society, and on the whole they have. Malcolm has definitely made good. Hugo and his wife are at least supporting themselves after a fashion, even if they've handed over responsibility for their children to you. But the grandchildren, with the exception of Rollo, have always chosen your way of life rather than mine. I told myself that everyone deserves a second chance, but Gideon and Grey and Venetia seem to think that whatever I've said, someone will always bail them out. I've warned you several times that they are out of control, but you didn't want to listen. And now you've made them accessory to murder.'

'What! No, I—'

'Yes, that's exactly what you've done. Not to mention their thieving, and their taking part in the scheme to destroy Sir Leon's reputation. I also believe they firebombed Mrs Abbot's house. So now they are going to have to take responsibility for their actions. Mrs Abbot, do you wish to stay to see the last act of this little drama, or would you rather retire?'

With a howl of fury Edith stooped to pick up the heavy crystal vase on the coffee table and threw it at Mona's head.

Rollo shrieked…

…and threw himself at Mona, who ducked but not quickly enough…

…Rollo managed to get between them…

…Bea yelled…

…Rollo fell on top of Mona on to the floor…

…in a tangle…

Blood spread out from under Rollo's head…

Bea struggled up out of her chair as…

…Hari leaped into the room, mobile to his ear…

'Ambulance!'

Mona didn't move, lying still under Rollo's sprawling figure.

Rollo's eyes were shut.

Was he dead? Oh, surely not!

Hari spoke into his phone, giving the address.

Bea saw that Rollo was trying to move, his eyelids flickering, blood running down his forehead on to Mona, lying beneath him.

Bea tried to help him up.

Failed.

In any case, wasn't it better not to move him? Suppose he'd been mortally hurt?

Mona, beneath him, was also trying to move.

One-handed and still talking on the phone, Hari helped Bea to pull Rollo off Mona and on to the carpet beside her. Bea knelt beside Mona, who seemed to be unharmed, but had had all the puff driven out of her. Mona tried to get her breath. She was breathing hard, as if she had asthma.

Bea helped her to sit, so that she could breathe more easily. Her colour improved. She opened her eyes and nodded to Bea, trying to say 'thank you'.

Hari was kneeling beside Rollo. 'Don't try to move. Keep still. Absolutely still. The ambulance is on its way.'

Rollo's eyelids flickered. He relaxed, muscle by muscle. He'd shot his bolt.

He wasn't dead, anyway, though that head wound...

The flowers that had been in the vase had ended up around him. The water, too.

Mona tried to speak. Moved her limbs feebly.

Bea bent down to her, repeating Hari's words. 'Don't move. The ambulance is on its way.'

Mona's eyes switched to Rollo. She mouthed, 'Is he all right?'

Bea nodded, though she wasn't at all sure that the boy was all right. That vase had hit his head with a clunk she'd replay in her next nightmare.

Mona struggled to stand. Bea helped her. Mona didn't seem hurt. Just temporarily winded. Mona looked around. 'Edith?'

No Edith.

Edith had gone. Scarpered. Made herself scarce.

Rollo opened his eyes, sent them round the room. Closed his eyes again. Began to laugh. He said, 'Gotcha!'

Hari and Bea looked at one another, bemused.

Mona wasn't. She said, in a tired little voice, 'Rollo is going to get Edith arrested for assault. That way, she can't get away with at least one of the bad things she's done. Not this time, at least.'

SEVENTEEN

Sunday night

THREE O'CLOCK IN the morning. Or was it four?

Bea felt dizzy with fatigue. She looked at the clock on the wall and couldn't make sense of what it was trying to tell her.

What time was it that she had trodden through the wreckage of her garden and across the barren space of the Admiral's house—or, rather, the house belonging to Mona Barwell?—in order to talk to that elderly lady?

It had been dusk then.

Mona had told the truth and Edith had accused Mona… Rollo had come to her rescue…and Edith had gone in for fisticuffs…

…which was why Mona and Bea now sat in the Accident and Emergency department of the hospital waiting for Rollo to be attended to.

Hari had taken them to the hospital and left them there, as it was obvious it would be some time before Rollo could be dealt with. Rollo, after all, was only one among many victims of weekend fights, shootings, drug overdoses.

Policemen hovered, trying to get reports from the injured people who littered the waiting room for the Accident and Emergency department. They asked a tired

Rollo, sinking now and then into sleep, how he'd come by his injury.

'My gran threw a vase at my great-aunt and I got in the way.' Which was the truth and nothing but the truth, but didn't give any of the interesting background to the case.

The policemen asked Bea and Mona if they could confirm this. Both nodded. Bea could see the police were going to class this non-event as 'domestic abuse', and wouldn't take the matter further unless they made a fuss, which they were not going to do at that time of night and in their state of fatigue. The policemen took their names and addresses and said they should report to the nearest station in the morning. Bea and Mona nodded, and went back to quietly worrying about Rollo, who kept dropping asleep on Mona's shoulder.

Eventually Rollo was processed, and X-rayed. The doctor said his brain didn't appear to have been affected, and there should be no permanent damage. However, they wanted to keep him in overnight because he had definitely been concussed and they wanted to be sure his condition didn't deteriorate.

Mona and Bea sat beside the boy while his head was stitched up, or rather, stapled. Bea thought Rollo's face was a fine advertisement for a rainbow, as the colour of his skin ranged from a livid yellow bruise on his cheek, fading to a nasty greenish-white around his mouth. There was black and purple in plenty around one closed eye, while a neat scarlet line showed where the gaping wound on his temple had been dealt with. All that was missing was some blue. Would his one open eye represent the missing blue?

Rollo tried to smile at them as he was wheeled off to bed. 'All hunky-dory, no permanent damage, but it's just as well they're not discharging me tonight because I can't see straight or work out what day of the week it is. Is it day or is it night?'

Mona sniffed and blew her nose. Bea put her arm around Mona and summoned Hari on her mobile to collect them. By the time he arrived, Mona had fallen asleep.

Bea woke her up, steered her into the back of Hari's car, and fitted the seatbelt around her…whereupon Mona leant back with a sigh, and proceeded to fall asleep again.

Bea got in the front with Hari. She kept her voice down. 'All quiet on the home front?'

'I went back and rescued the vase Edith thumped him with. I put it in a safe place to preserve any fingerprints that might be on it. The room is just as we'd left it. The house was empty.'

'Edith and the Admiral have scarpered?'

'The youngsters hadn't returned home by the time I left, but I went upstairs for a quick look around. There are signs that Admiral and Lady Payne packed a couple of bags and left in a hurry. There's no sign of jewellery, cash or passports. Drawers have been pulled out and clothes dragged off hangers. There was a square-shaped space in the top right-hand drawer of her dressing table, into which a cash or jewellery box might have fitted. Downstairs, behind the kitchen, there's an office area with a PC and a printer, and a couple of filing cabinets in it. Papers have been pulled out of the cabinet. Some have been left on the floor. There's no laptop in sight, nor any briefcase. Their car was a distinctive white Mercedes. There's a photo of the Admiral standing beside it in the kitchen. I saw the car outside the house earlier in the evening, but it's gone now.'

Bea sighed. 'They'll be out of the country by morning.'

'Probably. But what country will allow them to stay if an international warrant is issued for their arrest, and what will they use for money? How far will the Admiral's pension take them?'

And, Hari, we can't mention the fact that you've been trespassing on someone else's property. So we'll have to get Mona to contact the police to accuse the precious pair of murder and of covering it up. And then to report their disappearance.

Bea tried to clear her brain, which wasn't responding. 'You say the youngsters weren't back by the time you left? They were up to something, planning something?'

Hari said, 'Relax. Whatever it is, I've got it covered.'

Mona stirred. Bea reached an arm back to take the older woman's hand. 'Not long now. We'll tuck you up safely in your own bed with a hot drink. Do you have a hot-water bottle, or an electric blanket? We'll deal with the police tomorrow, after we've had a good night's sleep.'

Mona tried to smile and nestled back into her corner again.

Bea wasn't looking forward to the morning, either. She had a niggling feeling that they ought to have called the police in to deal with Edith the moment she'd smashed the vase into Rollo's head, but it had seemed more important at the time to get him to hospital. Anyway, wasn't flight considered an admission of guilt? Surely it would help their case that Edith had disappeared of her own accord?

Bea held her arm up to catch the light of a street lamp. She concentrated on her watch. Half past three. London never sleeps, and the traffic never ceases, though it does thin out a bit in the early hours.

Mona caught her breath on a snore. Hari and Bea exchanged rueful glances. Let her sleep. Life wasn't going to be easy for anyone in that house in the immediate future, was it?

They drew up outside Mona's house. No lights at the top of the house, but a couple had been left on in ground-floor rooms. Probably the youngsters had returned home, and gone to bed, not bothering to turn off the ground-floor lights? Typical.

Bea and Hari woke Mona and helped her down the steps to the basement. Mona was tottering with tiredness and it was Hari who managed to find her keys in her handbag and let them in. *And we won't refer to the times he's let himself in with skeleton keys or whatever they are.*

Bea made Mona a hot drink while Hari disappeared to reconnoitre upstairs.

Mona drank her hot milk, said she ought to brush her teeth, fell into bed and a deep sleep. That was probably the best thing she could do.

Hari returned to say there was still no sign of Edith or the Admiral, but that the youngsters were happily snoring away upstairs. He turned off all the lights on the ground floor, jammed a chair under the door at the bottom of the stairs leading up from the basement, but left a light burning in the corridor in case Mona got up in the night and wasn't sure where she was. Then he guided Bea over Mona's garden, through the barbed-wire barrier, across the mound of bricks and into the uneven ground of her own territory.

Her house was in darkness. 'What happened to Piers? Is he still here? I'd forgotten him.' She hadn't called him down to eat a pizza with them at supper time. She hadn't thought to brief him on what they'd planned to do that night. Oh well, either he'd gone back home or he'd dossed down in the spare bedroom on the top floor.

Oliver, too. They'd left him working on his laptop. He'd be tucked up in his own room up top.

Her brain zigzagged. The youngsters were safely in bed at Mona's house. So they hadn't been out doing anything awful to Bea's house.

Thankfully.

Hari opened the French windows into the cavern that had once been her office, switched on a torch, and guided her through the smell to the stairs, and up to the kitchen.

All was dark. And quiet. Peaceful. Bea had the odd fancy that the house was waiting to be brought back to life again on the morrow, with lights and sound and people working and phones ringing and clients arriving…

Hari disappeared for a moment to check that the front door was safely locked and bolted. 'It looks all right.'

She said, 'I suppose we might as well go to bed, too. Can you remove the blackout material from my bedroom window? I hate to sleep in the dark.'

He followed her up the stairs to her new bedroom. They both looked at the next flight of stairs. Hari said, 'Go to bed. I'll check everything's all right up at the top and see to your blackout while you're getting ready for bed. Then I'll catch a few hours on the settee next door.'

It seemed less trouble to obey him than to argue. As she brushed her hair, Hari tapped on her door. 'All's well upstairs. Both of them fast asleep. See you in the morning.'

She flumped on the bed, too tired even to yawn. In five hours' time or less, the agency staff would be arriving, to be helped to their new desks, with untested equipment, no landlines, builders and gas men to be dealt with and…the horrid mess at the Admiral's house… Rollo would need to be collected from hospital, provided he'd got through the night and…

A spot of prayer might calm her. She lay on her back and stared at the ceiling in the dark. Except it wasn't that dark. Birds were heralding the new day. Drat them! The sun would be up soon. Far too soon. It was all very well having long hours of daylight in the summer months, but when you wanted a good night's sleep…how odd of God to have arranged things this way. She supposed it showed he cared about us. We ought to be grateful for…

Aches and pains and an over-active brain.

Good friends. Her mind skittered around, thinking of all the wonderful people who had helped her since…

But not Leon, who'd bunked off.

No one would see if she shed a tear or two.

The birdsong was so sweet. Piercingly sweet. Thank the Lord for birdsong.

She was never going to be able to get to sleep, and would be good for nothing when morning finally came. She watched the ceiling brighten…

Monday morning

MONDAY MORNINGS ARE never easy. Bea groaned as she levered herself out of bed and stumbled to the window. She looked out over the ravaged garden and squeezed her eyes shut. What a lovely sunny day. Far too bright for her eyes. And ears. Too much birdsong. Too much of every-thing-being-jolly-in-this-best-of-all-worlds. The world wasn't at its best for her that day. Or for Mona, or Rollo, or anyone else who'd been dragged into this nasty affair.

Dear Lord, you know that I must be busy this day. If I forget you, please don't forget me.

There were sounds of men moving around. Water gushing.

Water? Did they still have water? Yes, they did.

Oh. Why did she think they might not have water?

She shook her head at herself. Her eyes wouldn't open properly. Her shoulder ached where she'd slept on her arm. And there were times when her brain responded with an answer to a question, and other times when it didn't. This was one of the 'Doesn't respond' variety.

She dressed in a severely business-like outfit. She didn't feel business-like, but imagined something might rub off on her if she pretended she was. Diamond ring on left hand. No diamond pendant round her neck. Enough was enough.

Someone raced down the stairs outside her room from the top of the house, making her jump. Her heartbeat went into overdrive. Oliver? Yes, only a young man would dive down two steps at a time. Piers wouldn't. He was older and more staid. Well, sort of.

Could she face breakfast? Someone was frying bacon.

Oh, wow! Triple wow! Hari…?

The scent of bacon cooking drew her down the stairs and into the kitchen, from which the blackout had also been removed. Piers and Oliver were already at work on their plates, Hari was cooking in the microwave. Winston was plump in the middle of the table, watching carefully to see that he got his share.

'Morning,' said Piers.

'Sleep well?' said Oliver.

'Coffee first, or juice?' Hari, ever practical.

'What news?' She grabbed orange juice in one hand and coffee in the other.

Oliver took the last piece of toast. 'I think I've got the link between the Admiral and the hanky-panky in the

Far East all sorted out. When they had an opportunity to meet, and so on and so forth. The Admiral is on the board of several companies, as I said. A fellow director, name and address supplied, is also on the board of another firm...company number two, as you might say. One of the directors on company number two is also on the board of the underbidder in the fight to buy out Holland Holdings in the Far East. According to the *Financial Times*, the deal was signed yesterday, all right and tight. The underbidder lost out, big time. There was a flurry of interest in their shares a couple of days ago, but now that the deal is signed and sealed, the underbidder's shares are hitting an all-time low. Which means that if Admiral Payne had been offered money to destroy Leon's reputation, he's failed big time and lost credibility as well. With any luck, he'd also invested in the underbidder and his shares will now be worthless.'

Bea nodded. It all made sense, in a horrid sort of way. Stupidity is not confined to the upper middle classes, or even to the middle classes, or even to...she told herself she was wittering and should stop.

Piers pushed his plate aside. 'A fine hostess you are, Bea. There I was, working away on your portrait—which you haven't asked about, but which is coming along nicely—and I didn't realize how time was marching along till the light went. At that point I was so tired I sat down for a bit and must have nodded off. When I woke up, it was dark but the lights wouldn't come on. Only then I remembered what had happened, and came downstairs to find you. At least the side lights work down here. Only, the place was deserted. You might have left me a note to say you were going out.'

'Sorry. A lot happened.'

'Well, I didn't know what to think. I was hungry, but there wasn't anything much to eat in the fridge, so I phoned round to see if I could get a pizza delivered, and eventually I got someone who said they would for double the price, which was daylight robbery, but I agreed, and I was waiting by the front door when I heard the delivery come, at least I thought it was them, and then there was a lot of crazy laughter outside, and a flash which I thought must be lightning. So I opened the door to find a couple of yobs on the pavement outside here, frozen in mid-step, mouths and eyes wide open, brandishing a tyre lever. So I shouted, they dropped the lever and ran off. I'd got my phone in my hand so took a couple of snaps, though I think they were too far away by that time to get a good picture.

'Hari heard me yell and came down to see what had happened. He'd rigged up a camera in the front window overlooking the pavement, so if anyone tried to interfere with the water meter, the camera would take a picture. Which was the flash I saw. He collected the tyre lever, which has such a rough surface I don't think it will take any prints, but it is marked with one of those invisible pen thingies, so we should be able to trace the owner. Or the police will. So Hari and I shared the pizza which arrived at that point, and then we went back to bed. So, what I say is, how soon do we call the police? Well, we should finish breakfast first, right?'

Bea accepted another cup of coffee and bacon sandwich. 'Yes, let's have breakfast first. It's going to be a long day.'

Ten frantic days later

BEA GOT BACK to her desk—which was now in a corner of the main office—in time to receive a voice message from Leon's annoying PA to say that he proposed to pick her up at eight and take her out to dine. With no apologies for not having contacted her for so long. Well, better late than never.

Bea wondered if she had time to get a manicure and hairdo? No, she hadn't.

Shrugging, she turned to the next item on the agenda, which was signing the wages cheques for her staff. None of them had defaulted except Carrie, who was still on sick leave and probably would never return. Bea hoped not, anyway. Betty was so much easier to work with.

At half past six Bea saw the last of her staff out, switched off her computer and went upstairs to shower and change her clothes. Hari and Anna had fixed her up some curtains temporarily, but it still gave her a sense of dislocation when she looked out of the window over her garden and into those of her neighbours. Mona's plot had been tidied up and swept, and her garden shed propped into an almost upright position.

The insurance company had agreed that the walls should be rebuilt using salvaged bricks, which was going to cost an arm and a leg, but would be in keeping with the surroundings. Bea had been interested to learn that even walls could be listed for preservation. However, this meant that every brick in the mounds of rubble between the gardens would have to be scrutinized and either rejected or set aside for a rebuild. Then new foundations would be dug and filled with concrete. Only after that would the work of reinstating the walls begin.

Bea was in consultation with a landscape gardener found for her by Maggie, who hadn't let childbirth interfere with work. The designer understood that Bea wanted an easy maintenance but pretty garden in which she could sit, and which would welcome all visitors, including Winston and any other cats that might come adventuring. And birds, of course.

Bea was still wondering whether or not to include a fountain. It would be a good opportunity to put one in, but…how would you keep Winston and other cats from eating any goldfish? Or perhaps you could have a rock thingy with water sliding over it and down into a pit below, to be recycled? But then, you wouldn't be able to have any fish.

Some people said that water added another dimension to a garden, and perhaps that was true, but didn't pools require maintenance? Would a water feature be more trouble than it was worth? Bea couldn't make up her mind.

Her garden was but a shadow of its former self, waiting for change.

Change could be good for one, keeping you alive and forward-looking. It could also be painful. Bea had steeled herself to accept the inevitable. You couldn't go back in time.

So, back to basics. What should she wear for dinner with Leon? Her diamond ring, of course. But apart from her ring? The odd item of clothing?

LEON WAS ON TIME. Bea let him in. She appreciated the aftershave which he was wearing, but was concerned about the slight thickening of his neck which had taken place since they last met. He put out his arm to draw her to him and she allowed that and a kiss on her cheek. But then she disengaged herself to shut and bolt the door. The electricity had been restored but the new alarm system wasn't working too well, and the men weren't due to come back to deal with it for another couple of days.

'It seems ages,' said Leon, going ahead of her down the hall.

It did seem ages. She'd rung him so many times to leave voice messages, but he'd only rung her once to say he was on his way from one place to another. Even then he hadn't stayed on the line to talk as he'd been interrupted by an important phone call. How long was it since they'd had a proper conversation?

The last time they'd met had been in the hospital... and then Leon had flown out to rescue his business...

'Hello, what's this?' He halted in the doorway to her temporary office.

'I told you, the basement was flooded after—'

'Oh, yes. I remember. I told you to close the business but—'

'I'm glad I didn't. It would have thrown my staff out of work, and we'd never have sorted out the problems at the Paynes'. My living room is one floor up nowadays. Follow me.' She led the way. 'We're all dried out down below, a new electrical circuit has been installed, the telephone system is back on and the decorators start in a couple of days' time. Then we'll put down new carpets and move the office back down again.'

He wasn't really interested. 'What a bore for you.' He surveyed her new living room. 'A bit cramped. I wish you'd come out to join me. I took the opportunity to have another few days in Japan this week. Amazing place. You'd have enjoyed it.'

When had she last had a holiday? Ah well. Soon, perhaps. When customers and clients had realized that a small thing like an arson attack hadn't affected the running of the agency, work had come pouring in. Word of mouth had it that the Abbot Agency—like the Windmill Theatre in the war—never closed. The link between Anna's College and the Abbot Agency had undoubtedly helped, and so had an article in the local paper, thanks to that inquisitive and ultimately helpful journalist.

Upstairs electricity had been restored everywhere, new panes of glass fitted where the old had had to be replaced, and although temporary curtains were up at the back of the house, replacements were on order and would be delivered as and when they were ready.

Leon walked around the room, touching this and that. 'I really missed you in Japan. There was so much to see.'

'I'd love to visit Japan some day, but I couldn't get away this time. Too much to do here.'

'I said I'd buy you out. You would have been free to join me.'

She shook her head. 'I couldn't shed my responsibilities so quickly.'

He didn't want to hear that. Restlessly, he went to look out of the back window. 'How strange it all looks from here. A moonscape. I understand the insurance are paying to replace the walls. I'll buy you another mature tree, of course.'

'When it first happened, I did want to replicate what I'd lost, but now I realize that the tree restricted my view. I can see so much more of the sky and the church now. So if I do get another tree, it will have to be smaller. A different species. Perhaps something with flowers and berries that the birds would like? I'm arguing with a landscape gardener about it at the moment. She wants me to have something exotic, but I'm not sure that would be in keeping with the house.'

They were talking as acquaintances, not friends. She shivered. Was the evening turning colder? She wanted to ask if he'd heard the latest about the Paynes, but he was not making eye contact.

He put his arm around her shoulders, and drew her to him. 'I've missed you, Bea.'

'I missed you, too. It's been a tough time. I wish you could have stayed.'

His smile disappeared. He didn't like being reminded that he'd run away. 'Well, we both had our priorities. But the deal has gone through and now I'm a free man. I can put the past behind me, and look forward to relaxing and enjoying life.'

She sighed. She wanted to talk to him about the Paynes. Yes, the police now knew what had happened, and were taking steps to extradite the Admiral and his wife from wherever it was in the Caribbean that they had taken refuge. And yes, the threat to derail the sale of Holland Holdings in the Far East had been countered, but the threat to Leon's reputation was still hanging over them, even if he didn't realize it.

Come to think of it, he really didn't know about it, did he? Or had she tried to explain and he hadn't been listening?

Rollo had said he'd destroyed the envelope containing the evidence Venetia had collected, but Bea wasn't at all sure that he hadn't kept it for use on a rainy day. There had been something about the way he'd told them what he'd done...

Mona hadn't seemed too happy about it, either. If that envelope ever resurfaced...? Or if Venetia decided to accuse Leon of abusing her, even if she now had no evidence to back up her accusation...?

Well, if the envelope did surface, Leon would have to

deal with it. She'd lost any appetite she'd ever had for a fight. Let him buy them off. He could afford it.

She grimaced. Was she becoming like the Paynes, reliant on money to get her out of a fix?

Leon pulled a jeweller's box out of his pocket and opened it. A flash of red. A ruby ring. He lifted her left hand to his lips and kissed it. He was about to slide the ruby on to her ring finger, but stopped when he saw she was still wearing her diamond.

He said, 'Isn't it about time you let me replace that?' A caressing tone. A here's-the-conquering-hero smile.

She held the ruby up to the light. A magnificent stone, worth a king's ransom, no doubt. But, she had never liked rubies. Diamonds, yes. Pearls, if it came to it. Rubies, no. She'd told him so, too.

He hadn't listened.

She held back a sigh. It was no good being angry with him. He hadn't listened in the past because he was a self-centred, self-made man. He wasn't going to listen now, and he wasn't going to change his ways, either. He was what he was and there was an end of it. If she liked what she saw, she could have it. Yes, she was pretty sure of that.

It was no good thinking you could change a man, because you couldn't. He'd had a hard upbringing. He'd told Bea once that he'd wanted to marry the woman who'd been his partner for many years, and that she'd refused. At that time Bea hadn't understood why. Perhaps she was beginning to understand now.

He had money. He wanted a companion and friend to whom he could talk freely. He'd found this in Bea, and wanted to make it permanent...on his terms.

'A ruby,' she said. 'Now, why did you choose a ruby?'

EIGHTEEN

'OH, FOR HEAVEN'S SAKE. Take off your long-dead husband's diamond!'

'Don't you remember my telling you that I exchanged this diamond for an ambulance to get you to hospital? I redeemed it later, for five hundred pounds. It's worth a lot more than that, of course, but it's priceless to me because of what it represents and for what it bought... which was your life.'

'What!'

'I told you, in the hospital. Don't you remember?'

He frowned, uneasy. 'Yes, I... No, not really. I wasn't really myself for some days after. Zoe kept having to remind me that... I really can't recall in any detail what happened, and so much has happened since... Is it important?'

'Yes, it is. You need to know what happened. You do remember that we went to a party at the Admiral's house? You were taken downstairs by the youngsters, were given a drugged drink and set up in a compromising situation. Fortunately, the lights in the house failed and you had just enough sense left to struggle out of the house, and through a gap in the side of the marquee into your own garden, where you passed out. Do you remember any of that?'

Still a frown. 'Bits of it, maybe. I'm not sure what was real, and what was a nightmare.'

'I found you in your own garden. You were in a bad

way. My one thought was to get you to hospital so I bribed some of the waiting staff, whom I happened to know, with my ring to get us out of there. They summoned an ambulance and covered for us. To this day the Paynes have no idea how we escaped, but I'm sure Sophy and Co. would be delighted to confirm their part in what happened. And, may I say, that the generous tips you've given them when they've done events for you contributed largely to their willingness to help us get away. Once at the hospital, you were pumped out. I was so anxious… I honestly thought you might die on me.'

He watched her, with painful attention, a frown line between his eyebrows.

Men don't like being rescued by their women-folk. They prefer it the other way around.

She managed a smile. 'I wish it had been you doing the rescuing. It was all most unpleasant! I'll never forget those hours at the hospital, and…' playing for a laugh, '…my outfit was completely ruined.'

He relaxed. 'I'll buy you another in Paris.'

'No need. What I'm trying to say is that we were so fortunate that night, because Sophy recognized me and decided to help. Afterwards, she might easily have decided to keep my ring, or to charge me more for returning it. But she didn't. She's a nice girl.'

'I'll send her a cheque.'

Bea was silent. She didn't think Sophy expected anything from him. Would she appreciate getting a cheque from him? Perhaps. But she wouldn't expect it.

Bea scolded herself. Why shouldn't he reward Sophy if he wished to do so? Was she, Bea, becoming resentful of his generosity to others? And if so, why?

He produced his chequebook from his pocket. 'It

seems I'm beholden to you, again. You always seem to be rescuing me.' And yes, he did resent that. 'Tell me how much you are out of pocket for saving my life, and I'll write you a nice big cheque, too.'

She pushed his chequebook away. 'I didn't do it for money, and neither did Sophy. The insurances have covered almost everything, and there's been an expansion of business since which will offset any additional expenses, updating of new equipment, and so on. Yes, I'm going to have to redecorate the basement, and this room, too, when the office finally moves back downstairs—'

'Well, you can let me pay for that.'

'No need. Maggie's got it all in hand. The inconvenience has been considerable, but what I've gained from my friends, from the loyalty and, yes, the love of my staff, is beyond rubies, or diamonds. Throwing money at a problem is easy, but doesn't always solve it.'

He reddened. 'Is that what you think I'm doing?' Defensive. Ruffled.

She said, 'I worry about you.'

'Money opens doors.'

She felt frustration coming on. She smoothed back her hair, trying to think what words she could use to make him see the situation through her eyes.

'Yes, money helps. But, getting involved in someone else's life is something else. For instance, earlier this week I took time off work to visit your niece Dilys and her husband Keith, who'd dropped everything to help me when I was in trouble. You can't believe how hard Keith worked to get us back on line, and Dilys kept everyone fed and watered right up to the very moment that she went into labour. You, Leon, sent Dilys some flowers, didn't you? Or asked your PA to arrange for some to be sent? But you haven't been to see them yet, have you?'

'Well, I've been busy.'

'So have I. But I made time. They're living in a pink cloud of bliss. The baby's the spitting image of Keith. He's gone all fumble-fingered with delight, and she's worn out by a hungry baby who demands to be fed on the hour every hour. The house was a mess. I took them a fluffy toy and washed up everything in sight and vacuumed. I took pictures of the baby and sent them to Dilys's aunt and her daughter because Keith hadn't got round to doing so. And they rang back, screaming with joy, wanting to know why you hadn't let them know. They're coming over on the next plane. I held the boy's fingers, and did a pile of ironing and sewed a button on Keith's shirt and restocked their fridge. I arranged for her to have a cleaner to keep them straight for a while. I was away from the office all morning, and everyone managed perfectly. Dilys said thank you for the flowers, and when were you going to see them. So when are you?'

'I can't this week because I have meetings up to—'

'Cancel them. You're the boss. You said you were retired now. Why can't you rearrange your—?'

His mobile rang. He fished it out of his pocket, and listened to a message. He said to Bea, 'My chauffeur's outside. I suggest we go straight away. It was hard to get a reservation at this new restaurant and I'm looking forward to the meal.'

Bea shook her head. 'Cancel the reservation. This is important. If you're hungry, we can either get something locally, or have something brought in later.'

He didn't like that. 'Come on, Bea! This isn't like you.'

'That's just the trouble, Leon. I don't think you know what I am like.'

'You want to rule the roost. You want everything done your way.'

Ah, do I detect the fell hand of your new PA? She's been working against me, hasn't she? Got her eye on him for herself?

Bea caught back the hasty words that were on the tip of her tongue. 'No, I don't want to rule any roost. I want to be treated as a good friend, as an equal, as a partner.'

'Well, you are. That is what we are, good friends, helping one another out.'

'Define "good friend". Someone you can rely on to help you when you're in trouble?'

He narrowed his eyes at her. 'That goes without saying.'

'I was in trouble, but you left me to it. My friends were...' her voice broke. 'I can't tell you how much they did for me.'

He flushed. 'You're twisting everything.'

'All right. Let's look at friendship, and how I define it. You know that there was another baby born last week? Maggie's. She was here, yelling at the electrical contractor when her waters broke. She was so furious with him for not having finished when he'd said he would, that she told him it was all his fault that her baby was coming early. Betty and I had to carry her off and put her in my car to get her to hospital, with her on the phone all the way. Boy, can Maggie yell when she gets going! Her husband met us at the hospital and removed the phone from her grasp as she was taken off to the delivery room. A couple of hours later she was sitting up in bed, cradling little Abigail, and telling us all that childbirth is a piece of cake.

'Maggie's fine, the baby's fine, but the only way we can get her to slow down is to have her come over here every morning to act as project manager while little Abigail has a nap in her Karricot. After Maggie's breast-fed the baby and had some lunch, I force her to lie down on my settee for an hour while someone takes the baby out for a walk round the block in her buggy—my staff are fighting for the privilege—and then I take them both home. She adores the baby, who luckily takes after her placid father, but she's determined not to stop work. It's entirely due to Maggie's efforts that the house and garden will be back to normal soon.'

'Good for her.' An uneasy laugh. 'Well, Maggie's always been a one-off.'

'So she has. The child is being called Abigail because "Abby" is the nearest they could get to "Abbott", and I objected to their calling her "Bea". It's a bit dated as a name for a baby nowadays, don't you think?'

He was not enjoying this. 'You think that's friendship? There's surely more to it than that.' His phone rang again. He answered it, frowning. He said to Bea, 'Mind if I take this call?'

'Yes,' said Bea, 'I do mind. We're at crisis point here, and if our relationship matters to you, then you will give it priority.'

He sighed, shook his head, then spoke into the phone. 'Cancel the dinner reservation. And, you can go home now.' He ended the call and turned back to Bea. 'I've told my chauffeur to go home.' He rubbed the back of his neck. 'Look, we're two different sorts of people. Business: that's fine. I know where I am. But I don't find it as easy to interact with people as you do. I've learned that money can smooth paths in life, so when I see a need I do something about it. I'll send—'

Bea said, 'If you say that you're going to send Maggie a cheque, I'll… I'll clock you one!' She swiped at her eyes, right and left. 'Sorry, sorry. It's been a terrible couple of weeks and I'm overtired and I haven't eaten since breakfast and you have every right to conduct your life as you think best, and I shouldn't have sounded off at you like that. What I'm trying to say, rather badly, is that I'm worried for you.'

'For me?' Uneasy, frowning.

She let herself down on to the settee and patted the seat beside her in an invitation for him to join her while she tried to sort out her thoughts. 'When you have as much money as you do, it can build a wall between you and the rest of the world. The people who work for you will insulate you from the slightest draught. But it's not the real world of mortgages and dirty nappies and struggles with transport and broken toys and over-the-fence quarrels with neighbours. It's nothing to do with the weekly shop, or somebody's pet dog fouling your front lawn, or the heartache of your son stealing from your purse and lying about it. Your brother's housekeeper and staff separated him from the real world by featherbedding him until he ended up dying in a gilded cage. I'm worried that this is happening to you, too. Now, tell me I'm an interfering old whatsit, and I'll agree with you.'

He pinched in his lips. 'Now you're on about my PA. You've never liked Zoe, but she has my best interests at heart. She knows that you don't care for her. She said so, right from the start.'

Bea felt remarkably tired. It would be good to cry…but

not yet. 'Friends are not afraid to help one another out, even if it means getting their hands dirty. Friends try to be honest with one another. It seems to me that you are gradually withdrawing away from your old friends and yes, that hurts.'

He reared his head back. 'Why should you care? You've got your portrait painter husband back, haven't you?'

Bea tried to work out what Leon meant. 'What! But... I told you all about that, didn't I? In one of my voicemail messages? When you weren't able to take my call? Piers saw I was in trouble and took action. He moved in with his oils and canvas and he was a tremendous help and, what's more, he actually managed to paint my portrait. Now! Of all times! After promising he'd do it for years, he had to start on it there and then! Once he'd started, we couldn't dislodge him, so he and Oliver and Hari... Oh, what's the use! Yes, Piers did help, too, in his own way. He moved all my sitting-room furniture up here and created a place for me to sit and rest. I am grateful to him. It was thoughtful.'

'Shall I buy your portrait off him?'

'No.' Crossly. 'It's not for sale. But you can see it in the Summer Exhibition at the Royal Academy if you like. It's a triple: me as a young girl in the distance, as an older woman coming through a door and then as a crone, reflected in a mirror. Very odd. Not at all flattering, but good. Even I can see that.'

His phone trilled again. He turned away from Bea, frowning. 'Yes? What...? No, I sent him home because... No, I'm not expecting any more calls this evening. I'll see you in the morning.' He shut off his phone. But continued to stare at it. Slight annoyance?

Bea wanted to say something like, 'Doesn't Zoe allow you to go out at night without checking up on you?' She refrained. If your opponent makes a misstep, don't crow.

He said, 'I was hurt, too. I expected you to ring me every day, to tell me how you were getting on. I asked Zoe to give you my new number, but all I got was messages through Zoe that you were coping just fine and had refused to join me.'

Bea breathed out, gently. *Careful, now! Don't fly off the handle.* She made her voice soft, and reasonable. 'Oh dear! What a misunderstanding. I kept ringing the number she gave me, only to get voicemail. You only rang me once, but you were in such a hurry, about to go into another meeting, you said you couldn't stop to chat.'

'But you gave Zoe a message to say you were out most nights and...' He took a deep breath. 'What number did she give you?'

'You know how bad I am at remembering numbers. I wrote it in my diary.' She found her handbag, extricated her diary, and showed him the page.

He said, 'She gave you the wrong number.' A frown. 'By mistake, of course.'

Bea kept her mouth shut. With an effort. Had Zoe been trying to ensure that Bea didn't speak direct to Leon, and that Leon didn't speak direct to Bea? A neat way of coming between them. Of separating them.

His move.

He took a turn around the room, ending up at the window overlooking the gardens—and his empty house. 'Those bones...they know whose they were now?'

'Yes, a warrant is out for the murderer's arrest, but she and her husband have fled the country.'

'You should have told me.'

She held her tongue with an effort. She'd tried to keep him updated, hadn't she?

She knew what he was going to say before he said it.

He said, 'I don't fancy living in a house which hides such a dark secret.'

It wasn't that house which had hidden a secret. But any excuse would do. He's backing out of the deal.

She said, 'You planned to head up a worthwhile charity which had been going through a bad time. You said their offices were going to be in the basement of your new house.'

'I've been rethinking.'

'You've decided against going into the charity business.'

'Well, maybe. I've been asked on to the board of a firm investing in IT devices for the future. Exciting.'

Bea almost bit her tongue. *Zoe was going to divert him from charity work because there wasn't enough kudos in it? Or because she hadn't suggested it?*

He said, 'In fact, I've had an offer, an excellent offer, for the house as it stands. From some Middle Eastern oil potentate. They want my house and the one next to it, to throw into one. I'm considering it. A nice profit, and what do I need with something so large? I've been looking at some penthouses in the City. They're amazing. Stupendous views. I'll have to take on a housekeeper.'

She stiffened. *I didn't see that coming. Will Mona be pleased to have an offer for her house? Possibly.*

How do I feel about him selling a house he'd bought only to be closer to me? I'm...devastated? Angry because he didn't consult me? Heartbroken? No, not that, but...upset.

He was waiting for a reaction from her. She kept the

lemon out of her voice. 'Congratulations. I'm sure Zoe can provide a housekeeper for you.'

'She did suggest someone. I've met her. Thirtyish, blonde, victim of an abusive first husband, ready to start tomorrow.' He turned away from the windows, but didn't meet her eyes. 'You think I can't see the trap, but I can.'

'It's baited with honey.' She took a deep breath. She must not show hurt or jealousy. 'It seems to me that you are at a crossroads. On the one hand you can live in a gilded cage, cushioned from the world by your money, with a staff who will fulfil your every whim. Perhaps you will marry someone suitable from this world. If you do…' She tried not to grind her teeth. 'If you do, I'll… I'll send you a cheque.'

He looked shocked…and then spurted into laughter. 'I deserved that, didn't I? On the other hand, I suppose you would say that I could choose to rejoin the human race and suffer blood, sweat and tears like the rest of humanity.'

He had intended to take over/join a charity whose officers had been shown up as incompetent, if not corrupt. It would have been a mammoth task to clean it up and set it on a new footing, but he'd been prepared to do it before all this happened.

She said, 'I suppose there'd be the usual business lunches and expenses if you decided to go into charity work but, if I know you, you'd want to do it properly. To go the extra mile. People will call on you at inappropriate hours; they'll traipse mud—figuratively and physically— all over your nice clean carpets. You'll be misunderstood by the press and your staff will go off sick at the most inconvenient moments. You'll wonder, at the end of the day, whether you have made the slightest difference to the world. You'll waste energy trying to help people who want your money but won't lift a finger to help themselves. You'll miss meals because you stopped to listen to someone in trouble. You'll lose weight.'

He was smiling, if wryly. 'A consummation devoutly to be wished, wouldn't you say?' His smile faded. 'I lost sight of the ball, didn't I? I was tired. Feeling my age.'

'Yes, I know. I understand.' And she did. She looked at the ruby. 'I'm sorry I overreacted about the ring. I did tell you once that I didn't care for rubies, but you weren't listening, and I knew you weren't listening. It's a beautiful ring.'

'But not for you?'

'Buy me a tree for the garden. Something that fits in with my lifestyle.' She smiled. 'Actually, you don't even need to do that. Because my staff have been using my kitchen here as well as my living room, and they're so grateful about keeping their jobs, they've clubbed together to re-stock the garden and my freezer! Amazing!'

'You really don't want a ring?'

'Not yet. Perhaps not ever. Perhaps I'm too old. I don't know.'

Someone rang the doorbell. Someone who intended to be admitted.

Bea said, 'Your chauffeur? Or Zoe? Or both?'

He subsided into a chair and stretched out his legs before him. 'This is your house. It's more likely to be someone visiting you. Piers or Oliver. Or, what's-his-name, your last tenant, the one with the orange trousers. Whatever happened to him? It's your house, and your front-door bell. You answer it.'

Was he opting out? Letting her decide his future? 'My

instinct tells me it's for you and, if so, you are going to have to deal with it.'

'Whatever. You'll have dinner with me afterwards?'

'No, but I'll see if there's anything in the freezer I can microwave for you, if you like.'

He picked up the day's newspaper and hid behind it. *Just like a man!*

She went downstairs and opened the front door. She'd guessed correctly. There in the porch stood Zoe, wearing a sweet little black dress and a determined expression. At her side was a willowy blonde with a lot of teased-out fair hair which had recently had some extensions added so that it tumbled forward over her astonishing cleavage. The girl was wearing, just, a gold and white strapless tube that was two sizes too small for her, held up by willpower and a heavily underwired bra. She was also wearing a lot of luscious red lipstick on her pouting, Botoxed mouth.

'Yes?' said Bea, in a voice loud enough for it carry up the stairs to the first floor.

'He's late for his surprise party!' said Zoe, thrusting Bea out of her way. She turned into the office. 'Oh, but…'

'He's upstairs,' said Bea, looking up and down the street to see if Leon's chauffeur was still hanging around. And yes, he was. Which meant he'd disobeyed Leon's instructions to go home. Which meant he was for the chop…probably.

'Yoohoo, Leon!' The blonde tottered up the stairs. Heels too high. Ditto skirt. She wasn't wearing any pants, was she? Perhaps a thong?

'Surprise!' trilled Zoe, locating the right room at last. 'To celebrate! Our treat! And of course Mrs Abbot must come, too, if she's not too tired.'

Translation: if she's not too old and decrepit.

Leon had taken off his tie and opened the top button of his shirt. *A good move to show he felt at home here, but these two were going to take some getting rid of.* He stood up as they came in, folding the newspaper, frowning.

Zoe wagged her finger at him. 'It's been in the diary for days.' She had a tiny camera in her hand.

What for?

The pneumatic Blondie cast herself on Leon's chest and clung around his neck. 'Aargh!' Bea dived forward, knocking Zoe off balance.

Flash! But, the camera had ended up pointing at the ceiling.

'Oops!' Bea held on to Zoe, to regain her balance. 'So sorry. I caught my heel in the rug.' There was no rug, and she was wearing medium heels.

Leon twisted around, dropped the paper, and un-hooked Blondie's arms. She tried to cling to his arm, and he dropped her on to her bottom on the floor with a thump.

Heavy breathing all round. Cross expressions.

Leon said, 'Zoe, I think you have my spare phone. Would you let me have it for a moment?'

Zoe placed her handbag behind her.

Bea reached behind the woman, opened her hand-bag, and picked out a couple of the latest phones. 'This one? Or this?'

'Doesn't matter,' said Leon. 'They're both owned by the company.'

Zoe snatched at one and missed. 'You can't...!'

'No,' said Leon, '*you* can't.' He clicked one phone on. Listened to Bea's voice asking for him, and then leaving a message. Clicked the other phone on. Looked at the list of recent phone calls. Bea remembered how good he was at remembering phone numbers. He only had to see them once to recognize them. He said, 'Zoe, I believe you gave Mrs Abbot the wrong number on which to contact me. A foolish mistake.'

'Did I? I certainly didn't mean to do so. If she thought there was something wrong, she should have queried it.'

'And I see your recent phone calls include the managing agents for the penthouse I've been thinking about buying, and for my house in the next street. These calls could be legitimate but I do wonder…if I contact them, will they confirm you are getting a commission on both sales?'

Zoe blustered. 'That is normal procedure.'

Leon sighed. 'Bea, will you see if she's got any office keys on her? They'll be on a ring with a lion tag.'

Zoe made a convulsive movement as if to hug her bag to her, then shrugged and handed it over.

Bea found the keys with the lion tag on them, and held them up for Leon to see.

Leon said, 'Zoe, I'm keeping the keys and the phones because they belong to me. Don't bother to come into the office tomorrow. If you have any personal property there, I'll have it bagged up and sent on to you. I will also send you a cheque for three months' pay in lieu of notice. Understood?'

Zoe went pale. 'I was only thinking of your best interests.'

'That's for me to decide, not you. Now please remove this girl you've brought with you, and tell my chauffeur I'll speak to him in the morning.'

'Oh, Auntie!' Blondie was in tears, which didn't improve her looks. 'I thought you said…'

Bea had had enough. 'Let me show you out.' And did so, bolting the front door after them.

She went into the kitchen and started to rummage in the freezer. She called out, 'My staff have been bringing me home-cooked dishes to save me trouble. I don't know who cooked what. Would cottage pie and frozen peas do you?'

'Ah, domesticity.' He reappeared, with the newspaper, and settled down in the kitchen to read it. 'As I've said before, why don't you take the *Financial Times*?'

'Perhaps because I don't read it? Why don't you get it on your iPad?' She checked the microwave timings.

'You do realize I now have nowhere to lay my head? May I stay the night here?'

'Certainly not. And you must be living somewhere. What about your flat in the Barbican? No, wait a minute, you've got a suite in a hotel somewhere.'

'It's cold and impersonal.'

'That's an easy problem to solve. Throw some money at it.'

He laughed, and concentrated on reading the paper.

She put the cottage pie and the peas on the table and served up. She tasted and chewed. Frowned. Whoever had made it...not Betty?...hadn't been a particularly good cook.

He said, 'Perhaps some ketchup with it?'

She pushed it aside. 'Tell you what, let's go out for supper, shall we? There's plenty of good restaurants locally. You can choose. I'll dispose of this in the recycling box, to avoid hurting anyone's feelings.'

NINETEEN

Later that month

THE SPECIALIST BRICKLAYERS had almost finished sorting
the fallen bricks into 'discard' and 'reuse' piles. Palettes
of reclaimed bricks had been delivered to make up for
those which had been lost. The workmen had dug out the
channels for the new footings, and soon the new walls
would prevent Bea from stepping from her garden and
into Mona's, but on that particular day it was still possible to do so. There had been a lot of argument about replacing or not replacing the wall between Mona's house
and the one which had belonged to Leon, because the
new buyer was going to throw the two houses—and
gardens—into one. So, for the moment, that part of the
rebuild was on hold.

Bea stepped carefully across the newly dug foundations 'ditch' and made it safely to the table in Mona's
garden. The two women had fallen into the habit of having coffee or tea with one another whenever they could
snatch a moment in their busy lives, but this was the first
opportunity they'd had to meet for over a week.

Today, as Bea approached, she smelled wood smoke
from a sluggish bonfire. A heap of the torn-down ivy
plants which had strangled the wall for so long, were
being incinerated. Householders were not supposed to

light bonfires in London, but no one seemed to have objected, yet.

Mona was struggling to put up a striped umbrella over a rickety table. Bea helped her. Neither umbrella, nor table, nor the chairs around it were in the first flush of youth, and looked as if they had been playing 'house' with spiders in the shed. Mona was wearing an old sun top and a rather decrepit pair of Bermuda shorts. Bea was in office gear.

'Instant coffee,' said Mona. 'Milk, no sugar?'

'Bless you.' Bea produced a tin of biscuits. 'Somebody's home-made shortbread biscuits. Not bad.'

Mona said, 'Neither of my husbands could get enough of the sun. Personally, I turn red rather than brown.' She seated herself in the shade.

Bea closed her eyes and lifted her face to the sun. 'Ten minutes, and I'm happy. After that, I'll join you.'

They sipped coffee, and ate a biscuit each.

Mona said, 'How's it going?'

Bea shielded her eyes from the sun. 'Leon's buying a pretty little town house not far away. In a small close. It's nothing like the grand penthouse suites or the mansions he was looking at before. Much cosier. More realistic. There's a loft conversion for his office and bedrooms en suite for his elder sister—the one who mostly lives in America—and for his great-niece for their holidays. The girl's going to boarding school here in the autumn. They're both over here now, alternately cuddling Dilys's baby and "helping" Leon to decide on decorating and what furniture he needs to buy for it. Their interference was driving him frantic, so he's handed the project over to Maggie to manage. He wants a new kitchen. He says he intends to learn how to cook.'

Both women smiled at that.

Bea said, 'I think he's finally worked out what having a family means. He's been to visit Dilys and held her little boy for five minutes, which is one minute more than I'd expected. But he's besotted with Maggie's Abby; carries her around and coos at her. I'm amazed!'

'And what will he do to pass the time of day?'

'I really don't know. I don't think he does, either. He's had offers…' A shrug. 'What about you?'

'I'm signing the contract for this place next week, and moving into the same block as Penelope. It's a nice, sunny flat, and there's a balcony to sit out on when the weather's good. There's only two bedrooms, one for me and one for Rollo in the holidays. You must come round and see it when I'm in.'

'I'll do that.'

They relaxed. So much had happened over the past few months. So much was still going on. The Admiral and Edith had turned up in Jamaica. Despite the fact that they must have known Mona's phone was being tapped, Edith rang her sister every few days begging her to send them some money, saying it wasn't her fault, and so on and so forth. Mona had refused and told Edith to return to face the music, but they hadn't done so, and probably wouldn't till either their money ran out or the police succeed in getting them extradited, whichever was the soonest.

Bea held out the biscuit tin to Mona, and took another herself. 'Has Edith actually admitted killing your husband in any of her phone calls?'

'A couple of days ago, yes. And the police recorded it. She says it was an accident. She tried to throw him out, he took a swing at her, she reciprocated, he stepped backwards, fell and cracked his head against the bottom step in the hall. The police have actually found traces of blood there. After all this time. Who'd have believed it?'

'Did the Admiral admit to having helped Edith bury the body?'

'He says "no". She says he did. I tend to believe her. It'll be manslaughter, I expect. I don't suppose she'll have to serve much time, if any, due to her age and so on, but…' She shrugged. 'As for him, even if he's convicted, as he's a first-time offender, he probably won't even get a custodial sentence.'

They considered this. Bea said, 'But, if what Oliver tells me is true, he's lost a packet by backing the wrong horse on the stock market.'

Mona took another biscuit, brushing crumbs from her top as she did so. 'Edith says he's gambled away his pension.'

'How…satisfying,' said Bea.

'They won't have much to live on when and if they return,' said Mona. 'A council flat, perhaps? Living on an old-age pension?'

'What about his car? It was an expensive one, as I recall.'

'They left it in the airport long-stay car park. Edith wanted me to retrieve it, sell it and send them the money. I knew it was a leased car because I'd had to come up with the monthly payments for them now and then. They were in arrears on it, so I told the finance company what had happened, and they've repossessed it.'

'Good for you.' Bea was slightly surprised that Mona had held out against Edith's demands so well. 'It's a pity we couldn't get them on their plan to entrap Leon—but, as he can't really remember much about that evening, and as the only evidence we have is the hospital records saying he was drugged…well, I can understand why the police think it's safer to concentrate on the long-ago murder—or manslaughter—or whatever it might actually have been.'

If the envelope containing the evidence Venetia had taken ever came to light, it would be a different matter, but Rollo had said it had been destroyed, and perhaps it was best to leave it that way. Unless, of course, Venetia tried to bring it up some time, or Rollo did?

Bea didn't want to think about that. She moved round the table into the shade. 'What's the latest on the children?'

'My dear Malcolm came over from Australia, last week. Trying to sort the boys out, but he's gone back now. The boys have been refused bail because the arson was such a serious crime, and their fingerprints on the paraffin container clinched the evidence against them. It was proved that they ran up the charges on your phone, but that's a minor matter, according to the police. Malcolm says he'll be back for their trial.'

'Ah. I'm sorry, Mona. I know you'd have liked me to drop the charges against the boys, but the arson put so many people's jobs at risk that I couldn't.'

'Not to mention their attempt to have your water turned off. No, you were right to stick to your guns. They've both been in trouble before and it cost me an arm and a leg to bail them out then. I'd told them that was their last chance—'

'But they didn't believe you.'

'Malcolm is paying their legal fees. He says that if they get a custodial sentence, which is very possible, he'll take them back home with him when they're released.' Mona took another biscuit. 'I've put on weight.

Comfort eating. I'm a bit worried that Australia might not take them back.'

'They have dual-nationality passports?'

'No. Australian.'

'Should be all right, then. There's a long history of Britain sending convicts over there.'

'True.'

'And...' Bea felt brave enough to speak of the elephant in the room. 'Venetia?'

'The Crown Prosecution Service decided they wouldn't pursue the matter of her "borrowing" your purse and watch as, technically, she's not been in any trouble before.'

Bea said, 'I get it that they can't prosecute her for trying to trap Leon without evidence, but what about "borrowing" and crashing other people's cars? Oh, those cases never came to court?'

Mona winced. 'I ought not to have bailed her out. I know that now. She's doing all right for herself. You know she went back to live with her parents? Well, her father introduced her to all the "right" people at the golf club and she's moved in with a man who's divorced two wives already. How long that will last, I don't know.'

So Venetia got off scot-free? Bea could foresee a career for Venetia in which the girl continued to sell herself in pursuit of a good time...ending in another smashed car? Or perhaps a marriage which would be featured in *Hello!* magazine, to be followed the next year by divorce...?

'Families,' said Mona. 'You worry about them till the day you die.'

'Mm. And, families aren't just kith and kin. Even extended families aren't just that. I see less of my own son than I do of Maggie and Dilys and their husbands and children. They're family, too. Then there's Oliver, who insists on coming back home frequently under the pretext of seeing if I'm all right and not up to any more shenanigans, but in reality to touch base with the only family he's ever known. Then everyone at the agency acts as if I'm their foster mother and wants to tell me all their problems. Don't get me wrong; I like being mother hen, but sometimes I want to be shut of the lot of them.'

'Pelicans,' said Mona. 'I don't know if it's true but they say that, in a drought, pelican mothers will offer their own blood to their brood to feed them.'

Bea took another biscuit. 'And it doesn't always turn out well. I know. But, you've rescued Rollo.'

'He's a nice lad and I shall enjoy having him around. His parents are delighted not to have to worry about him. I've persuaded him that I have enough money to keep him at his private school, provided he settles down to working hard. He's promised me he will, and I think I believe him. He's even been doing some work this holidays. I can, almost, believe in a good future for him.' Mona delved into a back pocket and produced a rather crumpled envelope. 'Here. Rollo gave it to me last night. He said you'd been so decent to him that he wanted you to have it. You know what's in it?'

'I do.' Bea weighed it in her hand. If she handed this over to the police, they could go after Venetia with a vengeance...but also drag Leon into a difficult situation. And, the chain of evidence had been broken not once but several times...from Venetia to Rollo...and from Rollo to Mona...and from Mona to Bea. Which meant that a defence counsel could rip the evidence to pieces.

'I do like a bonfire,' said Bea. 'I know we're not supposed to have them in a built-up area, but it's good to see the ivy disappear.' She got up from her chair to poke the envelope into the heart of the bonfire. Flame flared around it for a moment. The envelope blackened and shrivelled away.

Bea brushed her hands one against the other. 'Have we finished all the biscuits? I'll bring a different sort next time, shall I?'

*****